Holding the Perfect Hand

Taylor Squirek

DEDICATION

I dedicate this book to Serafim Baltić. Without you, the central messages of this story would have never been completed or told. Thank you for your friendship and leading with your certitude for the Lord. May the voice of the Serbs finally be heard!

DISCLAIMER

There are sections in this book that contain satire. Regarding the satirical elements of the COVID-19 pandemic, this book is not meant to be used to treat, cure, diagnose, or practice safety measures for COVID-19. Along with other situations in the story, it is intended to make points about the human condition and society.

CHAPTER 1

I t took Satan little effort to crush Roman's good spirit. He enjoyed getting inside Roman's head on a day like this. Satan made sure the weather was terrible to make his move. From there, he would let Roman do the rest. It was a cold mid-January day in 2021, with steady rain in the town of Neelyton, Pennsylvania. Roman Anderson was at home and decided to stay in due to the weather. So many thoughts would fill Roman's head as he detested days like this when it wasn't great to go outside. His best friend Miroslav was at work today, which means he couldn't visit with him. But staying indoors may have been his subconscious choice since he was used to carrying on in grief.

On a positive note, Roman could stay at home and finally make more plans for his future. He wasn't sure what he wanted to do. He had an idea to start up his own business, preferably opening one in the town of Neelyton or close by. A restaurant was one idea he had thought about, but he wasn't officially set on it either. Roman was quite an accomplished cook. His strength in the kitchen was baking, and he also had the skill to smoke all kinds of meats on his smoker. Growing up, his parents had shown him the ropes when it came to cooking, but he came into his own as he grew up. Roman also knew the methods for hot and cold pack canning, butchering, fixing up things around the house, landscaping, and drawing. He loved to draw and was quite an artist. He didn't consider anything too big of a challenge. He was a very talented person. His biggest challenge would be finally finding something that would stick. In a way, all his talents almost worked against him at times.

Roman would do his best to stay focused on this dreary January day. At the same time, he would even try to remember all the things he had to be grateful for. And he did have so much to be thankful for. His log cabin and land were things to be appreciated. He had a beautiful property with a little over nineteen acres with a generous mix of woods. Around six acres were open for his garden, a metal building, and a pond. His friend, Miroslav Kojić, and his wife, Theresa, were his neighbors and best friends. They also had a decent-sized property with a little over twenty-one acres. They were blessed with two beautiful children, Jason and Sarah.

Roman cherished the times he could spend with the Kojić family since they were very good to him. Roman, like Miroslav, was a transplant to Pennsylvania. Originally Roman was from New Seabury, Massachusetts. It was a cozy little town on Cape Cod where he lived all his life until he moved. He had only lived in Neelyton since the end of September 2019. Although it presented challenges living in a new location, he certainly didn't regret moving. However, no matter where he lived, there wasn't anything he could do to escape the personal demons that followed him. So, he figured that he might as well live somewhere that he would enjoy staying long-term.

The outdoors was always something Roman enjoyed. He loved being in nature, where it was quiet. It made him feel more at peace. Hunting was something he had done ever since he was a little boy. Roman had many warm memories of going hunting with his father. He and his father would mainly go duck hunting, as the opportunities were great growing up near the ocean and marshes. Since Roman always enjoyed nature, he randomly chose to buy the property in Neelyton so he could build his own house right in the woods. He also wanted to create some distance from where he grew up. He didn't have many friends growing up in New Seabury, so he didn't leave too much behind other than his immediate family. He had a steady job in the town of

Marion, where Roman and Briana had lived. Because of her passing, a regular job wasn't enough to keep him grounded in New England for the rest of his life.

He felt the pain from losing the love of his life, Briana Kennedy, and their unborn child. It was the pain he wanted to escape from so desperately by moving almost five hundred miles away from his place of origin. And yet somehow, it followed Roman to the mountains of Pennsylvania. On that rainy day, the mental anguish was suffocating. He saw the picture on the TV stand and picked it up. And there she was. She was still beautiful and still charming.

Briana stood in front of Roman with his hands on her pregnant belly. She was a few inches shorter than Roman. She had a voluptuous figure. Her skin was dark brown and smooth as silk. Her eyes were radiant and full of life and happiness, along with her smile. Roman had a clean-shaven face, a full head of hair, and a well-built figure in the picture. Now he had a modest-sized beard. His hair got long and was down to his neck. He had let himself go with his appearance. He was still well-built but now had a few extra pounds. He also picked up the habit of smokeless tobacco in recent years. His choice was usually either Skoal or Copenhagen pouches. The flavor would depend on his mood on whatever given day.

"I'm so sorry I killed you both. I hope you can forgive me. Please... please don't be mad at me," Roman said as he began to cry while holding and shaking the picture in his hands.

The tears were coming down hard now as Roman started to sob. Repeatedly in his mind, he would continue to blame himself for what had happened. The day Briana died, they argued over Roman's credit card bill because he ran it up again due to gambling away much of their finances. It's a day he wishes he could have back. If he knew it was the last time they saw each other, he would have done everything to resolve the conflict about his gambling addiction right then and there. Instead, he let her leave the house and left that conversation on a bitter note. Roman couldn't shake off that last memory in his mind as much as he tried to. Perhaps if he had taken ownership of the credit card debt he created in the first place, along with the compulsive gambling, maybe Briana would still be here today, and Roman would still be with the woman he loved. Perhaps he would have experienced the joys of being a father. He could have been a part of something extraordinary. He wished he could cultivate that love and bond with their child… *his* child that he sorely wanted to have back. He even missed his opportunity to pop the question to Briana. Those thoughts plagued Roman's mind today – what could have been, and possibly what would have been.

As he held the picture in his hand, he kissed Briana while crying and said, "I love you… I will always love you and our baby."

He then set the picture back on the TV stand and sat on the living room couch. Then Roman popped two tobacco pouches under his bottom lip. The nicotine helped relieve his stress, at least in his mind. The numbing rush in his face and hands made him feel more at ease. He took several minutes to relax on the couch and enjoy the inviting fire going on in the wood-burning stove, which was the means that Roman used to heat his house. The tears eventually subsided. He returned to his work at hand, trying to figure out what to do with his life.

As he spat tobacco juice from his mouth into his Gatorade bottle, he thought, *"Can I pull something like this off even with a pandemic?"*

It was a valid question. Even without the COVID-19 pandemic, he had never opened or owned any small business. He didn't even have a college degree. But what he did have was determination with a good work ethic. He also had money… tons of money. Roman was also the proud winner of the Mega Millions. He had won the jackpot from the random fortune cookie numbers he used. Roman had collected his colossal prize almost a year after Briana died. Although he hadn't won a world record-sized jackpot, he won about five hundred million dollars, which would be more than enough for him or anyone.

He knew living in Marion after Briana died would never be the same. Sure, he was independently wealthy now and debt-free, but he couldn't share it with his best friend. He also knew that sooner or later, he would have to do something with his life. Even though he hit pay dirt with the lottery, he knew that sitting around for the rest of his life wouldn't make him feel any better. Having a job would give him more purpose by working outside his house and allow for social interaction.

Finally, the wheels in his head were starting to turn. Time had passed since he initially sat down on the couch and relaxed for a bit. His Gatorade bottle was filled with dark brown spit at the bottom. But Roman felt like he was on a roll thinking of things now. He started talking out loud.

He said, "You know, I don't have a fancified degree or certificate in anything past high school, but I sure know how to cook. And I love to do it, too. I need to come up with something that has a unique quality. But what?"

He paused. He spat more tobacco juice into the bottle and set it on the coffee table. He glanced around the living room as he thought of ideas so he could answer his question. He had a mounted bull moose head over the wood-burning stove in the living room that he had shot and killed on a guided hunting trip in the Yukon. The antler spread was about five and a half feet. He looked at it and smiled. That was his favorite hunt, not only because of the size of the trophy but also because he got to go on a hunting trip with his father. His father also shot himself a good-sized moose during that trip. The antler span on the moose he shot was only a couple of inches more than the one Roman shot. The moose head made Roman remember that hunting trip, all the fun things he did with his father over the years, and everything his father had taught Roman growing up. Roman cherished the warm relationship he had with his father.

In the rest of the living room, he had a mounted white-tailed deer head he had taken on his property. It was a decent ten-point buck. There were pictures of himself in different stages of his life throughout his house in the living room – his parents, grandparents, his brother Craig and his family, and of course, Briana. He also displayed memorabilia from his favorite football team, the Minnesota Vikings. He had been collecting items from all the different eras of the Vikings. He had old-school players like Fran Tarkenton, Alan Page, Carl Eller, and head coach Bud Grant. He also had recent players like Randy Moss, Cris Carter, Daunte Culpepper, and Adam Thielen. He had several pictures of Disney characters hanging on the walls that he had drawn and framed. Roman's four-bedroom log cabin had the appearance of being cozy on both the inside and outside.

"Maybe what I could do," Roman thought, *"is like a variety of things. Barbecue and baking are my strong points in cooking, along with breakfast. But along with those things, I could pick Miroslav's brain for good Serbian-style dishes. I've never made Serbian-style food, but it couldn't be that hard to do, right? And besides, it's not like anyone else commonly serves it at restaurants, so that would be more unique. I bet I could also throw in wild game meat, too. The wild game would be a big seller in these parts."*

Roman felt satisfied with the nicotine high he had gotten off his tobacco pouches. So, he took both pouches out of his mouth and put them in the Gatorade bottle.

"What I could do is a restaurant, but maybe that's more like take-out style," Roman thought. *"Have a couple of tables inside but mainly make it take out. That way, I could stay open if the government enforces more pandemic guidelines regarding social distancing. I say outsmart them before they outsmart the American people."*

Roman was a staunch conservative, despite growing up in Massachusetts. However, Roman was not a believer in the Republican Party but was an independent voter. But because he was a conservative, many people didn't have a favorable view of him from where he grew up. It was honestly another reason he wanted to move. There was no point, in his opinion, in living in a place where he felt degraded and marginalized because he believed differently than the general public around him. He remembered Rhonda, a woman he dated for less than a year, briefly after Briana died. It did not work out due to sharp differences in political beliefs. If Roman were ever to get married, he saw very little chance of meeting someone up there, making him miss Briana even more because he looked at her as a rare find. Putting politics aside, he didn't hate people who were liberal. However, he didn't feel like they accepted him for his differences. Although it didn't provoke hatred, it placed distrust in his heart. He also saw Massachusetts as a tough place to make friends since he saw people in general as very standoffish.

"*It's hard enough to make friends up there, let alone find a date there,*" he thought. "*Plus, I'm not a Patriots fan, so that's another strike against me!*"

After thinking that thought, he chuckled as he remembered that he got heckled out in public on several occasions. If he wore his Fran Tarkenton and Alan Page jerseys with the Vikings hat to match, he knew it made him a target of ridicule. He looked up at the moose head again for several seconds.

"*I do miss my mother and father. I think I'll give them a call this coming weekend to see how they're doing up there in New Seabury,*" he thought.

Even though Roman wasn't a big fan of the politics and culture where he grew up, he missed some things about living on Cape Cod. The fresh salty air of the beaches during the summer and how the sun made the sand warm brought a smile to his face. He had many fond memories of his parents taking him and his older brother to South Cape Beach during the summer months when school was out for vacation. And the seafood! He loved the seafood. Fried clam rolls, whole lobsters, steamed clams, and battered fried cod fillets were some of his favorites. And all those times he and his family went to the Barnstable County Fair when it was in town toward the end of July was something he enjoyed. Also, going whale watching with his family was something that he missed.

"Someday, I'll have to make a trip up there now that I'm settled into my home. I also need to have the family over for a visit, too. I think it's about time I stop self-isolating myself. Even though I tend to blame myself for what happened, there's nothing I can do to change the past. It's not going to bring Briana or my unborn child back. And I don't think she would have wanted me to carry on like this," Roman said confidently.

It was getting close to dinner, and he was starting to feel hungry. He was feeling in the mood for some Chinese food. Living in the country caused him to drive a little extra to get to things. But that didn't bother Roman. It was something he accepted living where he lived. He put on his red plaid coat, camouflaged patterned cap, and country boots. Then he grabbed the keys for his Toyota Tundra and began walking to the attached garage.

"Ah, crap, my spit bottle and weapon," he said.

He found his spit bottle on the coffee table. He went to his bedroom and grabbed his .357 Magnum snub-nosed revolver from the nightstand and its holster. He secured the gun and holster to his pants belt, which went inside the waist on his right. After retrieving the items, Roman checked his pants pocket to ensure the tin of Copenhagen mint pouches was still there. Now he was ready to go. He made his way to the garage and got into his 2019 Tundra, which he had bought brand new at the time with his lottery winnings. He also had purchased a 2020 Rolls-Royce Ghost. He didn't want to use it today since the weather wasn't good.

Roman clicked the button on the garage door opener remote, and off he went. After pushing the button again to close the garage door, he placed his revolver inside the center console and popped two more tobacco pouches in his mouth, knowing he had a little while to get to Mandarin Gardens. He waited a bit before calling the restaurant with his order to time the pick-up just right. Plus, he could have more time to fill up his spit bottle without interruption.

Eventually, he made it home with his meal. As he made his way inside his house, he slipped off his boots, hung up his coat, and put his hat in his coat pocket. Roman set the takeout bag on the table as he made his way to the kitchen. He then grabbed a beer out of the fridge and opened the bottle. Pabst Blue Ribbon was his beer of choice. After getting his beer, he got his plate and silverware with a couple of napkins and placed them on the table. He was ready to dig in. The smell of the Chinese take-out made his mouth water, and he couldn't wait to feast. He was about to spoon the food from one of the take-out containers onto his plate but then suddenly paused.

"You know, maybe I'll try it," he thought. *"It will be my first time doing this, but what the hell… I guess you got to start somewhere. And I greatly respect the Kojić family and how they live out the faith. I don't understand nearly as much as they do, but they have most of it together. The small group has been interesting and fun, too. I like the way Miroslav runs the small group. And I kind of like some of the other people there. So, I think I'm going to give this a try."*

He closed his eyes and brought his hands together.

After he lowered his head, Roman prayed aloud and said, "Dear Lord… thank You for this food You have given me… and please bless the people that made this meal for me… amen."

After the prayer, he started to scoop the food onto his plate until it was full of sesame beef and rice. He also put a couple of crab rangoons, chicken teriyaki sticks, and an egg roll on his plate.

He thought, *"I don't know how some people can make a prayer long before a meal. I didn't know what to say. I got nervous. Did I even do the prayer right?"*

Roman ate a good portion of the food but still had some leftovers. He put the leftover food in the fridge and cleaned up his area at the kitchen table. Afterward, he stoked the fire with more wood. He went to his bedroom, put on his pajamas, and put his revolver on his nightstand. He was done for the day. Now was the time to relax and unwind for the rest of the evening. As he popped a couple more tobacco pouches under his lip, he made his way to the couch so he could watch some TV.

As he flipped through the channels, he saw a nature show about lightning on National Geographic. It looked like Roman had caught the beginning of the show. Nature shows and shows about historical events were things that would always grab his attention. Cooking shows, of course, were another thing he liked to watch. And when Sundays rolled around in the autumn months, he watched the Minnesota Vikings. He also enjoyed a good movie or a funny sitcom, but tonight, he was content with the nature show. He sat comfortably on the couch as he filled more of his bottle with tobacco spit.

The show eventually ended, and Roman turned off the TV. He got up and checked to make sure the house was locked up. Then he turned off the lights in the living room, returned to the bedroom, and climbed into bed. As he lay there staring at the ceiling, thoughts of the day ran through his head. Miroslav and his family, Chinese food, Briana, and potential businesses. He didn't want any negative thoughts to enter his mind before bed. So, he quickly turned the light off so he could find sleep. For he knew that tomorrow would be another day. It would be up to him how productive he would be. He decided that he would visit Miroslav tomorrow if he were available. Seeing Miroslav always made Roman happy. He closed his eyes and fell asleep, knowing that tomorrow would be a good day for him.

CHAPTER 2

t was half past seven the following morning when Roman woke up. He had a good night's sleep and felt refreshed as he awoke. The rain had passed, and the early morning sun was starting to show its face. He stretched his arms as he yawned.

"I think this will be a good day," Roman said as he got out of bed.

He made his way to the bathroom so he could urinate. He then washed his hands and made his way to the kitchen. He looked around the kitchen, thinking about what he could make for breakfast.

"I think I'll keep it simple this morning. A bagel and cream cheese it is," he thought.

Roman went to the cupboard and found the bagels and a paper plate. He took a plain bagel out of the bag and set it on the paper plate so he could cut it in half. He stuck both slices in the toaster oven and then went to the refrigerator to get the cream cheese and orange juice. He poured a generous amount of orange juice into his favorite Minnesota Vikings glass. After putting the orange juice back in the fridge, his bagel had finished toasting. Roman rarely skimped when it came to his food portions, so he loaded each bagel slice up with extra cream cheese.

"You only live once," he thought as he carried his food and drink to the kitchen table. He stared at the bagel for a couple of seconds and thought, *"Well, maybe I can pray again. After all, it will not hurt anything if I do."*

As he bowed his head and closed his eyes, he put his hands together and said, "Dear Lord, thank You for this breakfast, and let's have a great day today. In Your Son's name, Amen."

Roman ate his breakfast rather quickly. Not only because he was hungry, but he also felt motivated today. He finished his breakfast with ease. He brought his empty glass to the sink and threw his paper plate in the garbage. As he was leaving the kitchen, he was walking a little fast. He didn't realize that he would scuff his baby toe on the corner of the wall going from the kitchen to the living room until it was too late. He sure wasn't walking fast now. That motivation he had for the day quickly left as that shooting pain entered his baby toe and the side of his foot. He hadn't broken it, but it made him more awake than a few moments ago.

He grabbed his foot and shouted, "OUCH! That hurt! You son of a bitch!"

After he cussed, he closed his mouth and covered it with his other hand for a couple of seconds.

He thought, *"What a sight this must be. I probably shouldn't have said that. I know God probably disapproves of cussing. But man, did that hurt! I bet the liberals snuck up on me and did that to my toe. They're probably all laughing at my expense."*

After the incident was over, Roman slowly made his way to the bathroom. He was walking slower now because of what had happened. He then brushed his teeth and threw on some deodorant. After freshening up, he went to the bedroom and got dressed. He knew he would likely see the Kojić family today, so he secured his revolver in his gun safe.

"No sense in younger kids having access to a firearm," he thought.

As he made his way to the living room, he grabbed some more tobacco pouches and loaded a couple of them under his lip. Although Roman loved his smokeless tobacco, he felt it would be disrespectful to use tobacco inside the Kojić household. He admired them, and that was reason enough in his mind not to use tobacco in their house. So, he relaxed on the couch with a new plastic bottle, only to eventually fill it with tobacco spit.

Roman turned the TV on. He rarely watched the news anymore. It was too depressing for him. The pandemic, Antifa, Asian giant hornets, riots in major cities, and the social unrest among the American public made Roman uneasy. And who knew what was yet to come? Another civil war, perhaps? He also didn't enjoy watching professional football as much as he used to since it became more politicized, in his opinion. Even the thought of a potential government takeover was rampant in Roman's head. He quickly shook off his negative feelings as he skipped past the news channels. All these things greatly bothered him.

As he flipped through the channels, he came across Boomerang. He laughed out loud.

"YES! Frickin' *Johnny Bravo*," he exclaimed. "Be brutal, Momma," he said, impersonating Johnny Bravo. "Man, I didn't even know they could still play a show like this on television. That will probably get canceled by the liberals soon, you watch. Good ole' cancel culture… what a crock," he said as he scoffed at the idea.

He spat inside the bottle, and continued with his rant, "The liberals say they're accepting, yet *they're* the ones who want to censor everything. I guess liberals only accept others when people agree with everything *they* believe in."

After his tangent, Roman finally settled down and watched *Johnny Bravo* while enjoying his tobacco. A couple of episodes passed, and Roman felt satisfied with his tobacco pouches. He spat both pouches into the bottle and set the bottle down on the coffee table. He realized that he had forgotten to turn his phone on. He turned the TV off and went to his room to get his phone. He walked back into the living room and sat on the couch, waiting for his phone to turn on. Roman scrolled through his address book, wanting to call Miroslav. He placed the call and waited for an answer. He was in luck.

"Hello," answered the voice.

"Hey there, Miroslav," Roman said.

"Ah, hey there, Roman! How is your day going so far?"

"It's going well, my man. It's going well. How about yours?"

"So far, so good. The day is still young, though," Miroslav said as he chuckled.

"This is true," said Roman, "Say, I was wondering if I could stop by in a bit. Besides, I remembered you left your sweatshirt at my place from when you guys were over here last time."

"Oh, yeah, that's right, I did. I figured it was over there."

Miroslav paused for a few seconds and replied, "I'll tell you what. I'm about the change the oil in Theresa's minivan. We talked last night and wanted to ask if you would like to come over for dinner. We had plans, but they got canceled last minute. So, you're welcome to join us if you don't have anything to do. We're making ham pot pie and all the sides to go with it. I'd say stopover around half past four, give or take."

"All right, that sounds great! Thank you for having me over. Should I bring anything with me?"

"Just your appetite. We are looking forward to seeing you. Anyway, I need to get back to my work here. I'll see you in a few hours, my friend."

"You got it, brother. I'll see you soon."

"Okay, bye-bye."

"Bye," Roman said as he ended the call.

"I tell you, even with his thick Serbian accent, his English is always good," he thought.

Now that he wasn't going to the Kojić house until later, that gave him some downtime for a portion of the day. There wasn't much to do as far as house chores go. He had already done those a couple of days ago. He was tempted to throw some duck decoys in his pond and try his luck with duck hunting.

"No, it's too cold and damp. Besides, I would have had a better chance if I had gone right at sunrise this morning. I might go in a couple of days before the season ends," he thought. *"You know what? I think I'll FaceTime my folks."*

So, he did. He heard the connection go through and got a response.

"Hello," said his father.

"Hi, Dad, how are you?" asked Roman.

"Hi, Roman!" exclaimed his mother.

"Hi, Mom!"

"How's our son doing today? Good, I hope?" his mother asked.

"I'm doing good. I wanted to check up on you both to see how things are going."

"We're doing fine," his father said. "As you know, the winters are cold and uneventful up here on the Cape. It stays quiet until tourist season rolls around, but that's yearly. We didn't do much of anything over the holidays as far as traveling due to the pandemic, but that's how life is nowadays."

"Yeah, the whole world is different now. I don't know if things will ever get back to *normal,* so to speak."

"Me neither. Things are pretty much on lockdown up here still. But what can you do? Nothing... nothing at all. I thought we were going to get arrested last week."

"What do you mean? What happened?"

"Your mother and I walked into the store and got screamed at. I'm not talking about someone raising their voice at us. I'm talking about legit getting screamed at all because we didn't have our face masks on. But get this. I was in the middle of putting mine on, and your mother was going to ask if she could have a disposable one upon entrance."

"And they yelled at you guys for that? That's horrible! I tell you, it wasn't that long ago that people feared communism. Now it's a fashion statement."

"You're not kidding. Now, if that was your mother and I screaming and making a scene, we would have gotten thrown out of the store for disorderly conduct. But what do we know? Nobody has any respect anymore. I understand that the individual was doing their job, but there was no need to yell at us like that."

"I agree. It's some strange times we're living in. We're living through history if you think about it."

"Yeah, you got that right, for sure. But, yeah, there hasn't been much going on here. We miss you. We wish you were here, but understand why you're not."

"Well, I miss you guys also. Don't worry. Someday we can watch *Benny Hill*. That way, we can rile Mom up again!"

His mother rolled her eyes at that comment as she smiled. Roman's father laughed and said, "Yeah, you know she *loves* that show. Do you still have that *Benny Hill* collection on DVD that we gave you years ago?"

"Oh, you know it! But seriously, I thought of having you guys down again for a visit. I know you were here for Christmas before the pandemic hit, but I would love for you guys to come to Pennsylvania again if you want."

"That would be great! And once some restrictions are lifted, it will probably be easier for you to come up here for a visit."

"I would love that! I haven't been up there since I moved out in 2019. I'm not going to lie; I'm a little homesick. Mainly, I wanted to see you two, Craig and his family, and Grandma. On a random note, I'm thinking of going duck hunting before the season wraps up. I always cherish those times you took me out hunting as a kid, Dad. And I thank you for everything you and Mom did for me."

"It was our pleasure. And who knows, we can go hunting on your property together when we visit, if it's during the season. You know, your mother and I are proud of the two boys that we raised. We love you and Craig both."

"Well, I love you too, Dad. So how are you doing, Mom?"

"I'm doing great, Roman."

It gave Roman a warm feeling that his parents were excited and happy talking to him. He always had a good relationship with his parents.

"That's good. How's Grandma doing? I know things weren't going great the last time we spoke."

"Yeah, her dementia diagnosis is new, as you know. Unfortunately, it's only going to be a matter of time before we'll have to put her somewhere. At this point, I don't think having her travel would be wise."

"I understand. I'll have to reach out to her soon. As I mentioned to Dad, I wanted to have you both down for a visit, maybe for the Fourth of July, if things are open for everyone by then. You can't beat having fireworks in your backyard. And besides, in the communist Commonwealth of Taxachusetts, you can't even celebrate the nation's birth with fireworks. And yet, that's where the American Revolution started!"

Roman's mother laughed and said, "Well, you're not wrong about that. How soon people forget about their freedoms. They forget about all the people that served this country and sacrificed their lives to keep it free."

"You got that right. Dad served in Vietnam and Craig in Afghanistan. But anyway, we'll figure out a time for when you guys can come and visit. Dad texted me a few days ago and said you wanted to have a *Benny Hill* marathon with us."

"Oh, *that* Benny Hill… he's so raunchy! And all those women he has on his show. It's a man's kind of show."

Roman saw his father laughing on FaceTime. Roman said, "I figured I'd rile you up about that. But seriously, I'd love to have you all down for a visit. You can stay here if you want."

"We'll take you up on that offer," his mother replied. "Could Craig and his family come along too if we show up? You wouldn't mind if they came along, would you?"

"Are you kidding me? I hope they *do* come. Let him know if you see him before I get a chance to talk to him. We could all make this a family vacation for you guys. There's plenty of room for everyone to stay at my place. There's no need to book a hotel or anything like that. Craig's wife and kids would love to come down and do something different if they're available. And I'd like to get back up and see you on the Cape. I'm not going to lie; there are days I miss that pleasant ocean breeze. And you can't beat that fresh seafood either."

"You know, expensive as it is here, there is a charm about living on Cape Cod," his father said. "There will always be pros and cons to wherever you live. The Cape is far from perfect, but it's home for us. Kind of like Pennsylvania has become home for you."

"I couldn't agree with you more. And thank you for being understanding of… you know… me living farther away. I hope you guys aren't mad at me for moving far away."

"Roman, we would never hold that against you," his mother said. "When Briana died, we knew that tore you up inside. You had to do what was right for you. And your father and I know you didn't make a rash decision by moving. You took time to think it through. Besides, you're thirty-four now. We can't make you live somewhere you don't want to. You're a big boy. But you will always be our boy. Both you and Craig are our sons, and we love you to pieces."

"Thanks for being supportive, Mom. Sometimes I feel guilty that I left my family behind. But you're right. I had to do what I had to do. I will always be there for you guys."

"There's no need to feel guilty or ashamed, my son. And we will always be there for you, too," his father said.

"Thank you both. I'll keep this upcoming trip in mind. I hope you and Dad have a great day, and I'll talk to you later."

"You take care, Roman. We love you," his mother said.

"I love you, son," his father said.

"I love you guys, too. Take care," Roman said and then disconnected from the FaceTime session.

He felt satisfied after he was done talking to them. Speaking to his parents allowed him to reconnect with their warm relationship. He cherished that moment he had talked to them. And yet, part of him felt sad. Part of him wished he was still with Briana and that he could have added to the Anderson family. But he didn't. That's a regret he was stuck with.

He was longing for a purpose. A purpose that had been missing from his life; he was in the process of finding it. This restored his confidence. The idea of kicking around opening his own business was a big motivation for Roman. Or even something as simple as seeing the Kojić family later in the evening. Or the thought of having his family visit him at some point was exciting. Although it was a relatively new concept, he even wanted to try to make God a priority in his life somehow.

There was no telling if Roman would have what it would take to start his own business or if he knew what having a closer connection with God would be like. He had no idea where life was going to take him this year or if any of these things were obtainable or not. But he knew one thing. He was tired of the past defining him. Most of all, he was tired of getting into his head about it. And this would be a perfect way to end the day by seeing his best friends in the evening, the Kojić family. He was the kind of person who didn't make friends with many people. He didn't have many friends since he was new to the area. However, he was very close to the friends he did have.

Miroslav and Theresa introduced him to Christianity in greater detail, which is why the relationship aspect with God was a reasonably new concept to Roman. He considered himself an agnostic when he first met them at church. Even though that was the case then, he was interested in learning more and approached their religion with an open heart. He was mainly drawn to them because of their kindness to him. They made him feel at home shortly after moving to Neelyton. He knew true friends like that couldn't be found around the corner.

CHAPTER 3

Roman was looking to pass the time by until he saw the Kojić family. He wanted to draw something. He was very accomplished at drawing with the use of a charcoal pencil. He loved drawing many things, whether random objects, scenes in nature, or even other people. Mostly he loved to draw cartoons, primarily classic Looney Tunes and old-school Disney characters. He framed what he considered his best drawings from over the years in his house. He did have a few sketches of Briana that he drew of her from back in the day. He had a couple of her best ones that he drew of her in his bedroom, which he also had framed. He had other pictures of cartoon characters, his family, or nature scenes hanging on the walls throughout his house. The rest of them he kept in a safe place in his closet so the drawings wouldn't get smudged or damaged.

"You know, even if I go through with opening my own business, that could take a while. Until then, I could sell some drawings online. It would at least give me something to do in the short term," Roman thought. *"Maybe to pass the time by before I see the Kojićs, I can draw something, or at the very least start on it."*

After thinking it over, Roman went to his office room, which was next to his bedroom. He sat at the desk with a blank piece of paper, staring at it.

"What the heck can I draw?" he thought as he found his mind blank for the moment.

He stared at the blank piece of paper for a few more minutes while tending to his spit bottle.

"I think I'll draw a picture of Godzilla fighting King Ghidorah. That's something I haven't attempted before. I remember watching those movies growing up," Roman thought.

He then pulled up a picture on his laptop that he Google searched and used for his drawing. Roman always took his time when it came to drawings. He was very meticulous when it came to fine details. He believed in taking the extra time to make the picture look right rather than rushing through drawing a photo. That way, it wouldn't look sloppy and unrealistic. Roman began drawing at a very young age and had a natural talent. His parents and older brother Craig were always amazed at what he could draw and how well he did it. During his early years of drawing, he would give his artwork to his family or friends so they could have them as gifts.

Some time had passed, and it was midafternoon. He had decided to finish his tobacco and give drawing a break. He had a way to go to finish his drawing, but he wasn't in a rush to get it finished. He paused for a minute staring at the picture. So far, he was satisfied with it, but he felt something inside him that prompted him to look out his window.

He looked out the window from his office room and saw his backyard. The backyard was very generous in size. The yard itself was clear from most trees. To the left, his garden was fenced in to protect it from the critters. Nothing was in the garden now since it was winter, but Roman knew it wouldn't be long before he would have to start tilling the ground to prepare it for planting seeds. He had about a half-acre-sized pond that ran on the opposite side, which went a little further back into his property to the right. It was where he would sit during the days he would duck hunt. He thought about all the ducks he had harvested so far from hunting over his pond. Beyond the pond and garden were where the woods started.

It was a great setup since trees surrounded the house, which made it private. And yet, there was enough open space for both a front and backyard, which means the garden and pond were spaced out. The remainder of the back of the property was completely wooded. Roman had success deer hunting on the back of his property. This coming fall, he would give bear hunting another chance. Last year, he bagged his first bear using a .338 Winchester Magnum. There were multiple bear sightings on his property from what his trail cameras had revealed to him.

He was feeling peaceful now, thinking of the features of the property. Even though he didn't know anyone before moving to Neelyton, nature was where he could always find peace. That was a big reason Roman enjoyed nature so much. He could be free from the rat race and the politics of everyday life.

Roman continued to look out his window. He not only admired what he saw, but he looked at nature in a different light than he had in years past. He saw God and felt His presence. The beauty of nature that God Himself created and the majesty of it.

He bowed his head, closed his eyes, and prayed aloud, "God, thank You for what You have given me. This property and this house that I live in. Thank You for my family and for allowing me to hang out with my friends this evening. Please bless our time together. Amen."

He paused in his chair and thought, *"Wait, did that come out of me? That was no accident. The power of prayer is real. Even though it was more praise than prayer, it still counts for something."*

His relationship with God in the past was pretty much nonexistent. Although he was never overtly hostile toward God, there was no relationship present either. Roman's perception in the past was to live a good life and everything would be fine. As he looked back on it, that wasn't necessarily an evil philosophy. However, he felt like something was missing from that exact philosophy. He didn't know exactly what it was until now. He was very excited to share his day with the Kojićs this evening.

"I best get ready for the evening," he remembered.

Roman decided to hop in the shower. He knew the evening could be late, so he figured he would take a shower now to get it out of the way. Nothing felt better to Roman's bones than having hot water hit his body on a cold winter day. It was a refreshing feeling. He got out of the shower and dried himself off. After that, he put some deodorant on and went to the bedroom. He decided to wear casual clothes. He threw on a pair of blue jeans and a blue plaid shirt.

"I'll take a sweatshirt with me if I feel cold. Speaking of sweatshirts, I need to bring along Miroslav's sweatshirt," he thought.

Roman got one of his favorite sweatshirts out of the closet. It was a Pink Floyd sweatshirt with *The Dark Side of the Moon* album pictured on the front. The last things Roman grabbed were Miroslav's sweatshirt and a flashlight. Roman very rarely drove to the Kojić house since they were neighbors. But he knew it would be dark when he left their house. Bringing a flashlight along would be wise since he would be walking home in the dark.

He was ready to go. There was no need to bring any kind of games along. The Kojićs had a collection of them since they had two children. So off Roman went. He was smiling. Roman grabbed his key from the key hanger and opened the front door to exit. He took the key and locked the front door as he went outside. There was a light breeze in the air. There was also a mix of sun and clouds. The sun was lower in the sky since it was later in the day. But the sun made beautiful colors in the sky. Sunsets were one of Roman's favorite things. Briana and Roman would love to watch the sunsets on the beach back on Cape Cod. Seeing the sun reminded him of that, although it didn't make him feel sad. Instead, it brought a warm and fuzzy feeling inside of him.

"I miss her, but I must remember our good times together. I can't see being sad all the time anymore. I don't think it's what she would have wanted," Roman thought.

He confidently made his way to the Kojić house while keeping that motivation in mind. He was excited because it was always a good time when he hung out with them. He appreciated the friendship he had with them. They were his first acquaintances when he moved to Neelyton. It was about a five-minute walk since neither homes weren't right next to the property line. As he walked, he enjoyed the gentle breeze in the air and listening to the songbirds. He was halfway there when something startled him. He stopped instantly when he heard something stirring in the brush. As he paused, he saw a deer leap out from the cover. His heart was beating a little fast due to the element of surprise. Roman could feel the hair on his neck tingle as if it were standing up. He took a closer look at the deer.

"Ah, a shed," said Roman. He could tell the deer had shed its antlers because he had caught a quick glimpse of the top of his head.

"I hope to see you this coming fall. Until then, away with yourself," he said to the deer.

The deer stared at Roman and retreated deeper into the woods. Where he had seen the deer was just inside the Kojić property. So, he knew he didn't have much further to go to get to their house.

After another couple of minutes passed, he made it to their home. He was still smiling.

"Best friends are something you can't find around the corner or pluck from the trees," he thought.

He rang the doorbell twice. He heard someone walking to the door, and then it opened. Miroslav greeted him.

"Hey there, Roman," Miroslav said as they shook hands.

"Zdravo! Kako si?" Roman asked.

Miroslav laughed, "Ah, I see what you did there. Dobro, a ti?"

"Well, you got me there," Roman replied with a smile.

Although he knew some phrases that Miroslav had taught him, Roman was not fluent in Serbian.

"Oh, I brought the sweatshirt you left at my place."

"Thank you for that, Roman. Come on in, my friend. We're happy to have you over."

"I appreciate you guys having me over," Roman said as he walked inside the house.

"It's our pleasure. Make yourself at home. Hey, kids, guess who's here!"

Miroslav made his way to the kitchen where his wife Theresa was. Roman heard the fast-moving footsteps of the Kojić children making their way out of the living room to the front door.

"Hey, look, it's Roman!" Sarah exclaimed.

"Hi there, Roman!" Jason said, who was equally excited to see him.

Both children walked over and hugged him. Roman welcomed both children with open arms.

"Hi, Sarah. Hi, Jason. Are you guys ready to have some fun tonight?"

"We sure are," Jason said with a big smile.

"It's always fun when you come over," said Sarah.

"Well, it's always great seeing you guys, too. I enjoy it a lot," said Roman.

Sarah and Jason returned to the living room, where they had been watching *The Lion King.* Roman took off his coat and hung it in the closet. Then he took off his boots and left them at the entrance. He made his way to the kitchen. Miroslav was helping Theresa, who was preparing the rest of the meal for dinner. She heard Roman making his way into the kitchen.

"Hi there, Roman. Glad you could join us for dinner," Theresa said.

"I appreciate you having me over. I enjoy spending time with you guys, or as you people in this part of the world say, 'yinz' or 'yunz,'" said Roman.

Theresa chuckled. "Well, how faah did you have to paak your caah to go to the baah for a Budweiser?" she asked, trying to imitate Roman's Boston accent.

Roman smiled. He liked that he could joke around and have a good time with his friends.

"Well, I guess we all have different accents here. I got my Boston accent, yours is from this area, and Miroslav's is from either New York or Ireland."

"It's Northern Ireland if you want to be technical," said Miroslav sarcastically.

"Even though Miroslav's first language is Serbian, sometimes his English is better than mine," Theresa said.

"Really?" asked Roman.

"Well, I'm sure since you have hung around us, you've probably noticed I drop 'to be.' Instead of saying, 'the dishes need to be washed,' I'll say, 'the dishes need warshed.' Or 'we were eating ice cream' sometimes comes out as 'we was eating ice cream.'"

"Well, I know some people think it means they're stupid when people talk like that. But to me, it's a different way of talking. With so many different cultures on this planet, you'll have that. I don't think it's anything to be ashamed of either."

"You're preaching to the choir," said Miroslav. "Sometimes, when people hear me talk, they automatically think I'm from Russia or a former Soviet spy, and I have to set the record straight."

"Not to change the subject but do you guys need any help with anything?"

"We should be good. Theresa took the homemade dinner rolls out of the oven as you came in. I was tending to the pot pie, and the kids had already set the table. I'd say we're ready to eat. What would you like to drink? Wait, don't tell me… sweet tea?"

"How did you know?"

"Eh, wild guess. If you want, have a seat, and dinner will be served," Miroslav said.

He turned his head toward the living room and called for Sarah and Jason to come to the dinner table. Roman took a seat.

"You know, I never really had close friends like this. Not even in high school or during my childhood. Besides Briana, my brother Craig was the only one I felt close to growing up, but that was it. I don't know where I'd be if it weren't for Miroslav and his family," Roman thought.

For years he longed for faithful friends and had finally found what he was looking for in the Kojićs. They were the people he could go to if he needed something. He had that same kind of relationship with his brother and parents, but he wanted to make a connection from outside his family, too, since he didn't live in New Seabury anymore. A true friend was something that eluded him once Briana passed away. He was never as famous as his brother Craig in grade school. Roman was much more reserved than his brother and wasn't the life of the party like Craig was. Eventually, Roman grew out of his shell, but he had already been out of high school when that happened.

The kids made their way to the table and sat down. Theresa put the dinner rolls and butter on the table while Miroslav got everyone their drinks. Roman, along with Miroslav, had sweet tea. Theresa had water, while Jason and Sarah both had blue Gatorades. Miroslav finally sat at the head of the table. Theresa sat to his left while Roman sat between Miroslav and the children on the other side.

"Let us pray," Miroslav said. They all bowed their heads and held hands while their eyes were closed. "Heavenly Father, we thank You for this evening we could spend with Roman. We thank You that You brought him into our lives and that we could be friends. Thank You for this meal You have given us. Amen."

"Amen," everyone else said and began digging into the food.

Roman loved ham pot pie. It was something that he didn't grow up eating or had even heard of until he moved to Neelyton. And he knew from his cooking experiences that you could never turn down a homemade dinner roll hot out of the oven.

"This meal never disappoints," said Roman. "You guys know the way to a bearded man's heart."

Theresa smiled and said, "We're glad you like it. You know, you're a pretty good cook yourself."

"I do what I can. People think it's so hard to cook. If you can read, you can read a recipe. That's the way I see it. And with all the videos posted on YouTube, chances are you don't even need to read. You can watch a video."

"My favorite thing you made for us was the beef brisket," said Miroslav. "It wasn't dry at all. It was good, even without barbecue sauce. That smoky flavor made it good."

"It's a labor of love," said Roman. "I was out there for over seventeen hours, but it was worth it."

"You were out there for that long?" asked Sarah.

"I sure was."

"Well, that sure ain't like making ramen noodles!"

"Yeah, it's something that you can't rush. As I said, it's a labor of love. The same with this ham pot pie," Roman said with a smile.

"Why do you have to cook it for so long?" Jason asked.

"Well, brisket is a tough cut of meat. It's part of the cow's chest. Anytime I smoke a brisket, I do my best to keep the temperature between two hundred twenty-five and two hundred fifty degrees. I prefer to keep it on the lower end at two hundred twenty-five if I can. If you smoke a brisket and your temperature is too high, you could dry it out, especially if you don't wrap it in foil. Not to mention brisket is an expensive cut of meat. With that said, you want to get it right."

"Oh, I see. It sure was terrific."

"Well, thank you. I appreciate that."

"Guess what, Roman? Jason and I get to spend tonight at our Aunt Janine's!" Sarah said with excitement.

"Is that so?"

"Yeah, Theresa and I were originally going to see our friends, the Campbells, but they had to cancel at the last minute. And since Jason and Sarah were already planning on going to Janine's, we figured we could hang out, just the three of us," said Miroslav.

"That sounds good to me."

Everyone continued to eat dinner. The wheels in Roman's head were turning.

"This will be the first time I'm meeting Janine," he thought. *"I've only ever seen a couple of pictures of her. She looks like a nice enough person, though."*

"Come to think of it, Roman, I don't think you've ever met my sister Janine, have you?" asked Theresa.

"Funny you ask me that. I was thinking the very same thing in my head. No, I don't believe I've met her yet," he replied.

"She has started visiting more and more now, which is good. I know we've had our differences in the past, especially with the pandemic. I

29

will say that I certainly wouldn't trade her. Are you close to your brother?"

"Yeah, we have a good relationship. He's two years older than me. We had our sibling spats when we were kids, but what siblings don't? I feel like Craig is someone who has my back. I can't imagine not having him in my life."

"That's a good thing," Miroslav commented. "As I tell my children, and anyone for that matter, hang on to them if you have a sibling or siblings. The same goes for all family members. One day, they may be gone, and you'll never see them again."

Roman could see the calm composure that Miroslav had. But he could also see the pain behind those words in Miroslav's eyes. Not to mention he could feel Miroslav's pain surrounding the dinner table. It is a kind of pain you want to hide from and never experience again because it crushes the bones in your body. The type of pain where quietness becomes uncomfortably loud. He knew his wife and children felt and heard it, but more so his wife because Miroslav didn't tell his kids everything due to their ages. No one said anything for a few moments.

As everyone knew, growing up for Miroslav in the former Yugoslavia presented its challenges during the 1990s. Roman was aware that he had lost his family during the events in the Balkans. However, he didn't know all the graphic details of what happened through Miroslav's eyes growing up. He was tempted to ask about his childhood at that moment, but he decided to let it go. Roman did not grow up in the former Yugoslavia, but he had heard of the awful things that had happened there, mainly through the news highlights when he was a child. But he knew that the information he had seen on television was only the tip of the iceberg. Seeing it on television was one thing, but it was another to live through those events. He could only imagine the horrors that Miroslav had experienced growing up. Even during small group Bible studies, Miroslav only occasionally touched on those events, and when he did, it was never in any great length or detail.

Roman was afraid to ask him about what happened, mainly because he didn't want to make him feel uncomfortable or force him to do something he wasn't ready to do. Plus, dinner was almost completed, and Janine would be by any minute to pick up Jason and Sarah for the evening. He knew he would need an evening with the two of them alone to talk about something personal like that without the children around.

Roman realized that his curiosity would have to wait for another day. That way, he figured Miroslav would have a safe environment to share. In a way, Roman was looking forward to having that more profound connection with Miroslav. Mainly because Roman felt vulnerable, too. The pieces from the death of Briana and their unborn child had not been entirely picked up either. Roman was willing to wait for a better day to discuss that uncomfortable topic.

"You got that right," Roman casually replied. "I think I hear a car pulling up."

"That must be Janine. I'll go get the door," Theresa said as she got up from the dinner table.

"Make sure you guys are good for your Aunt Janine," Miroslav said to Sarah and Jason. "Do you both have your overnight bags packed?"

"Yes," both Jason and Sarah replied.

"Good. I'll load them up in a few minutes."

Roman could hear that Theresa let Janine in. Both Jason and Sarah left the dinner table to greet their Aunt Janine with hugs. Afterward, the children went to their rooms to get what they needed for the overnight. Theresa and Janine made their way to Miroslav and Roman at the dinner table. This was the first time Roman had seen Janine in person. He saw her as stunningly beautiful. She had an hourglass figure with an athletic body type. She stood six feet tall, half a foot taller than her sister. Miroslav was also in good shape and the closest to Janine in height but still two inches shorter, while Roman was only an inch taller than Theresa. Like her sister, Janine had long red hair and freckles on her face. Janine had some makeup on, but not much. She was also wearing a Green Bay Packers face mask.

"Wow, she's drop-dead gorgeous," Roman thought. *"Even better looking in person than from the couple of pictures I've seen of her. Not that there was anything wrong with her in those pictures. But yeah, she's way out of my league. She's seven or eight feet tall, and I'm only five foot seven inches. I know women prefer that the man should be taller than they are. I'll probably never know or understand why that is. If I remember correctly, she's four or five years older, which would be another strike against me. Oh, well, maybe we can be friends someday. I'm honestly not looking to date anyway, and that's the truth. I'm not ready for that next level yet. Too bad about the Packers face mask. Oh, well, that's not a big deal."*

"I don't think you two have ever met in person. Janine, this is our neighbor and good friend Roman. Roman, this is Janine, my older sister."

"Hi there, Roman. It's nice meeting you finally," Janine said as she extended her hand for a handshake. "Theresa and Miroslav have mentioned you from time to time. Word has it you threw a killer fourth of July party last year."

"It's a pleasure meeting you too," Roman said as he stood up to introduce himself as they shook hands. He chuckled and said, "Well, I like throwing a party or getting everyone together every once in a while."

"That's a firm handshake he's got," Janine thought. *"Pretty rough around the edges with that beard if you ask me. I can tell he's a man's man. He'll probably only be interested in my looks like all the other men. Maybe we can be friends someday and leave it at that. At this point in my life, I don't want anything serious after some of the arrogant men I've been with. He pronounced party as 'paaty.' That's funny. I like that."*

"So, you're from Massachusetts, huh?" Janine asked. "I could tell by your accent."

"Yeah, I guess that's a dead giveaway since I live in Pennsylvania now," said Roman.

"So, how long have you been here now?"

"Oh, almost a year and a half, I'd say."

"How do you like living here so far?"

"I like it. I like it a lot. It's allowed me to start fresh. I needed that."

"Well, that's good. My sister and I have lived here in Neelyton our whole lives. However, I live in Orbisonia now."

"Do you like living in Pennsylvania?"

"Eh, it has its pros and cons. There are certain things I like and don't like about it. But I guess you'll have that no matter where you live. It was very nice meeting you, but it sounds like the kids are ready to go."

She turned her head toward where she could hear Sarah and Jason making their way down the stairs.

"It was great to meet you too, Janine. Maybe we'll meet again at some point."

"In a small town like this, I'd say more than likely we will."

She looked down and saw the kids standing next to her, with Sarah on one side and Jason on the other. Janine didn't have any children. She never wanted children. Children were too much of a hassle, in her opinion. The idea of changing diapers and staying up long nights while trying to put a screaming child back to bed had never appealed to Janine. However, she loved her niece and nephew dearly. But she also enjoyed the luxury of returning the kids to Miroslav and Theresa when the time came. Janine embraced being a strong and independent woman and not having something like children or a husband to hold her back from being a go-getter in life. She prided herself on being very goal-oriented.

She had saved enough money during her teen years and as a young adult to pay for her education. She enrolled in a truck driving school for a couple of reasons. She knew that being a commercial truck driver offered good pay and benefits. Janine would also have an opportunity to work alone most of the time compared to being stuck in a cubicle at an office listening to everyone else's gossip or bantering about things she couldn't care less about. Plus, she knew that she could indulge in her habit of smoking a lot more with this type of job. Usually, a pack of cigarettes would last her a couple of days. However, she could blow through an entire pack of cigarettes in under a day if stressed.

Being alone, away from people, was the perfect escape for her, especially with the pandemic in full swing. She was never a people person and preferred to keep most people at arm's length even before social distancing. As a child in school, she was teased a lot for not wanting to go hunting or take care of animals on a farm. She thought farm life was gross. For that, the kids would call her a "city slicker." As she got older, the name-calling became more explicit. Insults such as "libtard," "bitch," or "dyke" were commonly used. The other students knew it made Janine's blood boil. But they knew not to overdo it. The fact that Janine was tall and athletic put her at an advantage. By the time she had gotten to high school, Janine had already been involved in several fights. Some fights were self-defense, but Janine was the aggressor in other situations. For that, she earned herself a reputation as a fighter and someone that shouldn't be approached. And eventually, the teasing gradually faded. But as it faded, Janine would also fade into obscurity after graduating high school.

To make matters worse, she didn't receive much support at home from her mother and father. Janine's father had his ideas of how a woman should act or behave, contrary to how he saw Janine with how she carried herself. For that reason, the two would always inevitably butt heads. Since their parents were Christians, her father and mother both intended to raise their daughters, Janine and Theresa, in a Christian home. Theresa gladly embraced making God the center of the household, whereas Janine didn't. Her father saw her actions as living in rebellion. And he had little patience when it came to what he thought was nothing more than nagging questions. Janine would go to her father inquiring about more information regarding religion. The fewer answers she got from her father, the more she desired to turn to other things in the world. Janine always embraced that she was the black sheep of the Flaherty household. Consequently, her heart was not on the best terms with God.

Her relationship with her mother was mediocre at best. Janine felt like her mother would never side with her on anything, especially if Janine felt personally attacked by her father. To make matters worse, she felt like her sister Theresa could get away with anything growing up because she was a good Christian girl. Janine hated it when her mother would tell her that Theresa only had good intentions when she did something that bothered Janine. For this reason, Janine's anger was only furthered.

As she was thinking of all these thoughts in her head of her past, she felt one of the Kojić children tugging on her shirt. She realized she must have been zoned out for several seconds.

"Aunt Janine, ain't we going to go now?" Sarah asked.

"Why yes… of course. Do you both have your things ready, along with your face masks?" Janine asked.

"Uh-huh, we can't wait to spend the night with you, Aunt Janine," Jason said.

"Aw, well, I love having the both of you over. And you know Disney Plus and donuts are waiting for you both over there."

"All right, let's go!" Jason exclaimed.

"I'll help carry their things," said Miroslav. He walked over to his children and got down to eye level. "You both be good to your Aunt Janine, all right? I love you both."

"I love you too, Daddy," the kids said individually.

Each one gave their parents a hug and a kiss. Everyone exchanged their "goodbyes" before they left. As they were going, Jason and Sarah put on their face masks. Although Theresa and Miroslav *did not* wear masks, they knew Janine did since she was much more concerned about the virus than they were. They made it known that their children were to respect the rules of their Aunt Janine's house. Miroslav and Theresa prioritized the Kojić household to teach their children to love and respect others even when they don't do the same things. Without the act of love, they knew faith without deeds would be dead. That's something they wanted to bestow upon their children. Despite coming from different cultural backgrounds, they knew the repercussions of what it was like when unconditional love was not displayed to others.

CHAPTER 4

Janine and the Kojić children were headed to Orbisonia. It was not far from Neelyton, which made things convenient whenever Janine was to visit her sister and her family. Janine lived in a simple house in town in a residential neighborhood. It wasn't a big city either. Janine started to think about Roman while driving home. She wondered what he was like since Theresa and Miroslav brought Roman up in conversation from time to time.

"I wonder if he's one of those types of Christians," Janine thought. *"I'm not big into the whole Christianity thing. They act like such goody-two-shoes. All these outdated rules they follow. Men control women in the household – no sex before marriage. I mean, really? How will you get to know the person you love or even have a little fun with if you must wait for sex until after you get married? Who gives a shit if people have sex before marriage if they're not hurting anyone else?*

"And the judging... God, how I hate that. I remember Jane at youth group. She came across as the typical preacher's daughter. She appeared sweet and innocent on the outside, yet she was the biggest damned slut in Huntingdon County! And then she had the nerve to criticize me for smoking cigarettes. Hypocrites are what they are. I don't know... we'll see what this Roman character is like. Maybe he won't be as bad since he comes from Massachusetts. I mean, they were the first state to allow same-sex marriage, I think. So maybe he's a bit more cultured than these country bumpkins around here. He would look

better without all that facial hair and a clean haircut. Oh, well, maybe it's because it's wintertime."

"Aunt Janine?" Jason asked.

Janine reflexed in her seat because her train of thought was interrupted.

"Yes?" she responded.

"Why do we have to wear these masks?"

"Because it's to help stop the spread of the virus. It's the best we can do before the vaccine is on the market."

"Oh… Aunt Janine?"

"Yes?"

"Do you think face masks work?"

"I do. Statistics have shown that it has helped to slow the spread of COVID-19. And I think if we as people can help slow the spread to protect others, then that's in our best interest to do so. And to do it not only as the nation but as people worldwide."

"Well, Roman said that they didn't work."

After Jason's response, Janine could feel that what he said struck a nerve in her and thought, *"Oh, great, just great. My sister and brother-in-law see that the new guy has moved into the neighborhood, and they're already indoctrinating him with their propaganda. Don't get me wrong; I love my sister. I'm happy we're close and have a better relationship than before, but for goodness sake, stop trying to change people!"*

Janine looked in the rearview mirror where Jason and Sarah were sitting. As her blood simmered, she didn't want to turn to intimidation toward her nephew. Instead, she realized she could overpower her five-year-old nephew with her own set of logic. This would cause Jason's young mind to stumble, resulting in a victory for Janine. Underneath her face mask, she had a grin on her face thinking she had her nephew right where she wanted him.

"Oh yeah? Is that so? Now, what makes Roman the expert on this matter? What is he basing his facts on?"

"Because Roman said a face mask can't stop a virus if a pair of pants and underwear can't stop a fart!"

Sarah started to giggle. Sarah and Jason got along remarkably well and were close in age. She was only two years older than her brother.

Janine shook her head as she scoffed at Jason's response and thought, *"This guy sounds like the rest in the backwoods of Pennsylvania. Probably a Trump supporter, no doubt."*

"Well, that's a complete lie, and you shouldn't believe such nonsense."

"No, it's true, Aunt Janine!" Sarah exclaimed. "He even proved it to us!"

"Is that right?"

"Yeah, he did it right in front of us. Roman went up to Mommy and asked her to pull his finger, and when she did, he farted! And the clothes that he wore didn't stop it either."

"That is the most childish and ridiculous experiment I've *ever* heard in my life," Janine said, trying to sound serious. Deep down, she wanted to laugh because the idea of someone blowing a fart around her sister *did* sound amusing.

"Maybe once we get home, you could pull *my* finger and see for yourself if you don't believe us," said Jason.

"No, I'm good with that," Janine said, still trying not to laugh.

She always got a kick out of how inquisitive her niece and nephew were.

"Aunt Janine, do you like Roman?" Sarah asked.

"What do you mean?"

"Like do you *like-like* him?"

"How should I know? I only met the guy for the first time tonight."

"I think Aunt Janine has a crush on Roman," Sarah whispered to Jason and then nodded his head.

"Maybe they'll even get married someday," Jason whispered back to his sister.

Janine smacked her hand on her forehead. Even though Sarah and Jason whispered to each other, Janine could hear both kids' words.

Janine thought, *"What on earth did I get myself into tonight? They are good kids, and I love them dearly. But I'm glad I can send them home when I'm done!"*

Janine finally made it to her house with the kids. From there, they got settled in for the evening. Usually, she would let her niece and nephew stay up a little late, whether playing board games or watching TV. Despite being a strong and independent woman, Janine enjoyed her companionship with her family. She disagreed with what her sister and her family believed regarding Christianity, but she accepted it. She knew that's how they did things as a family. Janine was glad that she and her sister finally found a way to get along after years of a strained relationship. She wished her relationship with her parents were better. But she also knew that at least she had a family. She didn't have to endure the horrors of the wars in Yugoslavia like Miroslav did.

Meanwhile, back at the Kojić house, Theresa and Miroslav sat next to each other in their living room. Roman sat across from them. Things were quiet now that small children's running footsteps and chatter were at their aunt's house. Roman sat silent for a minute with his head down as his hands were fidgeting. Miroslav and Theresa saw that he looked a little nervous or had something important to share. He was trying to find the right words. They both waited for him to say something. Neither one of them wanted to push him. Roman finally found the words that he wanted to say.

"Guys… I wanted to share something with you," Roman said as he finally raised his head to look at them.

"What's that?" Miroslav asked.

"Well, I have done much thinking lately. I appreciate what you both have done for me. The Bible study you both lead at the small group at church has been so good. All of you are like my family away from home… I really can't tell you both how much that means to me. The

40

way you two live out the faith and don't just sit around talking about it is what I like. What you both have is very real, and I see that. It's helped me understand our faith versus what the world says. Because of that, it's allowed me to grow within myself and know who Christ is. I want to tell you that I want to accept Jesus Christ as my Savior and Lord."

Theresa and Miroslav look at each other with excitement at first. Then they look at Roman.

"Really? That is so wonderful!" Theresa exclaimed with a big smile. "We are so happy that you moved down here to Pennsylvania. And right next door to us, for that matter. We love you, Roman, and our children do, too."

"I greatly appreciate each of your friendships. The more I think about it, the more I think moving down here wasn't an accident. I think God used this move so I could come to know Him."

"Well, we're happy to know that you've chosen to make this decision in your life and that you're doing it because *you* want to. I can tell that you're not doing it out of pressure or feeling strong-armed into it. This is worth celebrating, for sure. So, tell me, what brought you to this point?" Miroslav asked.

Roman thought for a few seconds about Miroslav's question. He didn't want to blurt out any random answer. Not to mention Miroslav was his accountability partner, so he knew he should tell him the truth. Even telling him a white lie was something Roman wanted to avoid at all costs because he didn't want to damage their friendship. He knew Miroslav well enough that trying to pull the wool over his eyes didn't work on him. He was too bright for such games.

"I would say that what I was doing before didn't work, which was trying to do things on my own, especially coping with the loss of Briana and our unborn child. After a while, I knew that this couldn't be it. There must be something better than what's been dumped in my lap. I'm tired of shouldering all that. I'm tired of carrying those burdens and hurts around. Nothing I did on my own changed it either, especially the gambling. You both know I had a gambling addiction.

But I haven't done it now in going on four years. June 30th, 2017, will be four years of no gambling. Now, do I wish I could buy a ticket and another and another occasionally? Of course. I have those days from time to time. But I know it will lead to failure and excessive debt again, as I had in the past. Our small group, especially you two, has been my biggest support group. Having Miroslav as my mentor has been a great help to me. And both of you taught me who Christ is versus what the world *says* He is. That's the kind of Savior I want to accept, and I'm all in."

"That's awesome, and I have to say you have quite a testimony. Overcoming addiction is not an easy thing. I don't know how things were for you growing up on Cape Cod, but so many people are addicted to heroin and opioid-type drugs in this part of the world. It's been a pandemic long before the COVID-19 pandemic was even a thing. True, you didn't do hard drugs, but addiction is addiction, regardless. I am glad you chose me as a mentor and an accountability partner. I've benefitted from it also. There's nothing like, as you call it in your language, bromance?"

"That's right," Roman said as they laughed at that.

"I don't know if I ever asked, and maybe it's none of my business, but how much debt did you have because of gambling?" asked Theresa.

"Well, I racked up a little over forty grand in debt."

"Wow!" Theresa exclaimed as her jaw dropped. *"Really?"*

"Briana was the only one who knew about it. I eventually told my brother about it, but my folks don't know a thing about it. I was honestly surprised that she never spilled the beans to anyone. If she did, I never had anyone approach me about it. But I paid for it with her anger. Unfortunately, we all suffered from it because of my lack of responsibility in the end. She was an outstanding woman and didn't deserve to be put through that. I know what's done is done, and I can't change the past, but sometimes I can't help but think about it."

"It's hard not to blame yourself for something you did," Miroslav said, "but I know from my own experiences that if we continue to condemn ourselves, that gives Satan a foothold in our life. That's exactly what he wants to do to people, especially those who choose to follow Jesus. The Devil wants to go after those people because walking with Jesus goes against everything the Devil wants for us. All he wants for us is to fail in life. So that's something to keep in mind since you've professed Christ as your Savior and Lord. Satan will be after you extra now. You're at the top of his list."

"I'm sure he will be, whether to tempt me to gamble again or anything I shouldn't be doing. Honestly, I'd like to quit using spit tobacco."

"How long have you been doing that?" Theresa asked.

"Oh... uh, let's see... I'd say pretty much not long after I quit gambling. Go from one addiction to another addiction. It's a way to ease my nerves, especially after all that happened. Now it's merely a bad habit. I like to smoke a cigar here and there and have an adult beverage. But honestly, I could completely stop either of those things and be fine. Smokeless tobacco, though, is a whole different animal. I hope you can still be my friends even though I do it. I am going to do my best to stop, though."

"Roman, unless you eat our children or something, we will *always* be your friends. We will always be here for you. We pray that God will show you how to kick this habit."

"Thank you, Theresa. So, I had an idea. I was thinking I'd like to be baptized at some point. I thought of having some people over at my house and getting baptized in my pond. When the weather is warmer, of course. I want to show people that what I believe is real. I'm not doing it to say I'm a church member or to look good. I want to do this because I want to proclaim that Jesus is the Son of the living God, and He is the One who saves us. I wanted to ask you, Miroslav, would dunk me in the water?"

"Why, that would be an honor. I will do that for you. Let us know when you would like to have your baptism, and we'll be there," said Miroslav.

"Absolutely. I think I will invite my family along if they can attend. My parents had only seen my house once after it was finished. Craig and his family haven't seen it, however. Maybe they could take a little vacation if they decide to come. Then they could meet you guys, too."

"We would be happy to meet them," said Theresa. "They sound like really nice people from what you've said about them."

"Yeah, they sure are awesome. Man, my brother and I used to fight like Hell when we were kids," Roman chuckled. "But I'll tell you what, eventually, we got older and more mature. I wouldn't trade him for anybody, and that's the truth. I wouldn't trade my folks, either. My mother is a sweetheart. She kind of reminds me of Sally Field from *Forrest Gump*. She's a very gentle person. My Dad is a great man too. He's also mellowed out a lot as he's gotten older."

"That's good to hear. It sounds like your family is close to each other. You may have heard me bring up my sister Janine from time to time, but we didn't always have the best relationship, especially growing up."

"Oh?"

"Yeah, some of it was her doing, but some was mine. I don't think either one of us was innocent. You didn't grow up in a Christian home, Roman, but Janine and I did. Our parents are super strict when it comes to the Bible and attending church on Sundays. This, in turn, made home life rigid as well. I think that's where there was pushback with Janine, whereas I went along with it because I wanted to do what our parents told us to do.

"Janine was always a strong and independent woman and did things her way, which isn't necessarily bad. Part of it, I think, was that she wanted to see how far she could take things or how far she could push the envelope so that she could have her way. She wanted to be in control, especially since she was the older sibling in the house. Sometimes her selfishness got her in trouble, so she looked at me as the favorite. But I think other times, she had legit questions about the Bible that my parents couldn't answer. And they would get upset when they couldn't answer her persistent questions, particularly Dad. And those two butted heads constantly.

"Looking back on it now, I can see why Janine felt pushed away from the faith. She had honest questions and sought answers with an open heart, whereas Dad thought she was annoying or stubborn or being a nag. Because I went along with things at home, that caused much tension between us. As I got older, I had to sit down and reevaluate things. Was I walking with God because I wanted to? Or was it because my parents told me to? That's where I had to grow in my spiritual walk. Not only following the Lord to do it but knowing exactly *why* I'm doing it, if that makes sense. I had to make it *my* relationship with the Trinity instead of someone else's."

"Wow, that's an interesting story," Roman commented. "I knew that you were born into the faith, but I didn't know the juicy details of the matter either. So how did you and your sister make peace?"

"It took a while, that's for sure. Even in our younger adult years, we didn't talk much. She'd come by occasionally on holidays and stuff like that, but that was it. She had a boyfriend for a while out in McKeesport that she lived with for a bit. Once that went awry, she slowly came back into my life. I knew she was at rock bottom at that point. I don't know all the details of what happened. She *did* tell me some things about what happened, however. But, since it's not my story to tell, I don't want to overstep. Things didn't end well for George and my sister. That's when we started talking more.

"Finally, over time, we buried the hatchet. After a long face-to-face conversation, we decided to put our differences aside and start fresh. Even though she identifies as an agnostic, I still love her. I will *always* love my sister and be there for her as much as possible. And it's great we have that understanding with each other now. Janine is a great person, even though she can be rough around the edges. But I think she needed someone who loved her and accepted her for who she was. I told myself years ago that I would do a better job loving people instead of passing judgment. I can still choose to love someone and not love what they do. And if Christ chose to save me and everyone else from their sins, I owe Him to extend that kind of love to everyone else. That's the way I see it."

There was a pause in the conversation. Roman felt peaceful now, and he could also tell the Kojićs did. Deep discussions like that are what

Roman liked with people he could have a deeper connection with. Being open and honest and not being afraid to share struggles was encouraging for Roman to hear. Roman had a notion before that somehow cradle Christians were perfect or without sin or hardships. He could see that people are people no matter what environment a person is raised in. And life happens to everyone, no matter what walk of life they come from.

"That's awesome you shared that. Thank you for doing that," said Roman. "I always thought people born into Christian homes had it together."

"It's a pretty common misconception," Theresa said. "I've discovered that a relationship with the Trinity isn't given; it's chosen no matter what kind of home a person grows up in."

"That's true." Roman looked at the clock in the living room. It was after nine o'clock. "Well, I probably should get going since it's getting late. But listen, thank you so much for having me over. Supper was awesome, as always, and I enjoyed the conversations tonight. I love you guys."

"Hey, man, we love you, too," Miroslav said. "We are so proud of you. If you need anything, we'll always be here for you."

"Same for you guys. I appreciate the hospitality. Say, now that the kids are gone, and you two have the house to yourself, you can… you know…" Roman said with a sly look on his face.

"Yes… I guess that's true," Miroslav said, smiling at Theresa, running his hand gently through her hair.

"Well, you talked me into it," Theresa said, smiling back at Miroslav.

"*I knew it!* All right, I'll leave you two love birds alone. For the next get-together, I'll cook at my place and have you all over," said Roman.

"That sounds good to us," said Miroslav. "See you in church tomorrow?"

"Sounds like a plan to me."

The three of them exchanged their goodbyes and hugs. Roman walked over to the closet to get his coat and boots. As he walked outside, he turned on his flashlight so he could find his way home in the dark. It was a cold and somewhat damp night with variable clouds and a light breeze. He returned to his place and settled in for the evening. As he lay in bed, he couldn't help but bask in the glow of the night that he had with his two best friends. He loved them for what genuine people they were.

"I know I've thought it before, but a true friend is something hard to come by, especially in this day and age," Roman thought.

He turned off the lights and went to bed. Before he fell asleep, he thought that maybe somehow, this would be his year. The year that things would start to look up for him. A year of positive change with a few surprises along the way. Surprises were always to be expected. Although life can throw curveballs, Roman had a feeling he was going to succeed regardless of whatever situation he found himself in. And with his new relationship with Jesus, Roman could get through anything if he put Him into his spiritual playbook.

CHAPTER 5

Winter had finally passed over. The cold and damp cloudy days eventually turned into warm spring sunshine. It was the middle of May. Roman found himself in the woods on his property before sunrise on a Friday morning. It was turkey season. He had the day planned accordingly. He would turkey hunt until about mid-to-late morning, depending on how his hunt went. After that, he would break ground with his tiller in the garden. It was about time to plant seeds. The last frost had come and gone. After tilling the garden, he would cook for the Kojićs. Steaks and marinated chicken were on the menu for tonight. But until then, it was game on in the woods.

It was quiet and still dark. The only thing that lit up the forest was the full moon shining brightly. That allowed Roman to see more than usual. He had all his equipment with him in his box blind – his backpack with hunting equipment that he needed and a nice cup of coffee in his thermos. He had strategically placed his turkey decoys in the food plot at around twenty-five yards away. He had two hens and a jake. As he sat there, he was startled a little bit. He heard the passing by of flapping wings that had gone right by his blind. He listened to what it was. It landed on the branch high up on a tree several yards in front of him. It was a great-horned owl. It started hooting, which was loud since the owl was close by. It didn't see Roman in his camouflaged box blind. He sat there in the dark, admiring the owl.

"These are the moments that I enjoy," Roman thought. *"There are*

days that I come up empty-handed when I go hunting. When you see something like this, I think taking the time to appreciate the little things in life are important. Take this, for instance. I'm sitting in nature, watching this big owl close to me. People nowadays seem to take so much for granted. When something like a tornado happens, people are all up in arms and blame God for everything. And yet, there's so much good in this world, and nobody wants to thank God for it. What a shame... what a shame."

The owl stopped hooting. It didn't hoot for a couple of minutes as it sat motionless on the branch. Then, it turned its head a couple of times. Roman assumed it was probably looking for a meal. It stood still and motionless for a couple of minutes again. Roman didn't know that the owl had locked its eyes on its target. Quickly, the owl flew down to the ground, pounced on its prey, and was gone in a flash.

"Wow, now that was cool. That's the kind of stuff you see on National Geographic. It sounded like he scooped up a mouse. Well, owls need to eat too. Speaking of eating..."

After Roman thought of eating, he unwrapped a granola bar and ate it. He then washed it down with a couple of sips of coffee. He looked at his phone to check the time. Another twenty minutes would be legal shooting hours.

Then the time came to hunt. This is what Roman had been waiting for. He used his diaphragm call to imitate a hen. He was skilled at using game calls since he practiced with them. After calling a couple of times, he waited. He knew you weren't supposed to over-call, as that wasn't a good technique for hunting. To Roman's surprise, he heard a response. He listened to a turkey gobble in the far-off distance.

"Now that was quick," he thought. *"Well, I guess we'll see what happens."*

He used his call again and got another immediate response. At about fifty yards, he saw him. The gobbler emerged from behind a giant maple tree, strutting his stuff. Roman remembered the time growing up when his father took him out in the woods as a teenager to go turkey hunting.

That was the day he shot his first turkey. He thought of that warm memory he and his father shared on that day.

Roman called to the turkey again, but this time not as loudly as he previously did. He wanted to give the turkey some time to walk in and discover the decoys he had put out. It saw them. It gobbled at Roman's call. He was excited to see what was going on but stayed perfectly calm. Over the years, he knew not to get too excited. The consequences of shaky hands could send a shot sailing way off target. He called again, and the turkey responded with another gobble. It was now in the ideal shooting range for Roman. The turkey was still strutting but came to a standstill. It stood there looking in Roman's direction. He knew this was the moment of truth. Roman needed to shoulder his shotgun quickly, or a potential Thanksgiving Day meal could disappear. He promptly lifted his Browning 10-gauge shotgun to his shoulder. The turkey stopped strutting immediately and extended its head to see the sudden movement. It didn't know Roman had that big bird right where he wanted him. Roman wanted the turkey to extend its head and neck so he could get a clean shot without damaging breast meat. He placed the sight bead on the bird's head and pulled the trigger. The shot rang out through the forest. The bird moved back about a couple of inches due to the impact of the shot pattern. Even though Roman was in better physical shape when he was younger, he still was solid and built big with broad shoulders. He could easily handle the recoil of a 10-gauge shotgun. He used that gun a lot for turkey hunting and hunting waterfowl over decoys at his pond.

The bird was done and didn't move after the shot. Roman knew it was a well-placed shot and a clean kill. He felt excitement now that he had got the bird. He had a big smile as he took another sip of his coffee. Minutes later, he got out of his blind and urinated beside a tree. He then made his way to the turkey.

"That's a pretty big one," he said. "I bet anything it's over twenty pounds. That will make for a great Thanksgiving Day feast."

He filled out his turkey tag and attached it to the bird's leg. Now it was time to collect everything and go home. He eventually made his way out of the woods. Now he had his work carved out for him. He had to clean his gun, pluck the feathers and remove the innards of his turkey. That way, it would be ready for the freezer. Roman decided first to put away his hunting equipment in the basement. He had to go down there anyway to get the items he needed to clean his shotgun. He also grabbed his scale sitting in the cellar to weigh the turkey. He made his way outside to the deck. He had cleaning supplies for his weapon, which he set on the table. Then he hung the scale on a sturdy branch. It was a sturdy fish scale, so it could easily handle a turkey. Roman took a small piece of rope so he could use it to tie the turkey's feet together. From there, he hung the turkey on the hook to be weighed.

"About twenty-three pounds," he said. "Yeah, this will be good eating. Well, time to go to work now."

He sat on his chair that was on the deck and cleaned his gun first. After he cleaned his gun, he put it back in the gun safe and got what he needed to clean up his bird. He got his big cooler and grabbed his propane burner with the fry pot out of his shed. He filled the pot with water from the spigot and lit the burner to heat the water. Roman was about making things as simple as possible. He knew that plucking a turkey was no small job. He took down the fish scale and hung a meat hook in its place to hang his turkey on it.

While waiting for the pot of water to heat up, he cleaned up the turkey. He did little things like removing the flight feathers, secondary feathers, the beard, and the fan. He then placed the turkey in his cooler. He noticed his big pot of water was close to the boiling point. He went inside and grabbed a homemade donut and a glass of milk while waiting for the water to reach the boiling point. He enjoyed the peacefulness of the mid-morning sunshine as he sat outside and ate his donut. He could tell the cool crisp morning would give way to a mild spring afternoon. As he finished his snack and drink, he noticed it was time. He put on a pair of oven mitts and took the boiling pot of water with him. He dumped it inside the cooler and closed the lid. He rocked the cooler back in forth in different directions. That way, the water could coat the entire turkey evenly. After a minute of rocking the cooler around, he took the turkey out and hung it back on the hook.

He could easily pluck the bird and make quick work out of it. He then got another cooler out of the shed and filled it with ice and water. He placed the bird inside the ice bath for about a half-hour. During that waiting period, Roman could clean up the area and get the rest of the things needed to finish the job. He also took that opportunity to pop another couple of tobacco pouches in his mouth. Once the time was up, he took the bird out of the ice bath and hung it back on the hook again so it could drain the excess. Then he placed the turkey on the cutting board on the table. He cut its head and legs off in a chopping motion. After that, he removed the bird's innards and discarded them in the trash bag where he had put the feathers.

"I can't believe this bothers some people," Roman thought. *"I mean, where do they think food comes from?"*

He was done at this point. After rinsing it out, he vacuum-sealed the bird and placed it in the freezer. He finished cleaning up the area and put things away. It was only about nine o'clock. He felt sleepy since he had gotten up early for the hunt. He wished he could nap, but he knew that he had more work cut out for him. He had to till his garden to plant seeds. The weather called for sunshine for today and Saturday. It was ideal for what he needed to do. He could plant all his seeds tomorrow after the tilling was done. Rain was in the forecast for Sunday. This would work in his favor after the seeds were planted. He got up from his chair and decided to go to work.

After his work was finished in the garden, he decided it would be best to take a shower. He had plenty of time before his company showed up. He didn't have to do too much preparation for dinner either. All he had to do was fire up the grill and chop the potatoes so he could roast them in the oven. He got done with his shower and sat on the couch in his living room. He took the opportunity to enjoy his smokeless tobacco while he had some downtime. His phone started to ring. Roman looked to see who it was. It was Miroslav.

"Hello," Roman answered the phone.

"Hey there, Roman, how are you doing?" asked Miroslav.

"I'm doing good, my friend. I'm relaxing for the moment. What's going on with you?"

"Well, as you know, our kids will stay at their grandparents for the evening. But we wanted to run this by you first to ensure it's okay. Theresa's sister wanted to know if it was okay if she tagged along tonight. I ask because I didn't know if you had enough food for someone else last minute."

Roman paused and thought, *"Janine wants to come and hang out? Now that's interesting. I don't even really know her. Eh, what the hell... I'm always up for meeting someone new."*

"Sure, that's fine with me. I didn't know she wanted to hang out with me at my place. I hope she knows that I'm not looking for any romance. I don't want this to be awkward, that's all."

"Yeah, she knows. I don't think she's looking for romance, either. Honestly, I think she's looking for something different to do for the evening. So, with that said, there won't be any pressure there."

"That's true. All right, that sounds like a plan. I have extra food anyway. I like to make extra, so I'm not cooking every day."

"I meant to tell you she *does* smoke cigarettes. If you don't want her smoking on your property, that's your call."

"No, that's fine. I smoke cigars every once and a while, as you know. If she goes outside, I'm good with it. Besides, I grew up around it. Both my parents smoke."

"All right, I'll let her know. Are you still planning on having dinner around five to six o'clock?"

"Yeah, give or take within that time frame. You're all welcome to come over earlier if you want."

"Okay, we got the cake made, too. We'll bring that over as well."

"Sounds good. We'll see you all in a bit."

"All right, take care."

"You too, bye."

Roman had pulled out an extra steak from the freezer. He did it so he could have steak and eggs for breakfast tomorrow. But he decided to make it for Janine.

Roman had never been much of a lady's man. But then again, he didn't have to be. He knew Briana from elementary school. They both decided to start dating when they got to high school. He always had that love in his life. Their love was true to each other. Neither one ever thought about straying from the other. They took their commitment very seriously, even though they never married.

After she had died, Roman didn't date too much. Sure, he went out on a few dates here and there, but nothing ever stuck. He dated Rhonda for a bit, only for it to become a total disaster. It was never the same after Briana died as far as the dating scene went. He was comfortable being single. He knew that if he were to meet another woman, she would have some large shoes to fill. That's why he didn't mind if Janine came over. He wasn't intimidated by her natural beauty. He knew that physical beauty would only go so far with him. It was the woman's heart he was more interested in. Roman knew that physical beauty fades over time with age, but true love doesn't. He saw the love that his parents had for each other. That tender and gentle love that he knew was real between his mother and father. He refused to settle for anything less if he were to enter the dating world again.

It was time to prepare the meal. Roman started chopping the potatoes and seasoning them. He also seasoned the asparagus. Next came the steaks. He seasoned each steak as well. Now it was time to fire up the grill. He dumped some charcoal in the chimney starter. He knew charcoal takes a while to get going, so getting a head start was his plan. He got the potatoes in the oven first because he knew those would take longer to cook than the asparagus. In between roasting the potatoes and asparagus in the oven, Roman would tend to the grilling. He thought of something. If Janine ate steak, he didn't know how she wanted it cooked. So, he texted Miroslav to see if he could get the information from either him or Theresa. Several minutes went by as Roman threw the marinated chicken breasts on the grill.

He received a text from Miroslav saying, *"She prefers her steak cooked medium."*

He kept that in mind as he continued cooking the chicken.

He texted Miroslav, *"I may be busy cooking. The front door will be open for you guys. No need to knock. Come on in."*

He sat down for a few minutes on a chair. He was outside on the deck where his grill was. He watched the grill while drinking a Pabst Blue Ribbon. He relished that moment of everything he had gotten accomplished. His morning hunting trip and then tilling the garden. Now it was time to have fun tonight.

Time passed by as he was cooking the chicken on the grill. When the chicken was finally done cooking, he pulled it off the grill so it could rest while it was covered on an aluminum tray. Now it was time for the steaks. But before he put the steaks on, he heard two cars making their way up to his driveway. He knew that company was here. He made his way to the kitchen to check on the potatoes. They still needed a little more time. He got to the door, and everyone was there.

"Hey, everyone," Roman said.

"Hey, my man," Miroslav said as he and Roman exchanged a hug.

"Hi, Roman," said Theresa.

"Hi, how are you?"

"I'm good. You remember my sister Janine, right?"

"I sure do. It's nice to see you again," he said as he extended his hand to shake hers.

Roman laughed a little inside, seeing Theresa and Janine standing beside one another. Janine had a lower-cut t-shirt with a pair of Daisy Duke shorts and country boots. She also had her Packers face mask on again. Roman noticed that Janine had a belly button piercing. He also noticed she had a couple of detailed tattoos on her body. Her right leg had a garter tattoo with a bow on it. At the center of the bow was a flower. There were also smaller flowers that periodically highlighted the edges of the tattoo. Her other tattoo was quite elaborate. He didn't know exactly what it was while looking at it. To Roman, the necklace tattoo appeared to be some design of a royal necklace that he thought looked elegant. It was a sizeable Aztec-style necklace wrapped around her neck with smaller fusions of tribal art on it. Theresa wore pants and a regular shirt.

But Roman wasn't laughing at the fact that Janine had tattoos. He liked her tattoos. He also wasn't judging either of them by their looks. He was amused that one sister was much taller than the other. Even though both sisters had red hair and freckles, Janine was much taller and skinnier, while Theresa was shorter and had a larger figure.

"I should name them the odd couple," he thought as he was still laughing on the inside. *"I must admit Janine is hot. Not trying to check her out, but I can't unsee Janine with her lower-cut shirt. However, I hope Janine isn't planning on seducing me or something. She'll have to move along if that's the case. Don't get me wrong, she is hot, but I'm no longer into the one-night stand business."*

Roman didn't particularly care how Janine was dressed. He was more neutral on the subject, even though he knew the Kojićs didn't like it. Mainly they didn't want their daughter to dress like that when she got older. However, Roman knew many girls dressed like that when he was in high school. In a way, he was desensitized by it. The way he saw it, being desensitized could be good or bad. Good because then one doesn't pass judgment as easily but bad because anything can become accepted over time.

"Well, this is awkward," Janine thought.

She noticed Roman's walls had memorabilia of the Minnesota Vikings. But she chose not to comment since he didn't comment about her face mask.

"It's nice to see you, too. Thank you for having us at your place," said Janine while shaking his hand.

"My pleasure." He turned to Theresa and said, "I'll take the cake for you and put it in the kitchen. Ah, chocolate cake! How did you know that chocolate cake was my favorite?"

"It was a wild guess, you could say," said Theresa.

"Well, come on in, everyone. I was about to throw the steaks on the grill. You want to chill outside with me, Miroslav?"

"Sure thing, pal."

The men headed out to the deck while the women stayed inside. Roman threw the four ribeye steaks on the grill and sat next to Miroslav.

"Hey, I need to ask you something," Roman said.

"What is it?" asked Miroslav.

"Does Janine usually dress like that, or is she doing it to get me to notice her?"

"No, she usually dresses like that when the warm weather shows up. I know she doesn't dress like that when she's at work. Her job won't allow for that. They make her wear uniforms that she can't stand. She says they're too heavy and itchy."

"Oh, I see."

"Personally, if she wants to dress like that, I can't tell her otherwise. But I don't want my daughter to dress like that when she becomes a teenager. I'm afraid she'll attract the wrong kind of men and send the wrong message to people. And we told Janine, if you don't pressure our daughter to dress like that, we don't care if you dress however you want. I have too many other things to worry about than how my sister-in-law chooses to dress. I have a family to raise and court cases to attend to for my job."

"Yeah, that's true. How is your job going, by the way?"

Roman got up from his seat to flip the steaks, then sat back down.

"It's going well. I don't share anything due to keeping my clients' cases in confidence, as you know. But being a criminal defense lawyer is a ton of work."

"I can imagine that. I respect you for what you do. I mean, everyone today is guilty before they even get a trial. People presume someone's guilt even though our Constitution states otherwise."

"That's the direction things are going. I remember growing up with the hatred I used to hear from people, particularly from my father. He *hated* the Croats. He thought they were all bad people. I think what people said to him before the wars broke out went to his head. His hatred was a bit over the top."

"When was the last time you were over there?"

"I haven't been back. I know if I were to go back, I would not be received well."

"Why is that?"

"Because I'm a Serb. There aren't many Serbs that live in that region of Croatia anymore. I'm not sure if there's any left, to be honest. I wouldn't know."

"I'm sorry those circumstances have made it hard for you to go home."

"It's okay. I've accepted it and made my peace with it. It's funny how people talk about being persecuted over here. Don't get me wrong; I know injustices *do* occur. But if only those people could have seen what I saw growing up. They may look at life differently."

Roman decided not to engage Miroslav further in that conversation. He wanted to do it when no one else was around. He got up and checked the steaks and flipped them over. After a couple of minutes, Roman pulled two of the steaks off the grill. Miroslav and Roman liked their steaks medium-rare.

"Take a look at this, my man."

"I'm sure it's done to perfection. You sure know how to cook. Speaking of work, have you found any work yet?"

"No. I'm still undecided about what I want to do. I'm not in a rush. I'm sure I'll find something eventually."

Roman threw a gob of butter on each steak and then covered it with aluminum foil so they could rest. He went into the house and put the asparagus in the oven while removing the potatoes. He came back out with two more plates. He pulled Janine's steak off the grill and let it rest.

"Your wife is great, don't get me wrong. But man, I don't know how anyone can eat a well-done steak."

"Me neither. You might as well eat one of my dress shoes. A1 Sauce couldn't even save that."

"Oh, well, to each their own. Speaking of shoe leather, I think it's finally done now."

He pulled the last steak off the grill to let it rest.

"I'd say it's time to eat!"

Both the men went inside. Roman discovered that the table was set and ready to go for dinner.

"Who set the supper table?" asked Roman.

"Janine and I did," said Theresa.

"Well, thank you both. That was very kind of you. You even put the vegetables on the table. What does everyone want to drink?"

"What do you have?" Janine asked.

"Let's see. I have water, sweet tea, milk, and adult beverages."

"He has booze in his house? I thought Christians didn't drink. Maybe I misjudged him," she thought.

"Um, what do you have as far as alcohol?"

"I have Pabst Blue Ribbon, Yuengling, Killian's Red, and hard stuff."

"Damn, this guy is cool, even though he likes the Vikings," Janine thought. *"Maybe he won't be so bad to hang out with, even though he doesn't sound informed about protecting others from COVID-19."*

"I'll take a Yuengling."

"All right. What do you two want to drink?"

"I'll do sweet tea," Miroslav replied.

"Water for me," Theresa said.

Roman served each of them the drinks that they wanted. He went to the basement fridge to get the Yuengling and Pabst Blue Ribbon. He made his way back to the dining room and sat with everyone.

"I'll say the prayer before we eat. Dear Lord, thank You for this meal You have given us. Bless our evening together. Thank You for my family and friends. Amen."

"Amen," Theresa and Miroslav said.

Janine did not say "amen." Roman didn't expect her to. He knew that she didn't go to church or anything like that. He would rather have a person choose the faith instead of faking it.

"Well, I must hand it to you, Roman. You outdid yourself again," Theresa said.

"Thanks, you can keep your dried-up shoe leather over there, and Miroslav and I will eat ours still mooing. I mean, you got to check this out."

Roman cut off a piece of his medium-rare steak and showed it to Theresa. He could tell she started to feel squeamish as she sat uncomfortably in her chair.

"I don't know how anyone can eat that. You might as well not even cook it!"

"Here, have a bite of mine," Miroslav said.

He had a piece of his steak on his fork and moved it toward her mouth. Janine started giggling. She always got a rise out of it when people instigated her sister.

"Get that out here!" Theresa exclaimed. She was annoyed yet holding back the laughter at the same time.

"What's the matter?" Roman asked. "I thought you liked his meat. See what I did there?"

Janine almost spat out her beer at Roman's comment while drinking it. She swallowed it very loudly and started laughing and coughing simultaneously. Everyone couldn't help but laugh; even Theresa started laughing.

"You two are *always* something when you get together," said Theresa.

Everyone settled back down and continued to eat.

"So Roman, I must say you have a beautiful house," observed

Janine. "And this is honestly the best steak I've ever eaten. It's cooked and seasoned perfectly. But yeah, I think it's cool that you live in a log cabin. So, tell me, what do you do for work?"

Roman froze for a second. He didn't know how to respond to Janine's question. He hadn't told a soul about his lottery earnings, not his parents, not the Kojićs, not a single person. He kept that a secret so nobody would try to take advantage of him. Then he felt calm and collected and decided to respond to Janine's question.

"Well, I haven't found what I'm looking for yet. I'm not sure what I want to do. I'm still trying to figure that out. In the meantime, I'm living off savings I've made in years past. But I'm sure I'll find something to do eventually. What do you do for work?"

"I'm a truck driver."

"Oh yeah? Do you do long distance?"

"No, I work for a company right in Orbisonia. We do residential trash pickup and roll-off dumpsters."

"Oh, that's cool. Do you like it?"

"Eh, it pays the bills."

"Yeah, I hear you there. Before moving to Pennsylvania, I worked for the Water Authority in Marion. It's a small town back in Massachusetts. It wasn't bad. It paid the bills as you said."

"How did you like living up there?"

"Honestly, I didn't care for it too much. I thought the people there were kind of rude and stuck up. Plus, I…"

Roman caught himself. He didn't want to have to explain the death of his girlfriend to someone he had recently met.

"I, um, I needed a change of scenery. I miss going to the beach and smelling the ocean air. I *do* miss my family very much. I can't wait to see them again. They are fantastic people, and I wouldn't trade them."

"They *aah?*" Janine asked, teasing Roman's accent.

"Yeah, I talk a little bit differently," Roman said as he chuckled. "Oh, I meant to tell you guys that I went turkey hunting this morning and shot a whopper of a bird!"

"I thought I heard a gunshot early this morning," said Theresa.

"Congratulations to you. How big was it?"

"Right around twenty-three pounds."

He pulled up the picture on his smartphone and passed it around the table so everyone could see it.

"Wow, that's a big one," Miroslav commented.

"Looks like you'll have a good Thanksgiving dinner then," Janine said.

"Yeah, I can't wait to eat it. It's the fourth turkey I've ever shot but the biggest one I've killed. So, how are Jason and Sarah doing?"

"Pretty good," Miroslav replied. "They're excited that summer is here. We're planning on going away for a week on a camping trip next month."

"Oh yeah? Where are you all going?"

"We'll be going to Monongahela National Forest in West Virginia for a week right about a month from now. It's something we've been looking forward to for a while."

"That should be a fun time. You guys need help tending the animals when you're gone?"

"Well, we had asked Janine to do it. But you two can work that out with each other if you want. Jason has goldfish, and Sarah has a rabbit that also needs care. Plus, there are the chickens, too."

"You can take care of the chickens, Roman," Janine said. "I can handle fish and rabbit, but I don't do farm-type animals."

"Very well. I'll take care of the chickens then."

"Thank you, guys, for doing that. We appreciate that," said Theresa. "We're excited to go on this trip because everything has been shut down for so long with the pandemic. It's nice to get out and finally do some things again."

"You think life will ever go back to normal?"

"I don't know. I don't know if this virus can be something that will ever be eradicated or not. We may be stuck living with it like the flu. If life goes back to normal, it will be long before that happens."

"I sure hope it does."

"I'm going to step outside and have a cigarette if you don't mind, Roman," said Janine.

"That's no trouble at all. I'm going to start cleaning up and getting ready for the cake. There's an ashtray out there for your butt."

"Cool, thanks."

Janine stepped outside onto the deck. She lit a Parliament cigarette and stood on the porch looking out into the back of Roman's property.

"You know he might not be much for looks, but he seems like a good guy," Janine thought. *"He has a good sense of humor. It was funny when Roman and Miroslav were razzing my sister. I can't say I've met a man who knew how to cook worth a darn. My previous boyfriend couldn't boil a pot of water, let alone fix a steak properly. I mean, that steak was cooked perfectly. Most restaurants can't even get a medium-cooked steak right. It's always either undercooked or overcooked. Roman sure has a nice house. It has a rustic charm to it."*

Janine finished smoking her cigarette and placed the butt in the ashtray that read "San Cristobal." It was a fancy-looking ashtray with the parrot insignia on it. She noticed ash and a butt from a previously smoked cigar. She made her way to the house and helped with the rest of the dishes and cleaning up. They eventually dove into the homemade chocolate cake. Theresa's homemade chocolate cake was always a crowd-pleaser. For the first time in a long while, Janine felt herself relaxing. True, she made amends with her sister long ago, but the trust wasn't always there. She felt that Roman and Miroslav together lightened the mood. While they were eating the cake, she thought it was funny that Roman asked Theresa to jump out of the cake for Miroslav. She saw that everyone was having a good time. She longed to join in on having fun with anyone in life. Having a deeper connection with people was something that eluded her.

CHAPTER 6

After dessert, the Kojićs had to leave. They had promised another couple from the church that they would see them after dinner at Roman's house. Roman knew about this before they showed up. He had planned to do some more drawing or watch TV. He didn't have anything significant planned for the evening.

Roman exchanged goodbyes with his guests. Then, he went to the garage to take the trash out to the garbage can. He returned to the living room and saw Janine sitting on the couch. She was wearing her face mask while looking at her smartphone. He had thought she had left with the Kojićs. She didn't. He was a little surprised yet cautious. He felt a little uneasy too. What was she still doing here? What did she want?

"Oh, hey," Roman said. "Are you all right? I thought you had left with Theresa and Miroslav."

She looked up at him and said, "Yeah, I originally was going to go home but didn't. Can I ask you something?"

"Sure."

"Are you doing anything tonight?"

"Um… I honestly had nothing planned for the evening. Why? What's up?"

"Do you think maybe we could hang out?"

"Oh gosh, I hope this doesn't get awkward. I wonder what she wants," he thought.

"What did you have in mind?"

"Well, I also saw in your living room that you have a Cribbage board. Would we be able to play? My grandfather taught me to play when I was a child. I used to play with him all the time, and I miss doing that. And not too many other people know how to play Cribbage."

"I don't see why not. Let's do it. Since we're already inside, I'll give you a quick tour of the house if you don't mind."

"Works for me."

Roman showed her the house. She again noticed all the Minnesota Vikings memorabilia that he had but didn't make any comments about it. She saw the big bull moose head over his fireplace, his trophy whitetail, and some drawings that he had framed and hung on his wall. There were photographs of his family and Briana and Roman together.

"So, these would be my folks. They're great people. My brother Craig and his wife Chelsea are with their two girls, Emily and Meredith."

"Who is this?"

Roman paused for a minute. Janine had pointed to the picture of Briana and himself.

"That would be Briana and me."

"Wow, you didn't have a beard then! You look like a completely different person!"

"Yeah, maybe someday I'll shave again."

"Was she your ex-wife?"

"No. We never got married."

"Oh. She looks pregnant in that picture."

"Yeah, we were supposed to have a child but didn't."

"What happened?"

"I… I don't want to talk about it right now. Maybe when we get to know each other a little better. I *just* want to enjoy the evening, if that's okay."

"Oh, okay."

Janine could instantly tell Roman felt uncomfortable as he started scratching the back of his neck. He avoided eye contact with her. She figured it would be wise not to press the issue at this point. There was an awkward silence as they walked down to the basement together. Roman could only imagine what Janine must have been thinking about him.

"She probably thinks I'm a deadbeat dad now or that I did something unethical. Oh well, whatever will be, will be," he thought.

"And finally, here's the basement," Roman said.

Janine's eyes lit up. It was finished with a pool table, a TV, and a bar.

"Wow, that's so awesome you have all this!"

"Yeah, I enjoy it. I've had people over from Bible study from time to time. I'll fix you a drink if you want. What would you like?"

She looked around and saw he had a modest selection of liquor.

"You know I usually go for a mixed drink. But I think tonight I'll take that Wild Turkey American Honey on the rocks."

"Good choice. I was going to do the same to celebrate my kill today since I shot a turkey."

He put a few ice cubes in each small glass and filled them with whiskey.

"I have a good cigar for you to try if you're interested. It's a Man O' War Virtue. It's a nice light smoke with a smooth draw to it."

"Why not? I've never had a cigar before, but I'll try it."

Roman also grabbed himself a cigar. It was a San Cristobal. He grabbed the Cribbage board and a deck of cards on their way out to the deck. There they sat across from each other once they were outside. The evening air was still. The remainder of the day still had some warmth to it. The sun was getting lower in the sky and would eventually create a beautiful sunset. In the distance, an eastern bluebird was singing. A raven could also be heard off in the distance, croaking. This set the mood for a peaceful evening. Roman dealt the cards once the pegs were in the holes of the Cribbage board. She took off her face mask to enjoy her drink and smoke.

"Well, are you ready to light it up? Remember, don't inhale it. Otherwise, you'll turn green as Pinocchio did."

"Yeah, I'll be fine."

The moment Roman saw Janine talk, he noticed she had the center of her tongue pierced with a golden barbell-style ring. Roman didn't say anything but wondered how he didn't see her tongue ring when they were conversing at dinner earlier. However, it didn't bother him that she had a tongue piercing.

Janine lit her cigar and took a couple of puffs of it.

She paused for several seconds and said, "You know, this isn't too bad."

"I kind of thought you would enjoy it. San Cristobal is a little heavier, but you can try it if you want."

"I think I'll stick with what I have for now."

"All right, I got to ask you something."

"What's that?"

"Why did you end up staying here? It's not that I don't want you here, but I'm curious."

"I'll answer that if you answer my question."

"I mean, I *did* kind of ask you first." They both stared at each other for a moment. Then finally, Roman decided to give in. "Okay, what is it?"

"Those pictures in your house. Did you draw those?"

"Why, yes. Yes, I did. Every one of them."

"Ha, I don't believe you," Janine scoffed at him. "You're telling me you drew those pictures and didn't trace them? Oh, and if you keep throwing me good cards in my crib, I'll surely beat you."

"Yes, I did draw those pictures myself," Roman said, annoyed. Roman also felt annoyed that their game of Cribbage wasn't off to a good start, at least for him.

Janine was looking for something to say. Then she smiled at him. She figured she had him right where she wanted him.

"All right, I bet you can't draw that moose head in your living room."

This tickled Roman to death. He smiled like he was already holding the perfect hand.

"All right, you're on," he said with a giant grin. "What's your wager? By the way, I scored sixteen points on my runs and fifteen combinations so take that."

"Hmmm... If I win, I get that bottle of Crown Royal in your basement."

"And if I win?"

"You get to pick. Ten more points for me, by the way."

"All right, let's see here... If I win, you have to comb my beard."

He instantly saw the look of dread on Janine's face and laughed.

"Don't worry. I won't make you do that. If *I* win, we go out on a casual date. I'm not talking about sex or anything like that – just a fun date. We'll go to White Castle at the drive-thru. You pay for my meal and have to talk like Yoda when ordering our food. After that, we can go to the park and eat."

Janine looked at him like he had three heads and then laughed, "Are you serious? I'm not doing *that!*"

"Hey, if you don't think I can draw that moose head in my living room, put your money where your mouth is. Besides, a bottle of whiskey versus a cheap date is more than a fair deal. So, what do you say? Do we have a bet? And look at this. I'm starting to gain on you. I have another good hand for twelve points."

Janine still couldn't figure out why Roman had such a big smile on his face the whole time.

"Is he that nuts?" she thought. *"This will be like taking candy from a baby."*

"Roman, you got yourself a deal."

The two of them agreed on it and then shook hands.

"Okay, now that I'm going to win – I mean, now that your question has been answered, it's back to my question. Why did you end up staying here after the Kojićs left?"

"You want to know the truth?"

"Yes, of course."

"I had fun hanging out with you. You seem different from other people I've known in my life."

"What other people?"

"Christians. They seem so stuffy. I know Miroslav can joke around, and my sister can. Well, *nowadays*, she can. But I feel like many of them can't have fun for some reason."

Roman didn't know what to say. He hadn't been a believer as long as other people he knew at church and Bible study. He took a sip of his whiskey and puffed on his cigar. She did the same. He decided to remain silent to see if Janine said anything more. And she did.

"So, why do you identify as a Christian? I can't and want to hear why and what you believe."

Janine moved her peg past Roman's peg on the Cribbage board. He could tell the way she asked the question and, with her body language, indicated she must have been hurt badly in the past. However, Roman was no stranger to pain. He had his share of disappointments and shortcomings. He thought about her question as he took another sip from his glass and a puff from his cigar.

"Let me make a statement to you first," he said as he paused. "I haven't been a *Christian* for very long. At the very beginning of this year, I accepted Christ as my Savior and Lord."

"Really? So, you haven't been a believer your whole life?"

"Nope. I didn't grow up going to church or anything. We didn't even go to church during Christmas or Easter. I'd say that I grew up agnostic for most of my life. I wasn't sure if God existed or not."

"So, what changed your mind?"

"Well… I hit some hard times a few years ago. Not only with Briana, but I was a compulsive gambler. I gambled to the point that it created massive debt. I also didn't have many friends where I lived either. I felt like the whole world was closing in on me. I don't know where I'd be if it weren't for my family. They've been so loving and kind and supportive of me.

"So, I was at the bookstore one day trying to figure out a gift to get for my mother's birthday. I was browsing the whole store. I knew she enjoyed reading, but I didn't know what to get her. And then, I came to the religion section. I saw multiple versions of the Bible on the shelf and decided to buy one for myself. Of course, I bought an easy-to-read version since I can't understand old Shakespeare-type English. I would read it from time to time, some of it I didn't understand, and some I still don't. As I said, I'm still new to this whole thing. I once got mad at what I read and threw the Bible in the garbage can. But about half a minute later, I decided to keep it. I didn't want to give up on it."

"What did you read in there that made you mad?"

"There's a section that talked about how we as people need to submit to the government's authority. That did not sit well with me because you have madmen like Hitler or Stalin killing innocent people. Not to mention that we fought for our independence from the British. But I didn't realize that the governments in charge of each nation are supposed to follow what God wants. And I think we could agree that the atrocities of the communists and the Nazis were wrong on many levels. True?"

"Yes, but why does God allow those things to happen to good people?"

"Well, I think there are some things that we must remember. I could say, 'Well, Adam and Eve and the fall of man' or 'Nobody is perfect and we all sin,' which *are* factual statements, but there's more to it. Saying those things only scratches the surface because what you're asking me is a legitimate question.

Many people have that question, which I also had at one point in my life. What part of the Bible says, 'God helps those who help themselves?'"

"Well... I... I'm sure it's in the New Testament somewhere."

"That phrase I told you is not in the Bible. Benjamin Franklin said that, which I believe he got from someone else. That's why it's important to know what the Bible says. Now back to your question. It's also important to know what the Bible *doesn't* say. We're not promised a good life on Earth. It even says that there will be fiery trials. We're not promised a happy marriage, 'X' number of children, a high-paying salaried job, or even staying cancer-free. It sure makes a person feel despondent when you look at it that way. Look at what God had to sit through when you think about it. He watched His only Son not only die but die a horrible death. I couldn't imagine having a child and watching people whip, beat, mock, and spit upon my child. I feel like God knows our pains because He has seen it all.

"This world isn't the end. Just because we don't get what we want or bad things happen doesn't mean God has forgotten about us, even though it seems that way sometimes. God's love is so much more than what happens to us *here*. Those who believe and seek His Son will be rewarded with eternal life. I don't know about you, but I think this world is screwed up. You have pandemics, people rioting, and divisions within families, sometimes to the point where people don't even speak to each other. Relationships anymore, I feel like, have become nothing but a checklist. You can't talk to someone because they're a Democrat or a Republican. Or this business can't stay open because the government says it's not essential. I'm going to tell you something, Janine. We're all *essential* in God's eyes! Regardless of how we vote, the color of our skin, or whether we sit on the deck and smoke cigars and play Cribbage or not.

"Now, I haven't known you for any length of time. However, it sounds like you got some scars from your past. And I'm not going to make you share those things with me. That's up to you when you want to share them. I'm not going to press you about it. If you have any questions, I'll be here if you need anything. Like I mentioned at the supper table, I'm not employed, so I got all the time in the world to give you a listening ear."

Janine was stunned. She was blown away by his responses. She didn't expect Roman to give her the answers that he did. She didn't know he possessed any sort of intelligence. In the past, he commented to the Kojić children about face masks being ineffective due to pants and underwear not being able to hold up against flatulence. What caught her off guard the most was his passion and the fact that she could sense he had respect for her. She saw him as a down-to-earth person, not putting on a show to impress her.

They both paused momentarily to let the conversation soak in. It wasn't an awkward feeling. If anything, it was peaceful. Janine was so used to being condemned in life that she expected Roman to get annoyed with her questions like her father did when she was a child. For that, it earned her a little respect for Roman. She took a sip of her whiskey and a drag off her cigar.

"I appreciate you and for your honesty. Can I ask you something else?

"Go for it."

"How do you choose to vote?"

"I prefer to be unaffiliated. Mainly I'm a strong conservative on most things. But seeing as I grew up in one of the most liberal states in the country, I was always the black sheep. And I know that ticked many people off."

"I'm kind of in the same boat myself. I'm a Democrat surrounded by Trumpers. I didn't vote for Trump. Did you vote for him?"

"Are you going to put that cigar out on my neck?"

"No, I promise," Janine said as she giggled.

"I didn't vote for him the first time, but I did the second time he ran. At first, I didn't know how serious about taking him if he were to be president. But he did many things that I liked."

"So, if you're a conservative and a Christian, do you think women are below men?"

"Goodness, no! Like men, women are also God's creation. Now I will say this, however. I'm not entirely on board with the feminist movement either."

"Well, what do you mean? I thought you said women weren't below men. Men have it *way* easier in this world than women!" exclaimed Janine as she snapped at Roman.

He could tell what he had said hit a nerve with her.

"They're not below men. Both are equal. But that doesn't mean I have to agree with feminists on everything, either. Some women hate all men for the simple fact that they're men. Again, not all women, but some. Well, what did *I* ever do wrong? My father and brother both served in the military to defend their freedom to hate men. What did my family ever do wrong? And not to mention, men don't *always* have it easier than women in *everything.* Most of the time, divorce courts favor the woman over the man simply *because* she's a woman. And then the man is lucky to have two pennies to rub together when the divorce is all said and done. Plus, anytime a man shares his struggles, he gets written off as less of a man for it. Not to mention women aren't forced to sign up for the draft like men are. Granted, the draft hasn't been used since the Vietnam era; my point is if they want to be equal to a man, let's make it *all* equal.

"Look, I fully appreciate what feminism has accomplished by giving women equal rights. Still, I don't like that some use feminism as a tool or a weapon to bash men because that's not right. The same goes for people who use Christianity and the Bible to manipulate others. People can use the Bible as a means of control. It's not right to do those things, nor is it how Jesus would have wanted scripture to be used. As you can see, not only has Satan pegged men and women against each other, but he can also use the Bible against people.

"But think of it this way. Do I agree with everything that my parents say or do? Of course not. But that doesn't mean I will stop loving them simply because we don't see eye to eye on everything.

"Or take Sally Field, for example. You may have noticed I had an autographed photo of her in the basement next to my bar. I may disagree with her political beliefs, but I admire her skills as an actress. She's my favorite actress. She's one of the best actresses ever to live! She's been in some great movies, like *Norma Rae, Smokey and the Bandit, Forrest Gump,* and the list goes on. If I ever met her in person, I wouldn't treat her any less because she has different opinions than I do. I'd treat her the same way I'm treating you, Janine. I would still be hospitable toward her.

"Anyway, I'm rambling. The problem with our society is that we have lost our ability to disagree with each other anymore. In turn, this means people can't even be friends. Sort of like how things have become a checklist, as I mentioned earlier. And I'm not talking about extreme examples like people who deny the Holocaust because there *is* overwhelming evidence that it did happen. People who do that are only looking to advance their political propaganda. I'm not talking about stuff like that. I'm talking about other things like whether we wear face masks or not or get the vaccine. Who would have thought a face mask or sneezing in public would put us on the brink of war? Who would have thought Mr. Potato Head would cause such a fuss because we're not sure an inanimate object can choose whether it wants to be referred to as non-binary or not? It's a toy, for goodness sake! I feel like we're living during wartime. We live in a society at war with one another. However, during this wartime edition, we're using other means to destroy each other instead of heavy artillery. I'll tell you this. I think this pandemic has brought out the worst in people, which Satan loves."

"Well, I can certainly see where you're coming from. I'm about fed up with all this hatred myself."

"Me too. I'm glad what I said to you made sense. For a minute, I thought we would throw the rest of your whiskey and the Cribbage board in my face."

They both laughed at that. Roman had finished his cigar a while ago while Janine was still working on hers. She had smoked about three-quarters of it.

"You want me to top off your drink?" Roman asked.

"I think I'm good," said Janine.

"How are you enjoying that cigar?"

"It's better than I expected. I see yours is already gone."

"Yeah, that's because yours was bigger than mine."

Janine saw that stupid grin on his face after he said that.

"You're a dork," she said as she shook her head.

"I was thinking, would it be okay if I got your number? The main reason being is because you'll probably be taking me out on my cheap date soon," said Roman.

"Yeah, you wish. Sure, I'll give you my number. Oh, and by the way, I already beat you before our official bet."

"How so?"

"Because I'm holding the perfect hand!"

She turned her cards around, and Roman saw what she had. She had the jack of hearts and three fives in her hand. The starter card was the five of hearts.

"Holy smokes!" exclaimed Roman. "In all my years playing Cribbage, I've never seen that happen in person. That's awesome! Not only did you score twenty-nine points, but you also beat me. And not only did you beat me, but you also skunked me!"

"That's right, I did," Janine bragged. "That's a sign I'm going to win our upcoming bet. While you're at it, take a picture of me holding my cigar and perfect hand so you'll always remember it. Then you can send it to me."

"Sure thing," Roman said with a wry smile.

He took a picture of Janine. She gave him her number so he could send the image to her cell phone. He also saved her picture under her contact information.

"I'll tell you what. If you aren't doing anything next Saturday, how about you come over again? You can watch me attempt to draw that moose head."

"That should work. I don't think I have anything going on that weekend."

"It's a deal then."

"So, what was it like going on that hunt? While you and Miroslav were sitting outside grilling, Theresa told me you shot that moose yourself. I've never met anyone who shot a moose before."

"Oh, it was incredible. It was a once-in-a-lifetime opportunity. My folks took my brother Craig and me up to the Yukon for a week at the end of September. The scenery was breathtaking. Craig was never big on hunting like I am, but he loves to fish. The package included fishing with the moose hunt. So, my father and I went hunting while my mother and Craig stayed behind to fish. We did a ton of walking in the woods with our guide. The one I shot was the first day we were out there."

"Oh, so your dad got one too?"

"Yeah, he got one on the third day of the hunt. His was a little bigger than mine."

"Well, it's like you said earlier about my cigar. Mine is bigger than yours. See what I did there?"

They both laughed at that. Roman knew she gave him a taste of his medicine, but he thought it was funny. He wasn't the kind of person to get sore, especially if something was being thrown in his face that he had done himself.

"Well, you got me there, Janine."

"Did you guys shoot the moose for sport?"

"No, we kept the meat. I don't believe in shooting something for the sake of it. Anything I shoot gets eaten."

"Did your mother and brother have a good time too?"

"They sure did. Each of them caught some good-sized fish which we all ate. It was a good time. I'd do it again in a heartbeat if I could."

"I've always been a city girl, but this is where I was raised, so it's home. I *did* live in the Pittsburgh area with a former boyfriend for about a year. We lived in McKeesport, to be exact."

"An old boyfriend?"

"Yes, but that's long and gone now, and it's better that way."

"What happened?"

"Well, I don't feel comfortable sharing that with you. The same way you don't feel comfortable sharing your story with Briana at this point."

"Fair enough. I didn't mean to pry."

"It's all good."

"Wow, check out that sunset."

They both looked at the sky and how the sun's light reflected off the clouds. There were beautiful textures and shades of red, orange, and yellow. They both felt relaxed. Each one felt satisfied with how the evening went. True, they were different people; this was only the first time they had hung out. But it was an excellent first start for them since they got to know each other and had fun along the way.

"I noticed it's starting to get a little cold," Roman said.

"Yeah, besides, I probably should be heading back home."

"You want to take home some of the grilled chicken?"

"Please and thank you. I can cut it up and use it to top off my salad tomorrow."

Janine had finished her cigar several minutes ago, and their drinks were gone. Roman took their glasses to the kitchen and placed them in the sink. She followed behind him and put her face mask back on.

"Well, I enjoyed getting to know you, Janine. I had a fun time with you this evening. I hope you did too."

"I did. It was good getting to know you also. You're a goof, but I enjoyed your company."

"Eh, it's what I do. Am I allowed to hug you? I didn't want you to feel uncomfortable due to COVID-19."

"Well, okay. I did receive my first vaccination, so why not? Maybe a quick hug."

They hugged each other. As she requested, it was quick, but the warmth felt good to them for that split second. Despite receiving her first dose of the vaccine, she was still a little cautious about things when it came to social distancing. As she picked her purse up off the floor, Roman noticed she had a tattoo on her lower back. A giant, colorful butterfly was at the center of her lower back, with vine branches on each side. Each vine branch contained three flowers.

On her drive home, she was at ease. At ease that she had a good evening with Roman. She saw that Roman believed differently than she did regarding God. Even though that was the case, she felt relief that someone was willing to sit down and talk to her about God. After all these years, someone was ready to answer some of her questions, or at least sincerely try. She didn't like it when her father and other Christians barked at her and talked down to her. It was the first time she didn't feel like a Christian was out to get her or condemn her.

She also appreciated that Roman didn't make comments about her breasts or was constantly staring at them. Part of her still felt like since she had piercings and tattoos, Roman would eventually judge her for those things. She couldn't wait to see him again, but she had a long way to go before fully trusting him and letting him into her private life. She returned to her house in Orbisonia and took a shower to eliminate the cigar smell. Then she climbed into bed, feeling a little more at peace for the first time in a long time.

On Roman's end, he was getting ready for the evening. He started the dishwasher since he had a full load after today's get-together. Even though he had taken a shower several hours ago, he took another to wash the cigar smell off him. Afterward, he got into his pajamas and headed to the bedroom. He stared at his bed for a moment. Then he realized what he was going to do. He would serve God one last time before he decided to go to sleep. He approached his bed and kneeled. He began to pray.

"Dear Lord, thank You for this day You gave me. A day full of laughter and joy. Thank You for blessing me on my hunt today and giving me the energy to prepare my garden. Thank You to my good friends and neighbors, the Kojićs, and all they have done for me. Please watch over them and their children. Thank You for allowing me to get to know Janine more. Please show her that You are the God of unconditional love, grace, and mercy. You're so much more than tradition. You are a relationship and the best relationship anyone could ever experience. Let her see that You are not out to get her or spite her, but You want her to follow You to Your glorious Kingdom. It's in Your Son Jesus Christ's name I pray… Amen."

Roman got up from where he was kneeling beside the bed. He grabbed his phone from his gym shorts pocket and found the picture he had taken of Janine earlier. He saw her physical beauty while she held her cigar and perfect hand from Cribbage. Her long red hair and beautiful blue eyes. Most of all, her smile. Her smile drove him wild. He saw the outward beauty that she possessed. He knew what he was going to do with this picture. Although she knew he had taken that picture of her, he would use it against her in a way she would never expect. By doing so, Roman would achieve what he wanted.

CHAPTER 7

t was quarter of six in the morning on that Saturday. Today was the day that Janine would go to Roman's house. She was confident she would get her payout on her bet with that bottle of Crown Royal she had her eye on. It was relatively humid outside. Scattered showers and thunderstorms were in the forecast for the entire day. It would be a perfect day to stay inside and draw.

Roman was awoken abruptly by a loud clap of thunder. The thunder happened about a second after the lightning, so Roman knew the storm was at his doorstep. He had wished he could have slept a little longer. He reluctantly got out of bed and made his way downstairs. He headed straight for the coffee machine. He sat at the table and drank his coffee while eating a bagel with cream cheese. Janine wasn't coming over until nine o'clock. He wished time didn't drag so slowly, mainly because he had a rude awakening earlier. The power flickered a couple of times due to the vivid lightning. Roman waited a few minutes before digging out his drawing supplies. He wanted to see if he would have to start the generator in case of a power outage from the lightning.

The storm eventually subsided after about twenty minutes or so. Roman got ready for the day and got what he needed for drawing. His paper, charcoal pencils, and his card table from the basement. He brought his comfortable office chair downstairs to sit on at the card table to draw. After getting set up, he popped some more tobacco pouches in his mouth. It wasn't even seven o'clock yet. Roman could feel himself nodding off despite drinking coffee.

Meanwhile, Janine was getting ready for the day too. Unlike Roman, she had slept through the thunderstorm and woke up feeling rested. The whole week she was thinking about this day. She could taste the Crown Royal. She wasn't an alcoholic but had no problems partaking in a good drink. She put on her track shorts and Green Bay Packers tank top. Afterward, she put on a little makeup. She always wore makeup, but it was never in large amounts. She was ready to go. She got in her Honda Accord, lit a cigarette, and drove away.

Roman was half asleep on his couch. He was startled when he heard the doorbell ring. He realized Janine was at the door. But he didn't know that he had dozed off with tobacco in his mouth. He almost swallowed all the nasty brownish-green juice but quickly caught himself so he wouldn't. Instead, his gag reflexes kicked in, and he ended up coughing it up all over the coffee table. He might not have been awake before, but he was awake now. He started to panic. He knew Janine was at the door and heard her ring the doorbell a second time. He didn't care if she found out he used smokeless tobacco. He cared about cleaning up the mess on the coffee table as quickly as possible. He ran frantically to the kitchen to grab some paper towels and all-purpose cleaner from under the sink. As he ran back to the living room, he stubbed the *same* baby toe in the *same* place he did a few months ago.

"OUCH! DAMN YOU! The liberals strike again!" he yelled as he held his foot with one hand.

This time he lost his balance and fell over on his side. He could only imagine what Janine was thinking standing outside. This time he heard her knocking on his door and calling his name. He knew he had to move fast. He quickly got the job done and disposed of the paper towels. He ran to the door and opened it.

"Hey," Roman said as he was panting with a sheepish grin.

Janine stood there with a disgusted look on her face and crossed arms. He knew he had been caught. He could tell she was less than impressed with him even though she was wearing her face mask. She had heard Roman running around like a maniac and his remark about liberals. She moved her eyes to the left and then to the right.

Then she looked directly at Roman and said, "You know… This is one of the rare moments I'm at a complete loss for words for stupidity. I hope I wasn't interrupting your playtime while you were masturbating to Fox News."

"No… no, it was nothing like that. Come on in and make yourself at home."

He didn't want to make a wise remark in response to her comment. He knew it wouldn't have done any good, and he didn't want to start a potential friendship on a sour note. They both went to the living room and sat together on the couch. Roman already had art supplies on a card table facing the moose head. He also had purposely put the bottle of Crown Royal on the table for show.

"I'm happy you were able to come over. I don't have too many friends down here yet since I'm still a little new to the area. I admit I tend to be an introvert, too," said Roman.

"The people down here are okay. Some are good, and some are bad. But I guess you'll have that anywhere," Janine replied.

"What do you think you dislike most about the people down here, Janine?"

"Um… Being in a small-town setting, everyone knows everyone, which can be good or bad. It's a double-edged sword, you could say. Not too many people, in general, want to be friends with a liberal like me. Plus, I have a couple of piercings and multiple tattoos. Christians tend to write me off as a whore because of that. I'm guessing being a Christian yourself; you'll pass judgment on me for my piercings and tattoos."

"You can do what you want to do. It's not for me to judge. I don't believe in looking down on people for stuff like that. I like your tattoos. I guess you're the one doing the judging this time."

She paused for a minute and then said, "All right… you got me there.

And thank you for the compliment, by the way. So let me ask you this. How come so many other Christians are judgmental?"

Roman paused for a minute. He didn't want to blurt out a response without thinking. Then he got his thoughts together and proceeded to answer her question.

"You know... I can't answer for every person. Everyone has a different experience in life. Since I didn't grow up in a religious home, I'm used to *things* in the world. I don't run wild like I used to, but it was simply the environment I grew up in. Some Christians have grown up very sheltered. Or maybe some of them think what they're doing is right by somehow protecting themselves. The problem today is that people don't have a good approach. Outright condemning someone isn't going to win that person your favor. It's love that wins out. Showing someone love is the best place to start. The fire and brimstone approach rarely works, especially in our world."

"Tell me about it. I used to go to a youth group at church. Another girl that attended was Jane. She used to be up to my ass constantly. She'd even get offended when I said, 'deviled eggs' because it has the word 'devil' in it. Yet, she was sucking and fucking every guy in town. I think Christians are such hypocrites."

"There are some out there like that. Not to mention we all sin. I know I get frowned upon by some other Christians for how I do business or even for reading a different translation of the Bible. Ironically, as a Christian, I've been persecuted by other Christians."

"Really? How so?"

"First, I'd say it's probably my sense of humor. You'll find that out the more you hang around me. But also my approach to how I share Jesus with people. Some people think I must strong-arm others into worshiping Him, almost like immediately planting the seeds in the garden. Since I have a garden, I know you need to till it first. You prepare it before planting it. You can plant all the seeds you want. If you don't have good soil, you're wasting your time. Or building a house, for example. You can build a fancy mansion or castle if you wish. But if it doesn't have a solid foundation, then forget about it. You see what I'm getting at?"

"I do. But why even go to church then if the people suck? I wish more Christians had the approach that you take. I feel like it's Kathy Bates from *The Waterboy*. Everything was always the Devil."

"Well, unfortunately, you'll have that sometimes - good movie, by the way. To answer your question, I ultimately go to church to experience and serve God. I don't go for the people. It's important to be with supportive and loving people, but I go for God first. I also think about this too. Perhaps those people haven't experienced all of Jesus' love and forgiveness and don't know how to show that to someone else. They have the head knowledge about sharing the gospel but not the heart knowledge to do it. Not to brag, but sometimes I think I'm at an advantage because I didn't grow up attending church."

"It's almost like you have a different perspective on life."

"Maybe so, I don't know. I can't control those people, but I can control how I respond. So, you said you were in youth group?"

"Yeah, many moons ago. After finishing high school, I haven't returned to church much since then."

"What was home life like for you as a kid?"

"My parents are good people, even though they had a hard time showing love. They lived more sheltered. Don't do this or that, or God will punish you. That sort of thing. And Theresa and I weren't very close growing up either."

"Really?"

"No, she was kind of a snitch. A goody-two-shoes, if you will. Not anymore, but you better believe she was when she was a kid. If I remember correctly, you said you have a brother?"

"Yes, I have an older brother Craig."

"Cool, do you both get along?"

"Yeah, he's a great dude. I love him and my parents very much."

"That's a good thing. I was always sort of the black sheep of my family, but, oh well. I like to think my parents love me, but I don't know.

Anyway, enough about that. You sad to give up your bottle of Crown Royal yet?"

"Yeah, I suppose we better get this show on the road. I tend to listen to music when I draw. I usually like quiet music. Is that okay?"

"Fine by me."

"Oh, and are you going to get offended if I use spit tobacco?"

"Yuck… you do that stuff?"

"Yes, yes, I do."

"Gosh, you and all the other country bumpkins around here. Such a nasty habit, you know. I thought you were from Massachusetts, where people are more civilized."

"Well, nobody is perfect, you know."

"I know, but spitless tobacco? Anyway, I'll step outside and smoke a cigarette if you don't mind while you tend to your disgusting habit."

Janine grabbed the pack of Parliament cigarettes and a lighter out of her purse and headed for the back door. Roman paused momentarily and saw her light up a cigarette outside on the deck.

He scoffed and said, "Disgusting habit… did the pot call the kettle black? Never mind… time to draw a moose head."

He propped his phone up and got his music playing on his phone to focus better. The first song on his playlist was "Country Hymn" by Christopher Boscole. He popped tobacco pouches in his mouth, and then he got started. Janine came back from outside. She watched Roman as he was drawing. She sat down in the living room with him.

"I have one request," Roman said.

"What's that?" asked Janine.

"No peeking. I'll show you when I'm done."

"Fair enough."

As time passed, Janine settled in the living room, watching Roman draw. She enjoyed listening to Roman's music that he was playing from his playlist. "Elysian Fields" by Tingstad and Rumbel was currently playing. Although she didn't know that tune, she enjoyed it nonetheless. She also thought of their conversations about

Christianity and church. She still wasn't fond of going to church, but she had respect for Roman. She hadn't had that kind of respect for many Christians other than Miroslav. Although she didn't know his story in detail, she knew Miroslav went through much pain during the turbulence of Yugoslavia's breaking up. She admired Miroslav for overcoming such adversity in life and for the fact that he didn't belittle her. She was also starting to admire Roman because he didn't criticize her either. He didn't shame her for not attending church or having all her tattoos or piercings. In a way, she felt safe talking to Roman about her issues, which hindered her from having a closer relationship with her parents. She felt like she couldn't go to them with her personal life.

"He seems like a genuine guy, but I wish he didn't use spit tobacco. Plus, I wish he would shave that beard off," she thought. *"But he's been nice to me, so I have no reason not to be nice to him. He voted for Trump and attends church, yet he's nothing like the people I've run into at church. I hope I'm not missing anything in the fine print here. I'm glad he's not constantly staring at my boobs like all the other men. So many men want to have a romp in the hay with me and then leave. I hope Roman isn't like one of those other guys and isn't faking all this Christian stuff with me."*

"Which way is the bathroom, Roman?" Janine asked.

"Down the hall to your right."

"Thanks. If it's okay, I may look around your house, so I don't break your concentration."

"Fine by me."

After Janine used the bathroom, she went to the garage. It was the only place she hadn't seen when she was at Roman's house during her previous visit. She turned on the light and saw a Toyota Tundra but saw what appeared to be another vehicle next to the truck on the other side of it. She walked over to it. Her jaw instantly dropped as her eyes grew like saucers. She couldn't believe what she was looking at. It almost made her gasp. Next to the Tundra was a Rolls-

Royce Ghost in a royal blue color for the exterior. She ran out of the garage to the living room. Janine could see Roman was in the zone while drawing, but this was something she needed an explanation of right then and there.

"*Holy shit! You* have a Rolls-Royce?"

"Ah, I see you discovered one of my toys."

"How the *hell* did you get that?"

"I bought it."

"Brand new?"

"Bought it with a cash deal."

"Okay, I know you said you've been living off savings. Where on earth did you work before you moved out of Massachusetts?"

"I believe I mentioned to you before that I worked at the Water Authority."

"Bullshit! No way *anyone* could make that kind of money even if they worked a good job like that."

"I never said I got that kind of money from working there."

"So, how did you get that kind of money then, a rich uncle?"

"Let's say I eventually got disciplined with my money over the years."

"Uh-huh… investments, I take it?"

"Something like that."

"Well, someday, you'll have to let me know what you're investing in because, *damn,* that's one hell of a ride you got there!"

"Someday, I'll take you for a spin in it… or perhaps I'll let you drive it."

"You'd let *me* drive that thing?"

"Yeah, why not? Especially since you'll owe me a meal at White Castle after this."

"Very funny."

Janine saw the grin on Roman's face but chose to ignore it. She looked around more but stayed in the living room.

"I see you like the Minnesota Vikings, Roman."

"I sure do. You like my Alan Page jersey that I'm wearing today?"

"Yeah, right. I'm surprised you're not a Patriots fan since you're from up that way."

"Yeah, I've always stuck with the Vikings. I'm not a bandwagon fan either."

"Well, as you can see from my tank top, I'm a Packers fan."

"Yeah, I know. How disgusting that is. Completely immoral! It's *even* pure evil. I'm fine with you being more on the liberal side of life, but being a Packers fan?"

Janine could tell Roman wasn't being serious and was trying to get a rise out of her. She knew that two could play this game.

"Yeah, at least my team has Lombardi Trophies and didn't squander the Super Bowl on four different occasions."

"Well, I *did* ask for a taste of my own medicine. Say, you hungry for some lunch? I got leftover shepherd's pie in the fridge. I also have deli meat and cheese for grinders if you want."

"Grinders?"

"Yeah."

"What the hell are those?"

"You know, subs."

"Oh, I never heard it called that before. Now hoagies, I've heard but not grinders. Must be a New England thing."

"Probably so."

"Anyway, I'll try the shepherd's pie. Did you make it yourself?"

"I sure did."

"Cool. It's been a while since I've had shepherd's pie."

"Yeah, I made it last night. Anyway, I'll get the food out and the table ready."

Roman closed the book he was drawing in and turned off the music from his phone. Janine sat at the table while Roman heated the shepherd's pie in the microwave.

"What do you want to drink?" asked Roman.

"I'll take Crown Royal on the rocks, please!"

"Yeah, yeah."

"You got any more beer?"

"Yeah, I got Yuengling and PBR on hand. Also, Killian's Red. Same as what I usually have."

"I'll take a Killian's Red."

"All right."

When Roman got the beer from downstairs, the food was done in the microwave. He put the food and bottles of beer on the table and sat down with Janine. She didn't start eating because she knew Roman would say a prayer first.

"Dear Lord, thank You for this meal and for this time we could spend together. Thank You for my new friend, Janine. Amen."

"Amen. Thank you. It's nice getting to know someone who isn't from around here."

"Well, I appreciate you wanting to hang out with me."

They both started to eat. There were a couple of minutes of silence as they dug into their food. Janine noticed something different about the shepherd's pie but couldn't put her finger on it. It didn't taste nasty to her, but the flavor was unfamiliar. She decided to ignore it and engaged Roman in more conversation.

"So, what was your life like where you grew up? Cape Cod, wasn't it?" Janine inquired.

"Yeah, I grew up in a town called New Seabury. We lived right next to the ocean. My parents bought the house years ago, which they still live in today. I bet it's worth a ton of money by now if they were to sell it, especially how the market has currently been."

"Do you think they'll sell it?"

"I don't think so."

"Did you miss living up there?"

"I can't say that I do. I miss my family. I miss the smell of the ocean air and the fresh seafood, but that's about it. I'm not a big fan of the people there, mainly because they're not a big fan of me."

"Why do you say that?"

"I don't want to sound judgmental, but I feel like people up there can't be bothered with anything. They won't give you the time of day. You say 'hello' to someone, and they look at you weirdly, like, 'Why are you talking to me?' That sort of a thing. I'm a conservative and a Vikings fan, so they used those things against me. Shoot, I remember wearing my Vikings hat or jerseys, and people would be like, 'So what, you hate the Patriots or something?' And I'm like, 'Just because I like the Vikings doesn't mean I despise the Patriots.' I also remember getting harassed in school because people knew I hunted."

"Well, pretty much everyone hunts down here."

"Not where I grew up. I used to get labeled a murderer and things like that. In a way, I think maybe you and I have something in common."

"What's that?"

"Our childhoods shaped us. As you mentioned, you don't attend church because of the hypocrites. I'm probably who I am because all my life, I heard growing up that Democrats are for the people and more accepting of everyone. They sure weren't accepting of me because I disagreed with them. So, because of that, I was an outcast."

"You know, it's almost like we're on that Christmas show stuck on the island of misfit toys."

"You could say that again," Roman said as he chuckled. "People don't have the heart anymore, I feel like. It's like we're supposed to be progressing and moving forward as a society, and I feel like we're going backward instead. And the pandemic has made it worse, I think. I'd almost rather be a hermit sometimes because people are so angry anymore. It makes me feel uncomfortable thinking about it all. I tell you, Satan loves every minute of it. He loves the divisiveness."

"That's something I can agree with. I feel like so many people down here judge me because I wear my face mask out in public, and they're like, 'that libtarded bitch voted for Biden', which I *did* vote for Biden. But do you have to punish me for who I am? I see these people wearing MAGA hats, yet they don't want to include me in that equation. Kind of like how you felt pushed aside because of whom you are growing up in the part of the world you grew up in."

"I agree with you. Having friends or relationships anymore has become nothing more than superficial. Well, I think I'm done eating. You want some more bear?"

"Wait... are you offering me another beer?"

"No, I said, 'bear.'"

"I don't get it."

"I know you don't. You just ate ground bear meat."

She gasped and asked, "Are you for real?"

"Yes. I mean, you ate your whole plate with no problems."

"You know, I thought it tasted different, but you seasoned it just right, so it didn't have too much of a gamey taste. You're a hell of a good cook."

"Well, thank you for the compliment. I do my best when I'm in the kitchen."

"Did you shoot that bear yourself?"

"Yeah, I shot him this past year on my property. He was not quite four hundred pounds. This was the last bear meat I had in the freezer."

"What kind of gun did you use to shoot a black bear?"

"I used my .338 Win. Mag. That's the same gun I used on the moose in my living room. I have the bear hide on my bedroom floor if you want to see it. Until then, I think I will use the bathroom and start drawing again."

"Okay."

As Roman went to the bathroom, Janine planned to make her move. It wasn't to go check out the bear hide, however. She would do that later. She saw something that grabbed her attention. In Roman's living room, he had a bookshelf. She was eyeing what was on the bookshelf earlier. She quickly ran over to it and took the book off the shelf. It was the Bible. She stared at it for a couple of seconds and then looked around to see if Roman was watching her. She saw the coast was clear, ran over to her purse, and stuffed the Bible inside.

"How ironic, I know. The Bible says don't steal, and that's exactly what I did," Janine thought. *"Well, I did see that he had a couple of different copies on his shelf. Plus, I can always give it back if I don't like reading it."*

"You checked out the upstairs yet?" Roman asked.

Janine was startled a little and flinched. She didn't know Roman was standing behind her.

"No, not yet. I... I was going to help clean up the dishes from lunch."

"Sounds good. I'll give you a hand."

They both helped with the cleanup. Roman rinsed the dishes as Janine loaded them into the dishwasher. Afterward, Roman returned to the card table and got set up again. He propped up his phone and turned on the relaxing music as well. Janine went upstairs to see the bear hide. As she made her way upstairs, she saw pictures of his family. His parents, grandparents, brother and brother's wife, two daughters, and a picture of Roman and Briana. She looked at the pictures. Janine could sense Roman's love for his family and Briana. It was a genuine kind of love. Each of those pictures was worth a thousand words. Sometimes one sentence is powerful enough to make a lasting impression for ages. That's how Janine felt as she looked at those pictures. It's almost like she could feel their warmth and tenderness from them. That's something she longed for from her parents.

She also noticed other pictures hanging on the wall that were drawings that had been framed. All of them were drawn with the use of a charcoal pencil. Some were drawings of landscapes, and others were fun pictures of Disney characters. Janine was impressed with the artwork. She couldn't tell whose signature it was on the bottom right side of each drawing. The signature was chicken scratch at best. But she was starting to wonder if maybe Roman drew all those pictures. She wondered if she would have to go through the White Castle drive-thru, talk like Yoda, and make herself look like a fool. But then again, he could have bought them from an artist over the internet.

She finally made her way upstairs. She saw the bear hide. There wasn't much else to see, and she didn't want to be overly nosy either. So, she made her way back downstairs. Roman was focused intently on drawing while using his smokeless tobacco. While listening to "17 Seconds To Anywhere" by Liz Story, he concentrated on his work. Janine decided to go outside for another cigarette break. After she lit her cigarette, she stopped to look at the beauty of Roman's property. She admired it and took it all in.

Even though she favored city life more than country life, Roman's property had a certain charm. She felt relaxed and at peace within herself. She felt safe. Mostly because she could feel herself starting to trust Roman more. She also wasn't thrilled about her house either. She didn't mind where she lived, but it was the house itself. It needed some work, and she didn't have the financial means to pay someone to do it all. Even though she was a truck driver, the company she worked for didn't pay her a high wage. She liked the job but didn't like whom she worked for. She couldn't stand the management at Oglebay Brothers. She knew she wasn't the only one working there who despised it. But she knew that job opportunities in the area were lacking. She also knew the uncomfortable truth that not many people would want to hire a woman truck driver. She feared that employers wouldn't take her experience on the job seriously for the fact that she was a woman. For those reasons, she felt stuck at Oglebay Brothers. But coming to Roman's house was an escape from everything – the politics from work and her strained relationship with her parents. It was a breath of fresh air standing out on the deck while admiring the seclusion of Roman's backyard. She soaked it all in for a while since she knew Roman was busy drawing and didn't want to interrupt him.

It was getting closer to late afternoon. Janine finally went inside and saw Roman sitting quietly at the card table. His left arm was propped up on the card table, and he was holding his head up as he looked down. She couldn't tell if he had a headache or wasn't happy with something.

"Did Roman see me steal the Bible?" she thought as that question of guilt popped up in her head.

"Is everything okay?" Janine asked.

"Well, not really," Roman replied.

"What's the matter?"

Roman sighed and then answered her, "I guess you were right. I tried with all my effort and couldn't draw the moose as I wanted it to look. I'm sorry I wasted your time, but you get your prize now."

Janine didn't know what to say at first. She was happy to cash in on her bet but felt terrible for Roman. She knew he put in every ounce of effort on the drawing.

"Well, before you write your efforts off, let's look and see what you got first."

"All right, if you say so. Here you go."

She approached Roman sitting at the card table. Roman's hand was extended to her so she could take the drawing from his hand. She looked at it. Her heart opened. She was stunned. Janine was in awe of what she was looking at. She knew right away that it was their meeting last week. The drawing was complete. Her eyes, her lengthy hair, the low-cut shirt she wore that day, the shape of her face and her nose, her smile, the freckles on her face, and her holding the cigar between the fingers of her right hand with her perfect hand from Cribbage displayed in her left hand. Her tattoo necklace was drawn in exact detail. Even the jack of hearts was perfect.

"I… *I can't believe it…* You drew a picture of me! And it looks *exactly* like me! You did that all from memory?"

"I didn't. What I did was I used the picture I took of you holding your perfect hand. It's the same picture I sent to you that day. That's why I had my phone on the table so I could draw you. Plus, the music helps me focus, as I mentioned earlier. But anyway, after you went home that night, I examined the picture itself. Your beautiful smile and eyes and how you looked right into the camera. It was perfect. I *knew* I had to draw you."

"Thank you… I don't know what to say. Nobody has ever done anything like that for me before."

"It's my pleasure. I enjoyed it. I know it's not as risqué as that scene in *Titanic,* but you sure are beautiful, Janine."

"Well, I'll take that as a compliment since my clothes were left on for the drawing," Janine said with a smile as she blushed.

They both smiled at each other for a few seconds. Then Roman handed Janine another drawing.

"But business is business, you know. Here's the drawing of the moose head. I did that one a while back. So, I guess you better work on trying to talk like Yoda because our White Castle date is right around the corner."

"You *are* a big dope but a talented artist, I must say. Did you draw those pictures that I saw framed in the hallway?"

"I sure did."

"I'm a big fan of Disney, especially the old-school stuff."

"Me too. *Pinocchio* and *Snow White* are my favorites, and *The Jungle Book,* too."

"I figured when I saw a drawing of the seven dwarfs. Also, your drawing of Mowgli and Baloo and the other of Pinocchio standing next to Honest John and Gideon. Have you ever thought of being an artist as a full-time job?"

"I've thought about it, but I don't know. I don't know who would buy these pictures."

"I'm sure somebody would. They're so detailed. I can only draw stick figures myself."

"I have a whole bunch of drawings saved up. Maybe I could sell some of those. I don't know. I haven't figured out what I want to do with my life down here. But I'm sure I will. It will come to me at some point in time."

"I'm sure you will figure something out. Well, I do need to get going. I can't thank you enough for drawing me. It's incredible what you did."

"Before you go, hang on for a second. I'll stick the picture of you in a frame so you can have it."

He went to the basement to get what he needed. He stuck the drawing of Janine in the frame and made his way back upstairs.

"All set," said Roman as he handed the drawing to Janine. "Next time you come over, I'll share some of the Crown Royal with you."

"Awesome. I'm looking forward to it."

"Well, I'll catch you later, Janine. It was good spending the day with you."

"Yes, I enjoyed it a lot. Thank you again; I appreciate you."

"I appreciate you, too."

They both hugged each other. Janine could feel his fuzzy beard and his strength as he hugged her. Even though she was several inches taller and a few years older than Roman, his height and age didn't bother her as they would have ten years ago. She knew she was taller than many men she had been around. She didn't want to get married to any man tomorrow, but she appreciated Roman's friendship and was open to seeing where things between the both of them would lead.

"Be careful now," Roman said. "We didn't stand six feet from each other, and I'm not sure if you quarantined for fourteen days or not. So, I may have to get tested for bubonic plague."

Janine shook her head and smiled. "Roman, you're such an idiot."

"Well, I try my best."

"I don't even think you have to try. Anyway, thank you again for everything."

"Absolutely. You're welcome here anytime you want, Janine. Bye now."

"Goodbye."

Janine walked out to her Honda Accord. She put the drawing of herself in the trunk. She lit up another cigarette and sat down in the driver's seat. She felt good about the day. Not only about Roman's drawing but about Roman. She perceived him differently from the rest of the Christians and conservatives she knew. How down-to-earth he was instead of being uptight.

She remembered that Jason Kojić had left his Wolverine and Thor action figures at her house. She had them in her car and needed to drop them off. She started her vehicle and made her way to the Kojić residence. She finished her cigarette inside her car, headed to the door with Jason's action figures, and rang the doorbell.

"Oh, hi there," Theresa said.

"Hey, Theresa," said Janine.

"Come on in. I figured you would be over about now."

"Yeah, I got the toys for your son."

"Awesome. Yeah, Jason has been asking for those."

Janine entered the Kojić house and sat in the living room. The two children and Miroslav greeted her. Jason, of course, was excited to get his toys back.

"So, what's been going on?" Theresa asked Janine.

"I've been busy with work and stuff. Enjoying the weekend even though the weather wasn't great today. Life's been good."

Everyone sat in the living room and stared at Janine for a few seconds. Nobody knew what to think. The smile on her face was as big as a crescent moon. Even the kids noticed it and stopped playing their game of chess together. Janine's look on her face was smitten.

"Janine, are you okay?" Theresa asked.

"Yeah, I'm fine."

"Oh… because I haven't seen you smile like the Cheshire Cat in a long time."

"Today was a good day."

"Why do I see hearts floating around your head?" Miroslav asked.

"Well, you know how it goes," Janine replied, brushing off the observation.

"Janine… did you… well… go out on a date?" Theresa asked.

"Not exactly."

A pause of silence filled the room briefly. Nobody knew what to ask next since Janine's details were vague.

"Well, what did you do then?" Theresa asked.

"I went to Roman's house."

"You did? Now, *that* is interesting," Miroslav said.

"I don't know. I know he's got that ugly beard and is shorter than me and a little younger, but there's something about the guy…"

"You like *Roman?*" asked Theresa. "But he's the total opposite of all the other men you've gone for in the past."

"I know, but he's easy to talk to."

"*I knew it!* I knew Aunt Janine *like-liked* Roman! I knew it all along!" Sarah exclaimed.

"Does this mean we'll have a baby cousin to play with someday?" asked Jason.

He had a big smile across his face. Everyone laughed at what the kids said. Janine then got up and started walking to the door.

"You're not even going to believe what Roman did for me," she said to everyone. "I must show you this. It's incredible!"

Janine quickly put on her shoes to grab the portrait out of the trunk of her car. She raced back inside as soon as she could. She set the picture down, facing away from everyone so no one could see it. She took her shoes off and held the portrait up, facing it away from everyone.

"Check this out," Janine said.

She turned it around slowly and showed everyone.

"Wow, that's truly amazing!" exclaimed Theresa. "Did he come up with that from memory?"

"No. What he did was he took a picture of me with his phone. We were smoking cigars and playing Cribbage together the evening we all came over for dinner at his house last week. After you and Miroslav left, I decided to stick around for a bit."

"Ah, you're a part of his special club," said Miroslav.

"What do you mean?" asked Janine.

"He'll only smoke cigars with people he's close to."

"How do you know?"

"Roman told me that once since I'm also one of those people. I'm not sure why it's like that for him, but he told me he'll only smoke with people he feels he can trust."

"Oh, well, I guess I'm a part of the secret club then!"

"Could you see yourself dating or being with him?" asked Theresa.

"Honestly, I want to see where it goes."

"I know he wants someone who goes to church and has that relationship with Jesus," said Miroslav.

"So let me ask you this," Janine said. "Do you think a Christian and non-Christian can be together and be happy with one another?"

Before he responded, Miroslav took several seconds to think about what he would say. Sarah and Jason took their chessboard and left the living room. He figured they knew the conversation would get boring from both their perspectives.

"I think a believer and non-believer can be friends. I also think that's a good thing. More people in this world need to see and hear the love of Christ. I think that's lacking nowadays, especially with the pandemic going on. There's too much hate being preached now on social media.

"Now, to answer your question that you asked me... I don't recommend that people be in a serious relationship or marry if they're a non-believing and believing couple. It's not that those two people are bad or anything like that. It's the fact that they each have two very different lifestyles. Unfortunately, instead of embracing those differences, the two people often end up not living in peace with one another. Now I have seen it where the non-believing spouse converts to becoming a believer. But I've also seen it the other way around, where the believer falls away to satisfy the non-believer because it's easier. Most of the time, the two live individually and not as a team. And trust me, marriage is worth it for sure. But nobody said it was easy. Even though *we're* both believers, Theresa and I have challenges because we're from different cultures and upbringings. Plus, men and women think differently and go about things differently. And I'm not saying that's a bad thing. It's a good thing, if anything. But it *is* something else to navigate in marriage. And we stick together *because* we put Christ in the center of our marriage. We also do the same for raising our children. Now could you imagine marrying a man that not only you would have to live with and deal with his quirks and baggage that he may have, but also the fact that your religious preferences are different?"

"Yeah, I guess that would be an undertaking," Janine said after giving Miroslav's question some thought.

"I know you've said in the past that growing up in our house and the religious aspect was not for you. And if that's what you choose in life, fine. We will always love you no matter what. But think of how that didn't sit well with you and then being married to someone who wants to have a relationship with the Trinity and live his life in that manner," Theresa said.

"I know, but Roman seems so different. He's not a grumpy Irishman like Dad or as strict as Mom and Dad. Roman can joke around about things and not get offended if I swear. He also doesn't mind the fact that I have tattoos and piercings as well."

"Well, Roman *did* grow up a lot different than we did. He didn't grow up going to church like you and me. And yes, he does have a bizarre sense of humor. But he still chooses to live a different life from how you live yours. I would hate to see you fall in love with him only to be disappointed or have your feelings crushed. I'd hate to see Roman hurt, as well. That's all I'm saying. I will not tell you what you can or cannot do. I'm merely giving you some of my thoughts. It's up to you what you decide to do."

"Well, I appreciate it. It's given me something to think about. How are Mom and Dad doing anyway?"

"They're doing good. We haven't seen them in a little while, but we'll probably stop in there before we leave for our camping trip."

"Well, that's good. Last time I saw them was over Christmas back in 2019."

"Yeah, I know things are strained between you and our folks. And I always kick myself that I wasn't there for you more back then and wasn't a better sister to you."

"It's okay, Theresa. You did what you thought was right during those moments, and it's water under the bridge for me. I wasn't always the best at being an older sister to you. But I'm glad at least someone in my family loves me."

"I know Mom and Dad love you. But they suck at showing it the way that they should. And I can understand your resentments about that."

Theresa knew that Janine was starting to feel bad talking about their parents. It was always a delicate subject with Janine.

"Well, anyway, I should head home. I got dinner sitting in the crockpot."

"All right, we'll see you around another time."

"Take care, Janine," Miroslav said.

"You, too. See you all later."

Janine took the picture with her and put it back in the trunk of her car. She lit up another cigarette and drove home. She had a lot to think about regarding her conversation with Theresa and Miroslav. She was also interested in reading the Bible she stole from Roman's house.

She wanted answers in life. She wanted something new. But would this be worth the time? Would having a relationship with God and doing what He does make things any better? Janine knew there was only one way to find out. Seeing how kind and gentle Roman was and that he didn't even grow up going to church, she thought that maybe there was something to this whole Jesus thing. If worse came to worse and she didn't discover God while reading the Bible, it's not like it would cost her a dime out of her bank account.

Meanwhile, Roman was settling in for the evening. He put on one of his favorite movies, *The Deer Hunter*. Since the movie was over three hours long, he had an excuse to sit down and get his nicotine high with some Skoal pouches. He enjoyed the day he had with Janine. He was glad he was getting to know her more and was happy about that. But he felt like he had to keep his guard up. Roman knew that dating a non-believer may not end well due to the differences in lifestyles. He still assumed he had no chance with her because he was shorter and not as old as her. He convinced himself she probably wouldn't be attracted to him. Therefore, he didn't want to invest that sort of love toward Janine.

Nonetheless, he looked at her as a good friend. Maybe someday, he could point her in the direction of following Christ. He still suspected that she might be searching for answers. He figured she wanted more than to smoke a cigar and play Cribbage with him that evening. He would wait for a later time to continue talking to her about it.

CHAPTER 8

Some time had passed since Janine and Roman had seen each other. Things had been busy for Janine at her job. They didn't even bump into each other when looking after the chickens and pets for the Kojićs. But now it was time for the first big date at White Castle. They had recently opened a new location in Chambersburg. Roman was excited since there weren't any White Castle restaurants where he grew up. He could see Janine pulling up the driveway.

"The door is open," Roman shouted so Janine could hear him.

"Hey, Roman."

"Hey, Janine. I was finishing up some house cleaning. I mopped the floors, cleaned the bathrooms, and did some dusting. All that fun stuff. So... you ready for some White Castle?"

"Yeah, I suppose."

"Let me ask you a personal question."

"Okay."

"How good would you say your driving skills are?"

"Pretty damn good, I would think. I mean, I drive a commercial truck for a living."

"You got a clean driving record?"

"Not even a parking ticket."

"Good."

He threw car keys at Janine. She grabbed them out of the air with no problem but looked confused.

"Ever driven a Rolls-Royce?" Roman asked.

She stood there looking surprised, not knowing what to say.

"I mean, it's a simple 'yes' or 'no' question," Roman said.

"No, I haven't," Janine replied.

"Well then. Today is your lucky day. Let's go. I'm starving."

"You're seriously going to let me drive your Rolls-Royce?"

"Yeah, why not? You told me you got a clean driving record."

"You're seriously going to let me drive your Rolls-Royce?"

"Is there an echo in here?"

"You mind if I smoke first?"

"Not at all. Thank you for asking too. I don't care if you smoke; however, I don't want it in my house or vehicles. Oh, I need to use the bathroom before we go."

"Okay."

As Janine stood outside, she lowered her face mask to smoke her cigarette. She was excited at the thought of driving a luxury car. She was a little nervous, however. What if the one time she drove Roman's car and managed to wreck it? Then there would be harsh repercussions to follow. But she wasn't going to think about it too much. She wanted to enjoy the day. She turned around fast, saw the garage door open, and heard a vehicle start. There it was. The Rolls-Royce Ghost was sitting next to his Toyota Tundra. The magnificent royal blue exterior shined, along with a silver Spirit of Ecstasy retractable hood ornament. She marveled at the sight of it.

"You ready, Janine?"

"Yes, yes, I am."

"Good. I'll grab that cigarette butt from you, and then we'll be good to go."

Roman threw the cigarette butt away and grabbed an empty sweet tea bottle as a spitter for his tobacco juice, along with his Vikings hat. He noticed Janine was wearing her Packers hat. He thought it would be fun hanging out together as opposites. Janine pulled her face mask up after she finished smoking. She opened the automatic door to the driver's side to take a look. The interior of the Rolls-Royce was pristine. The leather seats were a light cream color. She took a seat on the driver's side. She noticed the burr walnut veneer had a high gloss finish and an illuminated fascia on the passenger side. The ambiance of being inside the Rolls-Royce was breathtaking. It was better than she could have ever imagined. Seeing pictures or reading up on them in the past didn't do justice compared to sitting in one. Roman finally got in from the passenger side.

"Well, you ready to take this bad boy for a spin?" asked Roman.

"Absolutely," Janine said with a smile.

"Make sure you hit the button to close the garage door."

"Will do."

And away they went. It was about an hour to get to Chambersburg from Neelyton. Until they got there, they could enjoy each other's company along the way. It was a perfect day for going outside. It was warm but not humid. There wasn't a cloud in the sky either.

"So, do you like White Castle?" Roman asked.

"Their burgers aren't bad, but I like their chicken rings."

"I *love* White Castle! They're the crème de la crème of fast food."

"If you say so."

"Are you kidding? Where else can you order a bunch of little sliders, chicken rings, and fries?"

"I'm sure you can order fast food at any fast-food restaurant, at least the last time I checked."

"Yeah, but it's not the same. I'll tell you this. I would invite Snoop Dogg over to my house if I could. Then Snoop Dogg and I could eat a bunch of White Castle sliders and watch *Benny Hill* together!"

Janine laughed at that. "You're crazy."

"But I would! I would bromance Snoop Dogg with some White Castles and a *Benny Hill* marathon. I'd bromance him to the moon and back."

"*Bromance*… I'm sure you're at the top of *his* list for bromance, too! Do you know if Snoop Dogg eats White Castle or watches *Benny Hill*?"

"Well, I can't say for certain."

"So, you like Snoop Dogg?"

"Yeah, a guilty pleasure, I know, but I can't help it. Briana and I would listen to him together. I admit it; I'm a fan. Not what you would expect from a typical Christian."

"It's fine. I don't mind if you listen to his music. I can have a celebrity crush on Snoop Dogg myself."

"You do?"

"Yeah, I think he's pretty hot."

"That's perfect! You could join Snoop Dogg and me and partake in White Castle sliders! I don't know if you like *Benny Hill* or not. *Oh!* I got a better idea! Maybe Martha Stewart likes White Castle too. Then the four of us could go on what they call... a double date!"

Janine was laughing at all the outrageous statements Roman had made. She said, "You know, I must be frank with you. You are the most fun yet bizarre and over-the-top Christian I've *ever* met in my life."

"I'm just telling you the truth! Wouldn't you want to go on a double date with me if Martha Stewart and Snoop Dogg were there?"

"Well... maybe. If White Castle were my only option, I would go."

"I see... have you ever watched *Benny Hill*?"

"I haven't. I know who he is, however. My folks probably would have grounded me if I had watched him."

"I'm a big fan. My father and I would watch him together when I was in high school."

"What was high school like for you?"

"I didn't care much for it. People didn't care for me much, either. They liked my brother more because he tended to be more outgoing. I'm more introverted than my brother. People would tease Briana and me because we were an interracial couple."

"I wouldn't have expected that since you lived in New England."

"I guess people are people no matter where you live."

"Yeah, I didn't do well in high school with people, either. They mainly picked on me for my height since I grew tall early during my childhood. They would also call me a 'city girl.' Or the fact my..."

Janine cut herself off before she shared too much personal information with him. She feared that he would cast judgment upon her. She would tell him another fact about herself, but not the original one that had almost slipped out of her mouth.

"You what?" Roman asked.

"The fact that... I was never one to cave into peer pressure. The choices I made were the ones that *I* made. Not because the popular kids coerced me. And I know that infuriated them."

"Hey, you should make decisions on your own. That's the way I see it."

"Thank you. Thank you for not trying to change me. My boyfriend from McKeesport always tried to convince me to do things his way. I didn't want to listen to him because he nagged me too much. He couldn't accept me for who I am."

"What was his name?"

"His name was George."

"What happened with you and George?"

"I feel like he wanted the benefits of a relationship without the commitment. I know I didn't do *everything* right, but at least I wanted to work on us together. I wanted the benefits along with the commitment. Mainly I got sick of George looking at pornography. I mean, not to blow my own horn, but I'd like to think I'm somewhat attractive. I used to buy lingerie to wear for him in the bedroom. I tried to make the sex as fun and fulfilling for him as possible. I also did my best to do right by him when we weren't in the bedroom. But he kept going back to those porn websites to watch videos. He also thought drinking beer and watching a ball game or playing video games was more important than spending time with me. I don't know... I felt like I did even matter to him."

"That must have been hard to deal with. I'm sorry he didn't give you the attention you were craving and deserved."

"Well, thanks, but it was probably good that it ended. I found out he ended up cheating on me with some other woman. From there, I was done. So, I picked up from McKeesport and moved back to Huntingdon County."

"Do you miss living out in McKeesport?"

"Not really. I miss the city of Pittsburgh, but I don't miss McKeesport. It's so sad what happened there. McKeesport was a booming town with steel mills back in its glory days. Once they all packed up and left, it killed the city of McKeesport. What used to be nice mansion-style homes are now crumbling and falling apart. Plus, there's a good amount of crime in McKeesport."

"Maybe someday we can go to Pittsburgh together. I've never been to Pittsburgh or McKeesport before."

"That could be arranged. There's not much to see in McKeesport compared to Pittsburgh, but I could take you there for a spin so that you can see it."

"Sounds good to me. Oh! There it is! White Castle time!"

"Yeah, there it is."

Janine drove the Rolls-Royce into the drive-thru lane of White Castle. She pulled up to the menu sign right before the speaker so they could figure out what they wanted to order.

"I think I'll stick with chicken rings and share my fries with you if you want," Janine offered.

"That's a deal. I'll get a ten-piece mozzarella stick to share with you. Let's see. I think I'll do six sliders with a small, sweet tea," said Roman.

"All right."

"Don't forget you must talk like Yoda when you order."

"Yeah, I know… pain in the ass."

She drove forward to the speaker.

The voice through the speaker said, "Welcome to White Castle. May I take your order?"

Janine had her head down on the steering wheel. Roman was giggling.

"I can't believe I'm going to do this. Oh well, here goes," Janine said.

She thought about placing the order with as few words as possible so she wouldn't sound as ridiculous. She cleared her throat, lowered her face mask, and began putting the order in as Yoda.

"I'd like six sliders and a sack of chicken rings, I will."

Roman was laughing out loud now at Janine's best attempt to sound like Yoda.

"What else can I get for you?"

"A large fry and a ten-piece mozzarella sticks."

"Anything else?"

"Two small, sweet teas. Hmmm, eat the sliders, I will."

"What was that? I couldn't understand what you were trying to say."

"No! Try not. Do. Or do not. There is no try."

Roman was slapping his knee, laughing harder. He knew the person taking their order would have difficulty understanding what Janine was saying. He knew so not only because she was wearing her face mask but because she sounded ridiculous trying to impersonate Yoda.

"Shut up," Janine said in her normal voice as she shoved Roman on the shoulder.

"Two small, sweet teas," she said, talking like Yoda again.

"Is that going to be everything?"

"Yes."

"That will be twenty dollars and eighty-seven cents. If it's okay, I'll let you check your order once you get to the window since I had difficulty understanding you. I think the speaker might be going bad. It kind of made you sound like Frank Oz."

Roman would have been rolling on the floor with laughter if he wasn't inside the car.

After laughing, he said, "You see? Now that wasn't so bad, was it?"

"I swear I'm going to kill you. The next date is on you!"

"Back to White Castle again?"

"No!"

They drove forward, and Janine paid for their meals. Afterward, Janine went to a quiet park in Chambersburg, where they could eat lunch together. They got to the picnic bench with their food and sat across from each other.

"May I pray before we eat this time?" asked Janine.

"Oh, sure you can," said Roman.

"Dear Lord, thank You for this food, Rolls-Royces, and crazy friends like Roman. Amen!"

"Amen," Roman said with a chuckle.

Roman took a bite from one of his sliders and said, "Man, that tastes so *good!* It tastes even better because you're here, Janine. You sure you don't want a bite?"

"Yeah, I'm sure. I wouldn't want to deprive you."

"Ah, but you must marvel at that smell of yummy goodness."

He took the slider and held it up. Then he moved his hand, pretending to drive its fragrance toward Janine.

"You're obsessed with White Castle, aren't you?"

"I *love* White Castle! They're outstanding because they've been around for one hundred years, my friend! Mmmm-mmmm," he said as he took a bite and hugged himself. He kept making sounds, making it known that he enjoyed his food.

"Are you having a foodgasm over there?"

"Mmmmm, I can't help it, Janine. Just look at these sliders. They're... they're... *glorious!* Even *spellbinding!*"

"Oh, brother," she said with a smile. "You *are* something else."

"I enjoy the little things in life, you could say. Get it? Because the sliders are small. You see what I did there, right?"

"I sure do, Captain Obvious."

"Someday, I should visit White Castle headquarters because I have some big ideas for them."

"Oh, this ought to be good. Like what?"

"You know what I think? I think they should open a theme park! They could have a roller coaster ride called the Slider Rider. They could also have a play area for the little kids, calling it the Sandcastle. It's only a couple of ideas, but I'll think of more. What do *you* think?"

"I think you have too much free time on your hands. Anyway, changing the subject. Now that I told you about my ex-boyfriend, tell me about Briana. How did she put up with your antics?"

"I honestly don't know to tell you the truth. But we had known each other since elementary school. As I mentioned, I wasn't popular in school, but neither was she. She was on the heavier side, but I didn't care. She was my best friend. We pretty much did everything together. Shoot, we even got stuck in a tornado together."

"Whoa, seriously?"

"Yeah. You remember hearing about the Joplin, Missouri, tornado?"

"You both survived that *thing?* I remember seeing videos of that tornado. It was huge!"

"Yeah, we made it out alive."

"Well, what was that like? I've never seen a tornado in real life."

"We went out to Joplin to visit her brother. He eventually moved back to that part of Missouri after finishing his stint with the Army. Briana's father's family is from around that area, while Briana's mother's side of the family is originally from Mattapoisett, Massachusetts. They both lived in Mattapoisett before moving to the same school district I went to. Her father moved up to Massachusetts for work, and that's where her parents met."

"Oh, I see. So, did you see the tornado?"

"Not only did we see it, but we heard it and then some. Before the tornado, her brother Chris had kept the above-ground shelter stocked with food and supplies in case that day were ever to show up. That morning started as a gentle spring day. But toward the late afternoon and early evening, I remember he kept looking at the sky and telling me that he didn't have a good feeling. Eventually, the clouds turned an ugly black, and the sky had a sick green color."

"Not to interrupt, but did you say an above-ground shelter? I thought being underground was the safest place during a tornado."

"Well, out in that part of the world, I don't think many people have a basement. They can't build them due to the water table being too high or how rocky it is beneath the ground. I can't remember if it's either or both scenarios. Building a basement would be an expensive endeavor for most people. But above-ground shelters work very well. I believe companies that sell them put them through rigorous tests before selling their product. They bolt them down during home installation, anchoring them to something. Chris had his anchored to the concrete slab inside their garage.

"But going back to the story. Eventually, we heard the tornado sirens wailing off in the distance, and the lightning got bad. We gathered everyone in the safe room but couldn't find one of their children."

"Don't tell me their child got blown away."

"No, thank goodness, no. We left Chris' wife and son in the safe room along with Briana and their corgi. We weren't going to abandon Chris' daughter, of course. So, he searched the house as I looked outside. I yelled for her name. Her name is Rachel. I was starting to panic that I'd never find her. I saw the tornado off in the distance and knew I didn't have much time. I could see it carrying debris, and flying debris is the cause of many tornado deaths. That monstrosity of a tornado was headed right for Chris and his family's house on South Ozark Avenue. Eventually, I found her hiding in her plastic toy house attached to her swing set."

"She would have rather stayed out there in that?"

"No, but I know she feared the lightning. It caused her to freeze up; she was only four or five years old. I think their son was like three or four years older than her. But I eventually talked her into trusting me so I could carry her back to the house where the safe room was."

"So, then what happened?"

"Well, right when I picked up Rachel in my arms, I heard a noise. A pitchfork flew with such force that the tines were perfectly lodged into the tree right next to us. I looked at it and gulped as I trembled in fear. A lightning bolt struck an electric pole not far away. What a noise that made! That's when I knew we had to hurry. The tornado was more obscured by the rain, which made it harder to see. I knew it was getting closer by the second. I ran as fast as possible because I didn't want debris to kill us. The roaring of the wind was incredible. And then the rain came. The skies opened and rained so bad I could barely see the house as I ran toward it, even though I didn't have that far to go. I've never seen rain that heavy before.

"Chris finally got to the backdoor, where I was running to. He scooped Rachel out of my arms to try and comfort her as best and as quickly as possible. Chris also had to grab and pull me in as I got to the door because the winds picked up at that point. The weight of the air felt different too. I could also hear some shingles starting to pull off from the roof. Had it been any later, Rachel and I would not have made it. The wind or the debris would have killed us. There was no comfort for us on that day during that moment."

"Did the tornado pass right over you guys?"

"It did. A couple of minutes later, we took a direct hit around a quarter of six that evening, give or take. I can't even describe all the noises we heard when it was right on top of us other than it was so loud. That's merely an understatement. That tornado poured out its wrath right on top of us and over the community of Joplin, for that matter. We screamed like crazy. The children were bawling their eyes out. It was simply awful. And the word terrible only scratches the surface of the tornado's damage in Joplin that day.

"We waited a good while before we decided to venture out of the safe room. The children begged us not to open the door, but we had to do it eventually. Chris partially opened the door and peeked outside. He was lucky to get it as open as he did due to the debris scattered everywhere. The house, of course, was a total loss. Everything gone. But we were fortunate to have made it out alive and still have each other at that moment.

"Eventually, Briana's brother and his family got their house rebuilt. They're doing fine, as far as I know. I haven't stayed in touch with Chris as much as I should, but we talk occasionally. But living through that event made me appreciate life a whole lot more. I know over one hundred fifty people lost their lives during that tornado. I remember seeing cars scattered across the countryside since they got tossed by those brutal winds. I also saw a dead body. The individual was missing a head and an arm. I saw that and broke down and cried. I couldn't stand to see that kind of destruction done… It's something that I hope never to see again.

"For the remainder of our time in Joplin, we did our best to help others in the community while also helping Chris and his family. Chris' family lived nearby, and they stayed with them so they could get on their feet. The place looked like a bomb had gone off. It was devastating."

"That's an intense story. Gosh, I don't even know what to say. So, am I allowed to ask why you and Briana aren't together anymore?"

"Ah, I knew that was coming. Well, it's time that you know the truth, I suppose… she died."

"You mean the tornado took her?"

"No. We all made it that day. This happened a few years after the Joplin tornado. She died in a car wreck."

"Oh my God, Roman. I'm so sorry."

"It's okay. I think I've finally made peace with it, or to the best of my ability. She got into a wreck with a tractor-trailer."

"Man… I am so sorry. I know saying sorry won't bring her back, but I don't know what else to say. Were you able to file a lawsuit?"

"No, because it was her fault. She ran the red light at the intersection of a busy road. I guess she fell asleep behind the wheel, and that's when it happened. She was always exhausted during her second trimester."

"Your child didn't make it either; I take it."

"Nope. She was like five months pregnant. I lost her and our child, whom I'll never be able to meet, hold, feed, or play with. I'd give anything to change that child's poopy diaper or stay up late at night trying to put my would-be son to sleep. We tried for a couple of years to get pregnant. It was difficult going through that because the doctors couldn't find out why she couldn't get pregnant. There was also nothing on my end preventing it either. When we found out we were pregnant, we were so overjoyed. All that time we spent waiting for a child. Now they're both gone."

"You were supposed to have a boy?"

"Correct. We were going to name him James. I had put whatever was left of Briana in a casket since that was what she would have wanted. I know she didn't want to be cremated, but I chose to leave the casket closed due to the nature of her death. On top of the casket, I put pictures of her so people could see how she should have been. If only I had stopped my compulsive gambling sooner. If only we didn't get into a fight about it. She wouldn't have stormed out during our fight. She and the baby could have been here today. Sometimes... I feel like *I* killed her and the baby."

Roman put his head down on the picnic table and wept. All Janine could do was watch in despair. She reached out and ran her hand through Roman's hair several times. He looked up at her with teary eyes.

She said, "Roman... I want you to understand something. You *didn't* kill them. What happened was completely out of your control. I know you loved her and your child with all your heart. You're a good man, Roman. Don't let anyone tell you otherwise, especially yourself."

"I appreciate that, Janine," he said in a choked-up voice. "You've been a good friend to me."

"I know I am. It's not every day you'll meet a friend who will talk like Yoda at the White Castle drive-thru."

Roman laughed at that as a tear rolled down his cheek.

"Well, how about we start heading home since our gourmet lunch is finished?"

"Sounds good to me."

CHAPTER 9

Janine lit up a cigarette before they started their trip home. Afterward, they walked over to the Rolls-Royce after disposing of their garbage. It wasn't too far into their drive when there was a sudden interruption.

"Janine?" asked Roman.

"What?"

"I know you're going to kill me for this."

"What is it?"

"I have to take a *massive* dump."

"Are you kidding me? We *just* passed a rest stop like ten seconds ago."

"I'm sorry."

"Well, you shouldn't have eaten all that food in one sitting. What would Snoop Dogg and Benny Hill say about that?"

Janine saw Roman shifting in his seat with some degree of discomfort.

"Lucky for you, Roman. It looks like there's a gas station a couple of miles ahead. I need to buy myself a pack of cigarettes anyway."

Janine pulled into the parking lot of the gas station. Roman ran into the gas station as fast as he could while pinching his butt cheeks together.

"What a sight," Janine said to herself as she shook her head.

She got out of the car and went into the gas station to buy herself a pack of Parliaments. As she made her purchase at the check-out counter, she heard the performance of a lifetime. Both the cashier and Janine heard it. They both stared at the corner of the store where the bathroom was. Janine could hear Roman moaning loudly as she knew he was trying to go to the bathroom. They both heard that Roman had finally finished and could hear him sighing in relief. Even though it was muffled, they could both hear him talk.

They even heard him say, "Forgive me, Lord Jesus. I think I queefed myself!"

"I guess Roman has a mangina," Janine thought.

All Janine could do was close her eyes and turn her head down in embarrassment. She wished she could snap her fingers and make herself disappear. She wanted to laugh at his comment. However, she wished this situation wasn't happening in public. The cashier was a full-figured woman behind the counter and appeared to be in her early to mid-fifties. She continued to stare in the direction of the bathroom with no emotion on her face.

"Um… is that your man in there?" asked the cashier.

"No. No, it's not. I mean… I don't even know who's in there."

"Oh… I tell you what. He's hot."

"What?"

"Yeah, he is. I would tap that."

"Are you being serious?"

"Hell, yeah. I would sit on his face while he went down on me," the cashier said as she let out a thunderous belch that could have knocked a horse over.

"Please tell me you're joking," Janine said with disgust.

"Don't be ridiculous. I think it's every man's duty to let his woman sit on his face during the thrills of romance," the cashier said as she shoved a big wad of tobacco in her mouth.

"Congratulations. He's all yours, then. On that note, I'm going to smoke this entire pack of cigarettes in one sitting now."

Janine quickly exited the store after her purchase. She lit up a cigarette and waited for Roman next to the car. She figured he would be in there for a little bit. Roman finally emerged from inside the gas station and staggered toward the Rolls-Royce.

"Feeling better?" asked Janine.

"Janine, that was the dump of the century!"

"Good to know. Let's get going."

They both hopped in the car and restarted their journey home.

"Janine, I have to tell you something."

"What now?"

"That was seriously the biggest dump I ever took in my life. Like the kind that sticks to the back of the toilet. That must have been something from the Devil in the Book of Revelation."

"Would you please stop talking about taking dumps? It's disgusting."

"I mean, everyone does it. Don't you? It's nothing to be ashamed of."

"Can we *please* change the subject? Besides, it's the Book of Revelations, you know, plural."

"Um… I'm pretty sure it's not… Anyway… what do you think about this guy?"

"Who?"

"I'll show you."

Roman went on his phone and searched for a random image of someone wearing a face mask and then showed Janine the picture.

"Here, this person. What do you think?"

"What the hell do you mean?"

"You know, the wearing of the face mask."

"Oh… well, I think doing that during the pandemic takes a lot of strength and courage. I wish more people would take the guidelines to heart instead of making it all about propaganda. I feel like it saves people's lives if people would give it the benefit of the doubt. People at work laugh at me for wearing a face mask when I'm around them. My company is supposed to enforce face masking and social distancing, but they don't."

"Well, that wasn't my question. What do you think about this individual in the picture I showed you?"

"I thought I answered that."

"No, I mean, take a look at the picture."

"Does this conversation have any point?"

"What if he lets out a fart by accident and unintentionally performs a nonconsensual Dutch oven on himself? Or what if he's wearing a mask because something more is covered up?"

"What? Seriously dude? What's the matter with you? First, you go from talking about dumps to whether people are wearing a mask because they're hiding something. Right... speaking of *fake news*, that's a bunch of shit if I ever heard such a thing! There must be something extraordinary in that Cape Cod water you drank growing up. I can't even believe we're having a conversation that is so juvenile. This person is not trying to hide anything, so let's nip that in the butt now!"

"Wait... nip it in the what?"

"Nip it in the butt."

"I mean, I know what you said, but isn't it 'nip it in the bud?'"

"I'm pretty sure it's *'butt'* the last time I checked."

"Um... I'm pretty sure it's not."

"Roman, *everybody knows* it's 'nip it in the butt.'"

"Is this what they mean when they say *misinformation?*"

Janine scoffed at that remark and smacked her hand on the steering wheel. She knew he was going to start up again, and he did.

Roman continued the conversation and said, "So let me ask you a personal question. Have you or have you known anyone that's been nipped in the butt before? Or even the peanut gallery, for example. When is the last time anyone has seen a gallery of peanuts?"

"Roman, it's *just* a saying."

"I mean, I wasn't talking about taking it up the butt. I'm an exit-only sort of person, but to each their own. Anyway, let me get back on point. I meant on or around the butt, like on the part of the ham. A pressed ham, if you will."

"You are so freaking weird! Who would have thought I'd be driving an imbecile around in his Rolls-Royce someday? Besides, I'm sure the person you google searched for has many more important things to do, like protecting others instead of hiding ulterior motives or discussing pressed hams with a *simpleton* like yourself!"

"Oh, I see... so does getting nipped in the butt violate the rules of social distancing? And would it make a difference if it was a mandated nipping or not?"

"How should I know? It's just a saying, that's all!"

"Oh, well, why didn't you say so in the first place?"

Roman was trying not to laugh out loud. He covered his mouth so she couldn't see his mischievous smile. He thought it was funny, needling Janine with sheer stupidity. He didn't even care about the political aspect of it. He didn't even have a bitter hatred toward Dr. Fauci. Politics was something he never judged anyone else on. He wouldn't even be associating with Janine if that were the case. He was in the conversation only to be ridiculous. Simply to get the rise out of Janine was what he was looking for. Some time had passed before they engaged in another conversation again until Roman broke the silence.

"So, have you enjoyed driving the Rolls-Royce?"

"I sure have. It beats that little rust bucket I'm driving. It still runs great, but it is getting old, and I know the salt from the roads during the winters has taken a toll on it over the years."

"What year is your car?"

"It's a 2002. It's a stick shift."

"You know, I never did learn how to drive a standard transmission."

"Really?"

"It's the truth. It's not that I didn't want to. I never had the opportunity to do it."

"Well, maybe you will. Care to drive my car sometime? I'll give you some lessons on it."

"I could, but what if I stall it or roll backward on a hill and hit another car?"

"We'll start you off easy. Maybe like the parking lot of a Walmart on a Saturday morning. Besides, if you can let me drive this luxury vehicle, I'm sure I can let you learn how to drive my stick shift Honda Accord."

"I'd be up for that."

"Well, we can schedule a time in the future so I can teach you."

"Works for me."

They finally made it back to Roman's house. She parked the car in the garage.

"So, what do you have planned for the rest of the day?" Janine asked.

"I was going to do some work in my garden. I have to keep it properly maintained to do my canning toward the end of summer. It pays off in the long run. Garden fresh food is so much better than that store-bought crap."

"I agree with you there. I need to get going and do some stuff myself."

"What do you have going on?"

"Well, I need to do some cleaning in my house. I also need to go to my sister's house to tend to their pets since they're on their camping trip in West Virginia. Plus, I need to cook dinner too."

"Yeah, I need to go back and feed their chickens again. Thanks for hanging out with me and putting up with my shenanigans."

"Yeah, whatever, it was okay," she said with a smile.

They both exchanged quick hugs and went their separate ways. Roman ended up getting his garden watered and picking out the weeds. He also managed to feed the chickens at the Kojićs. After that, his work was done. He hopped in the shower. He didn't feel like cooking since he was gone for most of the day. He decided to do something quick and easy and heat a frozen pizza in the oven. The pizza eventually finished cooking, and Roman said his prayer before eating. As he was eating, his phone started to ring. It was his brother Craig. He wanted to FaceTime Roman.

"Hey, big brother! What's going on?" asked Roman.

"Hey man, not too much. How have you been?" asked Craig.

"I've been doing well. I've been doing very well. How's Chelsea and your kids doing?"

"They're all great. The kids are out of school for the summer, which means I'm done teaching at school for the summer. Chelsea is still working at the dentist's office doing the hygienist work. We've been hanging out at the beach and seeing the parents regularly. So, what's new with you, my man?"

"Well… I've met this woman."

"Really? Uh-oh! There you go, man. You both an item?"

"Well, not officially. We have been hanging out a lot, though."

"That's great, Roman. Good for you! If things are meant to work out, they will. So, is she a babe?"

"Yeah, she's stunning. She's taller than me too. I've never dated a woman taller or older than me. Janine is like six feet tall."

"Wow, that's cool. Yeah, most babes don't go for shorter or younger guys. But hey, if she notices you for who you are on the inside, you might have a keeper."

"You never know. That's why I'm going to see where this all goes. I'm kind of at peace with whatever happens to be honest."

"Yeah, man. Be who you are, and she'll see that. You're a good man, Roman, and you deserve only the best in life. How have you been feeling otherwise? You doing okay?"

"Yeah. Moving down here has helped a lot with the depression I had in the past. I miss you guys, but I couldn't live up there anymore. It got too depressing for me after Briana died."

"I understand. We all miss you like crazy, but we're proud of you. None of us are mad at you for moving to Pennsylvania, and I want you to hear that from me. We all got your back on this man."

"I appreciate the kind words, Craig. I can't wait to have you all down for a visit."

"Me neither. We're all busting to come down there to see you. We've seen pictures of your place. That property and the house you built on it look amazing."

"It *has* been good to me. I'll look at the calendar tonight and figure out when's a good time for everyone to visit. There's plenty of room, so there's no need to get a hotel or anything like that."

"That would be so much fun. I know my kids have been asking about their Uncle Roman. Everyone misses you, but as I said, we all support you. Have you been staying clean from the gambling?"

"Yes, I've been clean for about four years now."

"You're a brave man. Keep up the great work. I've said it before, but I'll repeat it: if you *ever* need to talk or need anything, don't feel bad about calling me. I don't care if it's after midnight. If you need something, call me anytime."

"Thanks, man, and the same goes for you, too."

"All right, Roman, you have a good night. I love you, man."

"I love you too, big brother."

Roman disconnected from FaceTime and pulled up his calendar on his phone. Christmas was something that came to mind. How cool would it be if everyone came down to spend Christmas with him? The more he thought about it, the more it made sense. Roman sent his parents and brother a group text about the idea.

After dinner, Roman spent the remainder of his evening going to the local ice cream stand and enjoying a sweet treat. After enjoying his ice cream, he went home to prepare for bed. The day ended on a good note for him as everyone he messaged about coming down for Christmas responded and said they would be there. He said his prayers before bed and then turned the lights out.

Over at Janine's house, she intently read the Bible she stole from Roman's collection of books. She randomly stumbled across the book of Ephesians.

She read one of the verses, "Wives, submit yourselves to your own husbands as you do to the Lord. For the husband is the head of the wife as Christ is the head of the church, his body, of which he is Savior. Now as the church submits to Christ, so also wives should submit to their husbands in everything."

She paused for a few seconds, could start to feel her blood boil, and thought, *"Are you kidding me? Does Roman believe in this shit? What woman wants to submit to a man when all men want is a booty call?"*

She picked up the Bible and threw it in the garbage beside her bed. She thought about what she had done. Guilt and shame overcame her conscience as she began to feel bad for throwing the Bible in the garbage. Not to mention it technically wasn't her Bible, to start with. She got up from her bed, got the Bible out of the trash can, and opened it again. This time she opened the Bible to the book of Romans.

Janine continued to read out loud, "But God demonstrated his own love for us in this: While we were still sinners, Christ died for us."

Reading this verse did not provoke the kind of anger like reading the verse in Ephesians did. Instead, it caused Janine to go deep into thought. Maybe she was still carrying around the hurts of her childhood and the lack of love she felt there. Perhaps she didn't love herself the way that she should have.

"I don't know if I can do this. How can God love someone like me? What do you think, Willow?"

Willow meowed at her and then jumped up onto the bed. She approached Janine to be petted. Janine reached out to pet Willow.

"I know, Willow. It's hard to figure out since nobody wanted to explain anything to me growing up. Then I got frustrated with it all and tuned everything out. Well, at least I have Roman. Sometimes, he might be a bonehead, but he isn't as dumb as he pretends to be. I know that for a fact.

"And I guess I have Theresa and Miroslav to talk to if I have any questions. But there's something about Roman that makes me feel more comfortable going to him than anyone else. But I still don't know if God can ever love me. It seems far-fetched at times. Not to mention, it sounds like the Bible wants the husband to control the wife. Seems outdated to me. Well, maybe I'll try saying a prayer before bed. I doubt it will make any difference, but what do I have to lose? Here goes nothing.

"Dear Lord, thank You for my friend, Roman, even though he's a bit of a clown. I appreciate the kindness and joy that he has. I'm glad he's genuine and not looking for a booty call. Thank You for my family and my cat Willow. Amen. Let's go to sleep, Willow."

Janine turned off the lights. She realized something as she was lying in bed and sat up. She turned the light back on and grabbed her phone, and google searched the phrase 'nip it in the bud.' It was there clear as day. She found out what Roman was talking about.

"Wow, I guess Roman *was* right. I still like using the word 'butt,' so I'm keeping it my way. Maybe now I'll look up a person wearing a face mask to see if... *Oh!* That pea brain Roman! I'm not going to buy into his outlandish theories. Time for bed!"

She slammed her phone down on her nightstand, turned the light off, and then cuddled up next to Willow. The next time she saw Roman in person, she knew she would have questions about what she had read in the Bible. But for now, it was time to shut off her brain for the night. It was time for sleep.

CHAPTER 10

The day had finally shown up. It was early morning, and it was time for Roman to learn something new. Roman was going to get an education in driving a standard transmission vehicle. It would also be the first time Roman would see Janine's house, as she had invited him to her house for lunch. He could feel the butterflies in his stomach because he was nervous about his lesson. He didn't want to look like a big dummy, unable to drive a stick shift car. But he also knew if he never tried to do it, there would be no way to get good at it.

Janine made her way up the driveway to Roman's house. He left his house and approached her car. He carried a small duffel bag and put it into her car's trunk. He sat there quietly, slightly fidgeting in the passenger seat. Neither one said much after they said "good morning" to each other.

"You mind if I smoke inside my car?" Janine asked as she cracked her window open.

"No, go ahead if you please," said Roman.

"Are you okay? You seem kind of quiet today."

"Well, I'm nervous about driving your car, that's all."

"Oh, you'll be fine. Trust me. I can promise you that you'll stall my car at least once. But don't worry. It's a beater. It's not a luxury car like the Rolls-Royce you have. This caah isn't fancy at all. Look, we're coming up to the Walmart parking lot."

Janine pulled into a parking spot. She turned the vehicle off. They both got out of her car and switched seats. Janine cracked the passenger side window open so she could smoke. Roman sat in the driver's seat. His body posture was rigid and tense.

"Relax, Roman. You got this. There's like no one here anyway. So, you want to put your foot down on the clutch pedal. Turn your key in the ignition to start it but keep your foot on the clutch pedal. I left the gear shifter in neutral for you and your emergency brake engaged, so you're good. Once you start the car, you can take your foot off the clutch."

"That wasn't so bad," Roman said as he started the car.

"I told you this isn't going to be awful. So now we're sitting here idling. Now for taking off. First, put your left foot on the clutch and your right foot on the brake pedal. Now you can disengage your emergency brake. Then you want to move the gear shifter to first gear while keeping your feet on the clutch and brake. See the number one on the gear shifter? That's the direction you want to move it to. Once you do that, take your foot off the brake pedal. You're not stopped on a hill or sitting in traffic, so you don't have to worry about anything."

Roman took a deep breath and did what he was told.

"Okay, let off the clutch as quickly as possible," Janine said.

He did exactly what she told him to do, and the Honda stalled out.

Roman gasped and said, "Oh no! I stalled your car!"

"It's all right. You don't have to make that much of a shocked face about it. I did that to mess with you and see how you would react. Besides, this clutch isn't exactly new. I'm planning on replacing it myself soon. So, as you can see, nothing happened. We're all right. Nobody got hurt."

"Well, how do I start up again?"

"We'll go back to the same scenario we were in. Engage your emergency brake and use your clutch to move your gear shifter back to neutral to start up. Always check to ensure the car is in neutral before turning the key. Now, foot on the clutch and start it up again… Good. Now, remember, put your feet on the clutch and brake pedal, and *then* disengage your emergency brake. Keep your feet on the clutch and brake while you select first gear. Now take your foot off the brake pedal. You ready for this?"

"Yes."

"Okay, now *slowly* ease your foot off the clutch. You will feel the car wanting to go as you're doing that. And as you do that, give it some gas. Not too much, however. You'll see it's a balancing act between the two over time."

Roman let off the clutch, but it was too much, and he stalled the car out again. Janine could see he was flustered. That look of dread and shock appeared on his face again.

"Oh no! I did it again!" he exclaimed.

She couldn't help but laugh. As she laughed, she choked a little bit on her cigarette smoke.

She said, "Look at the face on you! What the hell do you even call that look? Anyway, you're okay, all kidding aside. Relax and take a deep breath. As I said, there's no one here. Now start over again. You got this, my friend. And don't be afraid to ask questions."

Roman got back to the beginning. Once he was ready to go, he slowly let off the clutch pedal. He could feel the car wanting to take off.

"Do you feel that?" Janine asked.

"Yeah."

"Okay, now slowly give it some gas, and as you let off the clutch give it more gas."

Roman gave it some gas, and he didn't stall it this time. However, the take-off was a little rough.

"Not bad. A little rough, but you got it moving. Okay, see how your RPMs are getting high, and you can hear the engine's noise?"

"Yes."

"That means it's time to shift her into second gear. Push down on the clutch, move the gear shifter to second gear, and let the clutch out again."

Roman shifted the car into second gear with ease.

"Good job, Roman. That's good. I think we'll stay at this speed for now. There's no sense in going too fast in a parking lot. So, look up ahead now. You're eventually going to have to turn. You'll see your RPMs drop and hear the car's engine start to chug if you don't downshift."

He downshifted and made the turn that he needed to.

"Okay, now head to this parking spot and take off from a stop. Remember, if you stall, it's not the end of the world. As I mentioned, you can see that letting off the clutch and giving it the right amount of gas is a balancing act. It takes practice. Once you get it, it's like riding a bike. You don't forget it."

"Janine, did you stall out the first time you learned to drive a stick shift?"

"Oh, hell yeah! Of course, I did. And let me tell you something, my father was not a patient man when teaching us kids how to drive. Even Theresa will tell you that. But I'm not going to treat you the way he treated us. Getting all worked up doesn't make for a good learning environment."

"I agree with that."

"Well, get this car moving, big boy. Maybe someday you can drive me, Snoop Dogg, and Martha Stewart to White Castle for that hot double date in the future."

"Okay," Roman said with a smile.

He stalled the car again and huffed at what he had done.

"You're fine. No need to get flustered. Start her up and give it another try."

"Okay."

This time, Roman started up the Honda and smoothly took off from the parking spot.

"That's it, Roman! Just like that! Now drive around some more. Stop and take off from the parking spots as much as you want. It's all about repetition. That's what's going to build your confidence. Drive as slow on the driveway as you want, Rain Man."

Roman laughed at that comment. He was smiling now. His

confidence was shining all around him. He had a few more hiccups here and there with stalling the car out, but he could feel himself starting to grasp the concept of driving around in the parking lot. It was sort of fun for him now that he understood it. After about half an hour of driving, he eventually pulled into a random parking spot.

"You know something? That wasn't too bad. After I did it a few times, I felt like I understood why you were telling me *what* you were telling me."

"Exactly. And the more you do this, it's like riding a bike, as I said before. It becomes muscle memory, in a sense. Now, drive me to the store. I need to buy a pack of Parliament cigarettes."

"Wait, what?"

"Hey, Roman. You just did it in the parking lot, right?"

"Yeah."

"It's the same as driving on the road. You will apply everything you've learned here to drive on the main road. You can do this… You can do this. I believe in you."

"What about rolling on a hill?"

"If you feel yourself rolling back, give it more gas to compensate for gravity. And if you *do* stall, put your feet on the clutch and brake pedal immediately. I'm not going to steer you wrong. I'm not going to let anything happen to you. And I know you believe in God. So, trust in Him that He'll guide you."

"You know you're right. I'm going to do this."

"That's the right attitude."

"Well, here we go!"

Roman successfully made it to the gas station so Janine could buy her cigarettes. He even drove her back to her house without any problems. He made the car jerk a few times, but he didn't cause any accidents on the road. Janine was proud of him. She could tell that he had gained the confidence that he needed.

"Well, you brought us home safe and sound, Roman. And guess what? Nothing happened. Nothing happened at all."

"Yeah, that wasn't as terrifying as I thought."

"I knew you could do it. If you want to practice again, I'll be happy to go with you like we did this morning."

"I appreciate you taking the time to show me how to do this. So, what's for lunch today?"

"I got a salad with all the toppings. I got an assortment of dressings, shredded cheese, hard-boiled eggs, and even grilled chicken, to name a few things."

"That's cool."

"Now, you'll see my house for the first time. It's nothing special, but it'll do."

They both walked inside. It was a small house with an upstairs. Roman noticed the house needed some work. A window pane needed to be changed since there was a crack. A couple of the screens were busted. The living room carpet had seen better days. It gave Roman an idea. He sat at the kitchen table, thinking of his vision. Janine put all the items they needed to make their salads on the table. Roman said the prayer, and then they began to eat.

"I have an idea to run by you," said Roman.

"Oh yeah? What's that?" asked Janine.

"I'll fix up your house if you want me to. You're teaching me how to drive. You did something for me, so I'll do something for you."

"You know how to do home repairs?"

"Yeah, my father taught me at a very young age. He figured, why should you pay someone else to do it when you can do it yourself?"

"That's the main reason I haven't been able to keep up with it all. My job doesn't pay me worth a damn, and I got to save my money for other things, like maybe getting a different car someday, you know, things like that. Something always seems to come up. I make ends meet, but the money gets tight. Plus, I was never taught how to do home repairs. Now I can work on my car, like putting brakes on it and changing oil, but I've never mastered the art of doing home repairs myself."

"That's cool that you're able to do maintenance on your car. Earlier, you said you would replace your clutch at some point."

"Yeah, I taught myself how to do things. I got tired of men screwing me over at auto repair shops anytime I needed work done. So, I decided to take matters into my own hands."

"I understand that. I know that some men will take advantage of women in situations like that. So… if you trust me, I can make many home improvements when you're at work. You can pick out any materials and tell me what you want to be done. And I'll do it for free too."

"You would do something like that for me?"

"Yeah, why not? It's not like I'm going to work every day like you are. You can get your house fixed up, and I can have something to do during the day. It's a win-win situation."

"That would be great. Thanks for offering to help. I've wanted to get this house looking better for so long."

"No problem. How about next weekend we go to the home improvement store together? I'll bring my Tundra, and we can load it up with whatever you want."

"Sounds good to me. I do need to ask you something, if that's okay."

"Sure. You can ask me anything you want. What is it?"

"I was reading the Bible. It was talking about wives submitting to their husbands."

"Okay… what are your thoughts on that?"

"I can't stand that. So, what, the woman is a slave to her man? He orders her around while she does all the work, and he doesn't have to lift a finger to help. How entitled men are! Women already have a hard enough time in this world! I don't get treated with the same respect as my male coworkers because I'm a woman! They think a woman can't drive a commercial-sized truck, but I show my prick boss that I can do it like any other person. I do it day in and day out! And look at what the company does. I *still* get treated like dirt. They treat everyone like dirt, but I know I get harassed more because I'm a woman. I can't see being married to a man if the Bible wants to make women out to be less in life."

Roman was silent for a moment. He knew that this passage in the Bible had struck a nerve with her. He wanted to approach her professionally and still get the truth to her concurrently. He collected his thoughts and engaged her in the conversation she presented to him.

"What are some things you would say make it hard to be a woman in this society?"

It wasn't the response that Janine was expecting. She was expecting Roman to fire back with a snide remark. Roman's question allowed her to relax and not feel so tense. Roman could see her body language go from threatened to a more relaxed posture. This is what he wanted. For he knew a shouting match would get neither one of them anywhere.

"I'd say personally what I mentioned earlier about being a woman in that kind of work environment is one thing. People think you know nothing about trucking because you're female… I'd also say the way they make women's clothing is another example. A lot of it is a one size fits all type of thing.

"Like they make most clothing to fit women with 'C' cup-sized breasts. Well, guess what? One size *doesn't* fit all. If you have bigger breasts, your clothing might not fit at all, and if you have small breasts or are pigeon-chested like me, your clothing could fit weird too."

"What is pigeon-chested?"

At this point, Janine looked nervous, like she had been caught. She knew she would have to tell Roman about some of her past now. Roman could see that Janine was starting to tense up again. She was fidgeting in her seat a little bit too. Roman knew something was on her mind.

"Janine, remember how you told me you would be there for me when I talked to you about Briana that day in the park?"

"Yes."

"Well, I will extend you the same courtesy you've given me.

Anything you say to me stays between us. I give you my word on that."

"Okay… I, um… I've had breast augmentation…"

"Oh?"

"So many people picked on me during high school because I had smaller boobs. They used to call me 'flat chest.' I *hated* it. I hated it so much. I saved enough money for breast augmentation a few years after high school. The doctor said I was pigeon-chested, which caused my breasts to go more off to the side. The technical name for it is called pectus carinatum. My case was on the mild side but enough to be annoying. It made it annoying because my clothes would fit weird."

"Now that you mention clothing, I remember Briana would complain about clothes not fitting her because she was a bigger girl. I always felt bad for her because I know women's clothing shouldn't be a one-size-fits-all deal."

"Yes! Thank you! *Finally*, I'm glad someone, and a man, of all people, understands this!"

"Well, I try. So going back to the story… is pectus carinatum like scoliosis but not in the back?"

"Eh, kind of sort of, I guess. Although they say one in ten people with a pigeon chest has scoliosis. I also have scoliosis on the mild side as well. I don't know if I got these things from being six feet tall or because my growth spurts happened so quickly and young in life. I was tall even when I was a child."

"So, was there any treatment you could get for this?"

"No, because it's only bad enough to be annoying. Something that does help with both pectus carinatum and scoliosis is exercise. That's if I'm doing the *right* exercises, of course. Doing the wrong ones can make things worse. Exercise is a big part of my life."

"I can tell that you're in good shape. So, what led you to decide to get breast augmentation?"

"Primarily for two reasons. I wanted my clothing to fit me right, so I went up to a 'C' cup. It didn't feel too heavy when I tried the sample ones on at the doctor's office."

"Oh, they let you try on different sizes?"

"They do. I didn't want to go too big and have back problems later. You know, trade in one problem for another problem. I think anything more significant on my chest would have looked unnatural anyway. I wanted something comfortable for me, but also, I wanted to feel more feminine. I didn't do it to try to have sex with a bunch of random guys. I wanted to do this for myself.

"But once people discovered what I did, I got ridiculed for it. It's like when I had small boobs; I got made fun of. Then when I got bigger boobs, I got made fun of. Damned if I do and damned if I don't. It's like, what breast size *am* I allowed to have then?

"And boy, I tell you what. My folks were *not* happy with my decision, especially my dad. He even called me a 'whore' for doing what I did. And, of course, living in a small town where everyone knows or *thinks* they know your business, they're going to gossip. But as I said, I didn't make this decision to be promiscuous. That wasn't even on my mind when I decided to do this."

"Well... I appreciate you opening yourself up and sharing your struggles with me. I know that wasn't an easy thing to do. And I'm sorry you've had to put up with all that. You had to make this big decision for yourself, and I can tell you put much thought into it."

"Well, I thank you for your kindness. So, you don't think I'm a whore for doing what I did?" she asked Roman as her throat felt choked up.

"No, I do not. Honestly, I didn't even know they were fake. Well, I mean, I knew they were *there...*" They laughed when Roman said that.

"But, going back to what I was saying," Roman continued, "I don't look down on you for doing what you did. And if people can't accept you for who you are, they don't deserve to be in your company. I also think maybe you need to let yourself off the hook too. God loves you no matter what a person looks likes. He doesn't care about your breast size. He's interested in what's underneath your breasts... your heart."

And then it occurred to her. That verse she read in the book of Romans.

"Maybe Roman is projecting the kind of love God would show us. Maybe he's living out what God is commanding him to do. Maybe that's what love is all about. God's kind of love, not the ways of the world," she thought.

"Now, getting back to the whole submission thing," Roman said. "That's a very controversial topic in this day in age. The dreaded 'S' word infuriates many women. The word *'submit'* has received a lot of negative connotations. Before diving into this topic more, did you read the verses after the ones you read in Ephesians?"

"Well, I... I..."

"You didn't, did you?"

"All right, you caught me."

"It's okay. It's nothing to be ashamed of. So, if you read the verses following the ones that made you mad, it talks about the duties of the husband. He is subject to love his wife as Christ did the church. And we know that Christ's love is unconditional, right?"

"Yes."

"So that's how the husband is supposed to treat his wife. He is to love her unconditionally. He's supposed to be a servant leader. But some men don't look at it that way. They take that word *'submit'* and make it theirs instead of God's. They think it means the wife does all the housework and raises the kids while he gets to do whatever he wants. Or she must obey every command that he gives. He can do that if he chooses to, but that will not gain favor from his wife or the Lord. What wife would want to put up with that kind of bum?"

"Right? And that's how I feel. So, what *does* the word *'submit'* mean?"

"It means that the wife should respect her husband. Encourage the husband and come alongside him to build him up, not tear him down. Don't belittle him, either. Letting him know you are his partner and are in on this marriage together as a team. Let him know it's not 'happy wife, happy life' but 'happy spouse, happy house.' If he makes a simple mistake, go to him with love in private. Don't shame him, especially in public. That can cause discouragement. Treat him as you want to be treated. If there's an extreme situation like spousal abuse, the wife should separate for safety reasons."

"Hmmm, I never looked at it that way before."

"Believe me; I remember reading the Bible by myself. It can be hard, especially if you have no one to ask questions. If it weren't for Miroslav, I wouldn't be where I am, and that's the truth. So, you can see the word *'submit'* when used the right way, can be used for good and can also be used for evil when twisted around for selfish desire. Even the verse where husbands love their wives as Christ did the church can be twisted, believe it or not."

"How so?"

"Well, I wasn't a churchgoer back then, and neither was Briana. But looking back on it now, I noticed that it happened. Don't get me wrong; I was happy with Briana. I'm not talking bad about her, but this thing she would sometimes do would drive me crazy. For example, she said, 'Well, if you loved me, you would have remembered to make the bed today.' And I knew she wasn't kidding around either in that situation. I simply forgot. It wasn't because I didn't love her.

"Sometimes, she would use *love* to get her way or to belittle me. Sometimes she would even gossip about me to other people about my shortcomings. It didn't change my love for her, but I wish she would have gone to me in private instead of broadcasting things like that to the public. I *hated* it when she did that. I'm honestly surprised she never spoke about my gambling. She may have been too embarrassed.

"Anyway, let me get back on track here. Think of it this way. If you saw Sarah or Jason walking around with a butter knife when they were little, would you let them stick it in the electrical outlet?"

"No. Of course not."

"Exactly my point. You love them so much that you don't give them everything *they* want because you know it's not a good thing. Just because a husband is supposed to love his wife unconditionally doesn't mean he gives her everything she wants at her every command. That's not love. Sometimes I couldn't give Briana everything. It didn't mean I loved her any less. Sometimes, I felt like she wanted me to be flawless. No one is flawless. If love is based on a person getting everything their way, then they don't need a spouse; they ought to stick with a Magic 8 Ball. That way, they can get all the answers they want and not have to give any commitments in return. Then they can have their cake and eat it."

Janine chuckled at the Magic 8 Ball comment and said, "Yeah, I can see where you're coming from. I feel like our society has become so conditional. Not to change the subject, but I have seen that technology can be a double-edged sword. Things aren't as simple as they used to be. And we as people expect instant gratification right now."

"Exactly. And something I've learned over time is that God works in His own time. True, sometimes things happen quickly when He wants them to, but most of the time, it's prolonged. And that's something I struggle with at times – patience. I want things to happen right now, but that doesn't mean it's in God's timing. And that's something I need to do better with. I need to respect God more in that area by simply stepping aside and letting God run the show. Because it's *His* show to run, not mine; that, my friend, is easier said than done."

"Yeah, you got that right."

"But anyway, I hope that all made sense to you. And I'm here if you need to talk about anything. I won't blabbermouth to others either."

"Same for you. And again, I appreciate your kindness."

"Anytime. How about I look around your house to see what kind of building materials I need and how much?"

"Sure thing. There's not much to clean up at the kitchen table anyway."

Roman did some looking around in Janine's house. He made mental notes of everything that he needed to get for her. He knew what she needed, but he would leave it up to her as far as aesthetics go since it was her house. Roman returned to the kitchen, where Janine had finished cleaning up.

"Hey, do you have a tape measure, Janine?"

"I should. Let me go down to the basement and look for one."

"Okay."

"Here's one," she said as she headed back upstairs.

"Good. Can I bother you for something else?"

"Sure, what do you need?"

"I need you to put your face mask on now that you've finished eating."

"Um… are you feeling sick?"

"No, I don't have COVID. Humor me on this."

"Okay. I'll wear my Green Bay Packers one just for you, Roman!"

"Yeah, yeah, that will work. Now hang tight for a minute or two. I need to go out to the car and get something."

"Okay."

Roman stepped out of Janine's house for a few minutes. As she put on her mask, she wondered what he was doing, but she waited patiently. She couldn't believe what she saw once he stepped back into her house. She shook her head at the sight that she saw.

"And here I thought only the freaks came out at night," Janine said. "But *you're* out all the time. Where the hell did you get that thing?"

"What?"

"You know *what*, your plague doctor suit you're wearing."

"Oh, this old thing? Eh, something I had lying around. It was used back in Europe during the days of the bubonic plague outbreaks. I'm not sure, so don't quote me, but it may also work against tuberculosis, mesothelioma, and jock's itch."

"Is that right, bird brain?"

"Well, again, don't quote me on that. Anyway, I need you to hold the tape measure as I can walk out exactly six feet. I'm planning to put in a new drywall section for you."

"Oh, cool. I'd offer you to wear my Packers mask since I know you *love* the Packers, but you're dressed up like Big Bird's sociopathic relative."

"Trust me; it's part of the experiment – I mean plans for your house. We're going to start measuring from this point here. All I need you to do is stand here while I walk out the tape measure at approximately six feet."

Janine looked confused as to why Roman wanted her to follow his direction. Not to mention, he was wearing a plague doctor suit. But she tried to stay focused as she held the case part of the tape measure in her hand. She was happy to count on Roman to get her house looking better. She watched Roman walk with the tape measure out slowly.

"All right, I think that's good right there," said Roman. "Now I'm going to hold it right there so I can make my mark... believe me, I'm going to make a *big* mark."

Roman then turned his back toward Janine and squatted a little bit as he held the hook end of the tape measure. As he moaned, he let out the most giant, wettest, nastiest fart in the history of farts. As he farted, a giant blast of confetti burst into the air from out of his pants. As he let go of the hook part of the tape measure, he turned around fast to see Janine's reaction and immediately laughed. Janine, of course, was not amused as the tape measure quickly flew back into its case, almost hitting her in the face.

"Are you shitting me?" Janine asked.

"No, I only farted."

"You know what I mean!"

"Man, that was one of my better ones too! I didn't know a duck could sound so loud when you stepped on it."

"Damn you! That smells *so* bad! And shitting out confetti on top of that!"

Janine took the case of the tape measure and threw it as hard as she could. It hit Roman square in between his legs. Even though the impact of it made him reflex, he didn't care. Even though he felt uncomfortable, he still laughed about what he had done. Once again, Roman was trying to get a rise out of Janine, and it worked.

"You see that? We stood exactly six feet apart, and you could still smell my fart, even with your face mask. Plus, some of the confetti got on you. So let me ask you this. How can a face mask stop a virus if a pair of jeans and underwear can't block a fart? It's a valid science experiment if you ask me. I think I deserve a medal. Everyone at the CDC would be proud of me, *especially* Dr. Fauci! What is your opinion?"

"*My* opinion? I think Dr. Fauci would call you a *fucking idiot!* I think you need to do a pants check while you're at it, also. Now do whatever you were going to do with figuring out what you need for the house. I'll be with you in a couple of minutes."

"Okay, I do need to get a drink of water," Roman said as he walked to the kitchen table to get his glass.

"How the hell are you going to drink water while wearing that thing?"

"Well, if Darth Vader did it, there must be a way! I'm sure he had to eat and drink too."

"I swear every village has an idiot," Janine said as she huffed.

"Well, maybe the drink can wait after I get out of my new and improved doctor's suit of the future. I'll take this off and then get to work."

"Yeah, I think that's a good idea. OUCH!"

As Roman turned around to walk away from Janine, the beak of the plague doctor suit slapped her across the face. He did apologize, but she stood there with her arms crossed. Roman imagined the sound of a teapot making a whistling noise, knowing that's what Janine was doing at that moment.

"Sorry about that. Oh, it looks like you got some of the confetti on you. Let me..."

"Don't touch me, please. I'm good."

"Okay."

He kept walking away from her and then turned back to her and said,

"Say, you want to hear a joke about COVID-19?"

"No, I do not."

"Yeah, you're right. It would be tasteless. See what I did there?"

"Get lost!"

Roman decided not to poke at Janine anymore, at least for now. He stepped out of the house again to take his costume off. Then he went back inside and made his way upstairs. He was approached by Willow, who wanted to be petted.

"Well, hi there," Roman said gently.

He kneeled to pet Willow. She was purring, and Roman could tell she felt at ease around him. He continued petting her as Janine made her way upstairs.

"I see Willow has greeted you," Janine said.

"She's pretty. I like her rich blue coat. What kind of cat is she?"

"She's a Persian breed."

"Very nice. How old is she?"

"Five years old. She keeps me company. I love her to pieces."

"I can see why. She is very friendly. So back to business. Other than redoing some of the drywall, what else were you looking to get done?"

"Well, the upstairs bathroom needs a new toilet. As you can see from here, the linoleum on the bathroom floor is starting to peel up. The window downstairs has a crack. You don't have to do this either, but something I've always wanted was a garbage disposal in the kitchen sink."

"I can put one of those in if you want me to."

"Well, I don't want to trouble you with too much work. I mean, it does cost money for these things."

"Money is not an object for me. I'll modify my original deal. I'll buy the materials that you want. Instead of doing this for you when you're at work, maybe I could teach you what I know. The things that my father taught me as a child. I can pass down the knowledge I learned from him to you. That way, you can learn how to do it. Sound like a bargain?"

"I think that would be fun. I can learn something hands-on. Plus, we could do something together. In a way, it would be kind of like a date."

"Exactly. Who says a date must be going to a fancy restaurant always?"

"Yeah… I like the idea of keeping it simple."

"Speaking of dates, I was going to ask you on a date tonight. Maybe go somewhere a little fancier. The only reason I ask is that today is my anniversary."

"Anniversary?"

"It's been four years of no gambling, and I wanted to celebrate that with you."

"I think that would be great! A very noble thing, I must say. I'm honored that you want to celebrate with me."

"Thank you for saying that. I'm honored too. On that note, I will ask you for a lift home since you picked me up at my house. I need to see what kind of suit and tie I have lying around."

"Oh, we're dressing up for this?"

"Yeah, why not? Got to have fun occasionally, you know. Where's the nearest fancy restaurant around here?"

"Probably about an hour away in Altoona. There's a good place called Gold Mountain Estate. I've never been to it since it's so expensive. I'm sure the food is killer, but you'll pay like fifty dollars for a steak. It's fine dining, for sure. Plus, you're also paying for the view of the mountains."

"I say we do it. I'll call to make a reservation before we go. I'm not sure if it's still limited seating due to the pandemic. I can wear my suit and tie while you wear a pretty dress. We'll ride in style! It's the right occasion to use the Rolls-Royce."

"You know I've never really been on a hot date to a fancy restaurant. No man has ever taken me to one. I'm kind of excited to do this. If we do this, I'd better give you a lift home soon."

"Yeah, I need to get showered and cleaned up."

"Me too."

They both got into Janine's car. She let Roman drive home so he could get even more experience driving a manual transmission car. They made it back to his house without problems as far as stalling out. Roman got out of the vehicle, and Janine returned to the driver's seat.

"Thanks again for helping me out with the driving lessons."

"No problem, and thanks for allowing me to share myself with you without being judgmental and condemning."

"Hey, that's what friends are for. Could you do something else for me before you drive off?"

"What is it?"

"Pull my finger?"

"I'll give you something to pull on," she said as she stuck her middle finger up at Roman and fastened her seatbelt.

"Gee willikers, that's the nicest thing anyone has ever said to me. I know I'm number one. So, I'll pick you up around five, give or take?"

"Yeah, whatever," she replied, trying not to smile.

"Okay, if you ever change your mind about pulling my finger, you..."

"I'm not pulling your damn finger!" she exclaimed as she backed her car up.

"All right, well, see you later! Bye-bye!"

Roman was waving at Janine with a big smile on his face. He could see her shaking her head while talking to herself. Her dialogue was indistinct since she was off in the distance driving away, but he figured she was complaining about finger-pulling.

Now came the time to get ready for the big night. Roman made his way to the closet. He only had two different suits that he wore for special occasions. Tonight, he would wear his charcoal gray suit with a white shirt and black tie. He wanted to look good on his date with Janine. Roman was also going to surprise Janine with something big. A surprise not in the physical size of it but in the physical sense of it.

CHAPTER 11

The hour had come for Roman. This was the day Roman would shave his facial hair off entirely. He mainly grew his beard because he was depressed that Briana had passed away. But he wanted something different now. He wanted to live again. He didn't want to merely survive. He wanted to thrive. The hot summer air also made keeping a beard uncomfortable, especially when he had to work in the garden. He stood there in the bathroom and stared at himself in the mirror. He had his beard for a couple of years now. He also hadn't had a haircut for the same length of time. His hair was long and not well-kept. He officially decided to give himself a haircut and shave his beard off.

"It's now or never," Roman said and began shaving.

He shaved his hair first. However, he didn't shave it down to the skin. He used the number seven clipper guard that he attached to the shaver. Roman had only shaved his head once and didn't like how his head looked when he was completely bald. He used the clipper guard to leave hair on top. Then, he started to shave his beard. He used the clipper guard first to remove his beard's excess gradually. Then he took the guard off to shave closer to his face. He hopped in the shower to wash off all the hair clippings. After he was done showering, he could finish the job. He shaved the rest of his face with his razor and shaving cream. He had razors and shaving cream lying around for some time but didn't have a reason to use them until now.

He stared at himself for several seconds with his new look. He felt a wave of confidence upon him. He was starting to feel alive again. Not only for the fact that he was going on a date with someone he was growing to like, but for the simple fact that he felt like he could enjoy being social again. It was a feeling he didn't have for a long time.

Roman made his way to the bedroom and put on his suit. He looked at himself in the mirror again. Roman was never one to obsess about his appearance, but he *did* admire the fact that he could clean up nice when he needed to. Now he felt even more alive and was ready to see where the night would take him. He called Gold Mountain Estate to reserve a table for two and then went to the garage. It was time to ride in style with his Rolls-Royce.

Roman drove up to Janine's house. He didn't feel nervous at all. He had all the confidence that tonight would be a good night. Roman wasn't looking for an evening full of lust. He wanted a deeper intellectual connection with Janine. He walked right up to her door with his head held high. He rang the doorbell. Within several seconds, the door opened. He was in awe of her in her beautiful blue strapless dress. The strapless dress allowed her necklace tattoo to show. She didn't have too much makeup on. She wasn't wearing a face mask either.

From Janine's perspective, she thought whoever was standing at her door was very handsome, but she didn't recognize who it was. She only saw Roman without a beard in a picture with Briana. However, she had forgotten about that. She stared at him for a couple of seconds and then saw his Rolls-Royce in her driveway. Then she knew it was Roman. Her eyes sparkled when she made the connection.

"Hello, my lady," Roman said in a perfect British accent.

"Roman... I can't believe it! It's you! You look so different without that beard!"

"I take it you like the clean-shaven look more?" Roman asked, returning to his normal voice.

"Um, is the sky blue?"

"I'm glad you like it. I like it too. It was time for the beard to go. And you look beautiful, by the way."

"Why, thank you."

"So, may I escort you to our chariot?" he asked, using his perfect British accent again for the last time that day.

"You may, good sir."

They were both smiling as Roman escorted Janine to the car with their arms locked. Janine was glowing. She had never been on a high-end date like this before. She didn't expect a man to do this for her all the time, but she was excited. For once, she could finally dress up formally and share a romantic evening with someone. Even though she sometimes got annoyed by Roman's escapades, she appreciated that he wasn't in this for a one-night stand. Roman opened the automatic door for Janine so she could take a seat. He closed the door for her and headed to the driver's side. They were now driving to Gold Mountain Estate for their hot date. After a few minutes of silence, Janine decided to start a conversation.

"I noticed that something is missing," Janine said.

"What's that? You're even taller than me now, wearing your high heels?" Roman asked.

"No, not that," Janine chuckled. "I mean, I don't see you with that nasty spit bottle."

"Oh, that. Yeah, I've decided to quit."

"Really? When did you quit?"

"I started yesterday. I figured if I could quit gambling, I could quit this habit also."

"I think that's a great thing you're doing. I mean that."

"Well, thanks. It sure doesn't feel good now. I have a raging headache because of it, but God will help me get through this."

"Is that how you overcame the gambling?"

"Yes, it is."

"Well, you sure have my support on quitting the use of smokeless tobacco."

"I appreciate that. You're a good friend indeed."

"I try to be."

"So, have you ever been to Cape Cod?"

"I haven't, but I've always wanted to go. I hear it's beautiful. I would love to lie on the beach and soak up a tan."

"It is beautiful, especially during the summer months. The beaches can get crowded. Our trick was to go early to get a spot. Maybe someday we could see it together."

"I sure would like that."

"You know, I got thinking about something the other day."

"What's that?"

"I think it's time people expand on the topic of Critical Race Theory."

"Really? Do you mean that? I must be honest. I never thought I'd hear a conservative say that."

"I mean that whole conversation I had with you about going to White Castle with Snoop Dogg and bromance. I saw the light. I think there needs to be a federal holiday. I shall call it Interracial Bromancing Awareness Day!"

"Oh, sweet Lord. Here we go again."

"I'm just telling you the truth! If we study Critical Race Theory, we must explore *all* avenues of it."

"Well, I don't know if Critical Race Theory specifically touches on interracial bromance per se, but I think it thoroughly highlights the injustices that certain people in our country experience. I think African Americans need to be recognized more for their achievements and stopped being demonized."

"Exactly. I mean, look at Samuel L. Jackson. Now there's another one I would love to bromance at White Castle."

"Is that right?"

"Dude, he's like one of the best actors in history! If he could get rid of all the snakes from that plane in that movie, who's to say he didn't run off all the snakes from Ireland? I bet it didn't matter if the snakes were Irish Republicans or Ulster Loyalists."

"Well, I'm pretty sure Critical Race Theory doesn't specifically touch on the movie *Snakes on a Plane.* But I will agree that Samuel L. Jackson is a very talented actor. And speaking of The Troubles in Northern Ireland, it shows you that *those* disparities are among people simply because they're perceived as different, exactly like in our country. Those disparities *do* need to be addressed. Some of my father's side of the family fought against Northern Ireland for the cause to unite both Irelands as one."

"Really? I take it they were in the Irish Republican Army?"

"Yes, that's my understanding of it."

"You're not going to believe this, but some family members on my mother's side were in the Ulster Defense Association."

"Are you serious?"

"That's what my mother told me – ironic when you think about it. The two of us are going on a hot date. We're opposites on the political spectrum, we cheer for rival football teams, and our relatives from generations ago may have killed each other. And here we are, enjoying each other's company!"

"That is funny in a weird way now that I think about it."

A moment of awkward silence showed up. Janine and Roman had it planted in their heads growing up that each of their sectarian lineages was the correct way to believe. Roman decided to restart the conversation after the long pause.

"But yeah, I'm on board with that thinking when it comes to addressing the disparities in the world. Kind of like climate change needs to be addressed."

"You know, for the first time in my life, I honestly feel like I'm having an intelligent conversation with a conservative man. And I mean that as a compliment to you."

"No offense taken. We all know who's to blame here with the weather gradually heating up."

"Yeah?"

"Of course! Everyone knows the Heat Miser is to blame!"

And there it was again – that smile on Roman's face. Janine had seen that devious smile before driving home from White Castle. She could feel her blood boil since climate change was a hot-button issue for her.

"Well, so much for intelligent conversation," she said sarcastically.

"I mean, he's the one that didn't want any snow in Southtown for all the boys and girls during Christmas," responded Roman. "Or, as the Proletariats of Massachusetts would say, 'a non-specific celebration of a winter solstice holiday.' All these claims made by the alt-left about climate change are downright crooked. Not to be confused with crooked in the sense of Peyronie's disease. You know what that is, don't you?"

"And there he goes again," Janine thought. *"When I thought he had half a brain, the idiocrasies make their way out in the open again. Does he believe this shit, or does he like to be a troll?"*

"Okay, let's get something straight. The Heat Miser is not a real person, nor does this have anything to do with bent dicks."

"Did you say Dick's Sporting Goods?"

"No, I said *'dicks!'* The kind of dicks you see in Jonah Hill's notebook in *Superbad. Anyway,* climate change is occurring because people on this planet don't seem to give a crap about the environment, particularly conservatives in this country. I appreciate and respect you for being woke on racial injustices in this country, but you should take another look at the topic of climate change."

"Woke?"

"Yes, woke."

"What is woke?"

"It's being alert to injustices in society, particularly racism."

"I don't know. That doesn't make any sense to me."

"What doesn't?"

"Being woke. I already woke up this morning. Isn't it the past tense of wake?"

"Ah, I see what you mean. The word 'woke' describes someone aware of the injustices."

"Yes, but then wouldn't I be awakened? Woke is the past tense of wake, so that terminology is incorrect. So, it should be awakened. Not to be confused with AwakenWithJP, like on YouTube. Which, by the way, is good stuff."

"Roman *'woke'* is only an informal adjective for what I have mentioned."

"Right, so then I'm not sleeping since I'm awake. Aren't you twisting this *'woke'* thing a little bit to suit you? This sounds like the whole getting nipped in the butt thing again."

"Oh, son of a bitch," she said and put her hands on her forehead.

"I mean, I hope you won't judge me because some of my family had Ulster tendencies, but what kind of people can see the racial injustices in this country if they're all asleep?"

"That's what I'm trying to tell you! Being woke means you're vigilant of these issues!"

"Oh... well... you don't have to be such a poop about it. Not to be confused with the poop emoji. He looks like a jolly little fellow. *Oh!* Speaking of... pull my finger?"

"Forget it!"

Roman put his finger down and kept driving with that familiar devilish grin.

"I wonder if he likes to needle me on purpose or if he's that much of a doofus," she thought.

Either way, she felt like dropping the subject. As much as Roman got under her skin, she appreciated that he wanted to fix up her house and the fact that he respected her. Most importantly, she valued their friendship and felt that their differences didn't prevent them from wanting to spend time with one another.

————————————•————————————

They eventually made it to Gold Mountain Estate in Altoona. The restaurant itself sat partway up on a mountain. This made for a beautiful view from inside the restaurant. It overlooked the city of Altoona, which made for a gorgeous scene during sunset. They got to their table, and both sat down. Then they both took their face masks off since they needed to wear them upon entrance.

"This sure is a nice place," Roman commented.

"I know. I've always heard good things about it. It looks even better in person than on their website," Janine said.

"I agree with that. And just think, we have a great view when the sun starts to set."

"That's true."

It was time for Janine and Roman to order. They first requested a bottle of Cabernet and an appetizer of scallops wrapped in bacon. Roman ordered a fillet mignon medium rare, while Janine ordered rainbow trout for their main entrées. They would each would split a side of mashed potatoes and asparagus. Roman noticed Janine was looking around the restaurant with a sly look, but he didn't know who or what she was looking for.

"Janine, what are you looking for?"

"Hey… have you ever gone… people watching?"

"All the time! I love to watch people. Craig and I would do that a lot when we were teenagers. Then again, I can imagine what people might think of us since you're three feet taller than me."

"True, but we're the hottest ones in the restaurant. Get a load of those two over there. She doesn't look interested in him at all."

"Yeah, she looks bored out of her mind."

"His pants couldn't be much tighter than they already are. They don't look comfortable at all. Cripes, and I've seen better heads on lettuce, too."

"You know what they say about tight pants, don't you?"

"No, what?" she asked as she took a sip of her wine.

"Pants like that are like a cheap hotel, no ballroom."

She laughed out loud at that comment and almost spat out her wine. The couple they were both poking at looked at them in disgust. Then turned their noses up at them. The appetizer came out a minute later, and Roman said the prayer before they ate. This time they both held hands as he said the prayer. Then they started to eat.

"Boy, I tell you, Janine. There is nothing like the taste of bacon. I mean, you can wrap anything in bacon. Scallops wrapped in bacon, pork loin wrapped in bacon, bacon wrapped in bacon. Shoot, you can wrap Janine Flaherty in bacon!"

"I take it you like your bacon," Janine said as she giggled and blushed at his comment about herself being wrapped in bacon.

"I sure do! Come on, these people who don't believe in God. If He can create bacon, you know God is real."

"Ah, your faith lies upon a slab of bacon, huh?"

"Well, not bacon per se. But I am thankful for the food I have. And I love to cook too."

"I think that's awesome that you enjoy cooking. The guys I've met previously can't even microwave a frozen meal."

"Hey, maybe someday we can cook together, like during a rainy day or something. I'm particularly good at using the smoker and baking."

"That's great you can do those things. I know those aren't easy tasks to do. Did your parents teach you how to cook?"

"When I was young, they would let me help. Then over the years, I came into my own by experimenting. Like I've said to people, if you can read a recipe, you can cook."

"I wish I could do it more, but I always seem to run out of time. Between work and then exercising. And then I like to see Theresa and Miroslav and the kids when I can."

"That's great you got your family close by. I miss my family, but it was my choice to move down here. I can always go back to Cape Cod to visit them if I want to."

"Yeah, I'm still distant from my parents, but my relationship with my sister has improved over the years, so I'm thankful for that. And I think it was good that she met Miroslav. I think he sort of mellowed her out a bit. They're a good couple. They're good for each other."

"I agree. And I love spending time with them too. They're great people. So, am I allowed to ask how old you are? I'm thirty-four."

"I'm thirty-nine."

"Ah. I hope the fact that I'm younger doesn't bother you."

"As long as you're not bothered that I'm older than you."

"Not at all. Now, what do you think of kids? Do you want any?"

"I think if I did, I would want to adopt. So many kids need a good home."

"I can be on board with that viewpoint for sure."

"That's good. So not to change the subject. I am curious. Why do you believe what you believe?"

"Regarding what?"

"Your views."

"You mean with Christianity or the fact I'm a conservative?"

"Yes."

"I'll start with what I believe politically... I find it ironic that some liberal politicians want to take away my hunting rifle, but they have no problems with Iran having nuclear weapons. I always take my gun ownership seriously and responsibly, and so should everyone else. Don't get me wrong; I don't think guns should get into the hands of people that shouldn't have them, like people with a criminal background. But what did *I* do wrong? I don't have a criminal background. And to have the desire to confiscate my guns and allow a country like Iran to pursue nuclear weapons makes absolutely no sense. I'm pretty sure my bullets don't contain uranium.

"I also think liberals want the government to grow, whereas I don't. The government is lucky it can find its way out of a wet paper bag. And we're supposed to place our trust in Big Brother? These politicians want more government because they don't want us to make our own choices. They want us to surrender our freedoms. They can keep their government. I'll keep my Savior.

"But I think the other thing that did it for me was after Briana died; I tried dating this girl, Rhonda. I didn't meet her until about two years after Briana passed away. But I remember we had a long day driving and sitting in traffic to get home after leaving the casino in Connecticut. We were both super hungry. I saw a Chick-fil-A in Rhode Island and asked if she would prefer we stop there to grab a bite. And she lost it on me! Saying I was a homophobe and all this stuff. I tried to tell her that all I wanted was some food. That was it. My intention wasn't to make a religious statement. I *only* wanted to eat, and I know she did too. That's all. And I wasn't even a Christian back then.

"So, we had to keep driving to find another place to eat. She hated the fact that I went hunting too. She would always say it was animal cruelty, but I'll tell you something. You put a double-meat hamburger in front of her, and she could make good work out of it. That meat had to come from somewhere, you know. She sure talked a good game, saying that everyone should be equal. I guess she forgot about me."

"So, why did she even want to date you then?"

"I think it was primarily for the sex. She said I was good in bed."

"Oh... um... well, that leaves a lot for the imagination," Janine said as she laughed.

"Well, that *is* what she told me. Maybe I should have started charging her money for it."

They both laughed at Roman's comment.

"Anyway," Roman continued, "The lust is what kept us together. But check this out. Rhonda would always complain about men too. She was a feminist and a Masshole. As I've mentioned, I think women should have equality. But she took her feminist beliefs too far. She would tell me, 'I have no right to ever complain about stuff.' She thought men had no right to complain since women go through menstrual cycles, which means men have a much easier life. She never wanted me to be vulnerable or share my struggles with her. She didn't even show mercy that I struggled with Briana's death. She told me to get over my man cold and stop crying about Briana. She would get mad when I talked and then get mad because I wouldn't talk. I didn't talk much due to the fear of punishment. What was I supposed to do? I wanted to be vulnerable with her because I wanted a deeper connection.

I didn't do it to be a crybaby. But again, she was all about equal rights… unless you were male. I guess I don't matter, then. I guess a man is not allowed to have feelings, let alone express them."

Janine could sense the despair in Roman's voice and the look on his face. Something had occurred to her at that moment. The same adverse treatment she received from other Christians is the same treatment Roman had received from a self-declared liberal feminist. The treatment came from two different ideologies, but they left both Janine and Roman feeling discouraged and neglected. Both felt turned away from each of those schools of thought.

"I'm sorry that happened to you, Roman. I can promise you that not all of us feminists are like that. She sounded like an angry person and wouldn't be happy no matter what you did for her. I think she missed out on a genuine man."

"I appreciate the compliment. She's gone now, and that's all that matters. I had my revenge on her anyway."

"What did you do?"

"Well, after a conversation she had with me, I knew I had to leave. After she said all white men are terrorists and responsible for the world's problems, I knew I couldn't stay with her any longer. Plus, she said I was racist for voting for Trump even though Briana was the love of my life, and Briana was black. I would have walked through fire for Briana while stepping on spikes. I guess that's beside the point, in any case.

"Anyway, since she said I was good at sex, I made my move during sex. As we were orgasming together, I decided to call out my name a couple of times. You talk about watching smoke coming out of her ears!"

"You did that?"

"I sure did!"

"That's so genius!" Janine exclaimed.

She thought that was funny and was entertained by it since she didn't expect the conversation to go in that direction.

"Oh, an hour or so before we had sex, I did a double-decker in

Rhonda's toilet."

"What the hell is that?"

"It's when you take a dump in the toilet and don't flush it, and you also take a dump in the tank part of the toilet. You take the lid off from up top, get in position to squat, take a dump, then put the lid back on the tank and leave it there."

Janine tried not to laugh at that but couldn't help it.

"Leave it to you to do something like that."

"Well, she *did* dump on me enough times. By the way, did you hear about the feminist who crashed the helicopter?"

"No, I didn't."

"She got cold and turned off the fan."

She paused for a minute, then said, "You know, I could choose to be offended by that. But I have to admit, even as a feminist myself, that *is* pretty clever," Janine said as she laughed. "That joke is interchangeable. I could use that for some of the Trumpers I've known. I *will* say you have a brain, even though you voted for Trump. Well, sometimes you have a brain, anyway."

"I do have my faults. But anyway, back to what you said before. I agree that some people will never be happy, no matter how many good things go their way. And I'm guessing the way things are for you is why you believe what you believe."

"Yes, so many people would make fun of me because I didn't go hunting or I didn't like being around farm animals. And I didn't appreciate people's ignorance or close-mindedness. I'm not saying everyone down here is like that, but most people I've met are like that. And now, with the pandemic going on, they think I'm some sort of government official or city slicker because I choose to follow CDC guidelines to the best of my abilities."

"As you know, I don't wear a mask much and have no intention of getting the vaccine. But I'm not going to shame you for doing what you want. I'm not even angered by it, provided you don't impose your will onto me."

161

"Well, I *do* wish that you would get the vaccine. However, I've learned it's not my place to tell people what to do. And I appreciate you don't think I'm a wimp for doing what I do regarding this matter."

"I like you for who you are, Janine."

"Well, thanks. You're not so bad yourself."

The waitress brought their main courses out with the sides. They both thanked her and then continued their conversation.

"So, going back to your other question about my faith," Roman said. "For me, it came down to a couple of things. I wanted something better – the death of Briana and my unborn son and my gambling addiction were killing me. I knew there had to be something better out there than what was before me. Being a slave to gambling while dealing with severe depression was something I couldn't do anymore. I started to look to God for help so that He could take these things away from me. To give me a better life. A life with purpose and peace. It took a couple of years to finish reading the Bible and understand most of it.

"And you know what? There are still some things I don't understand. But I know that God is good, and He delivers His love to us. It may be in ways we don't expect, but He always stands next to us. It's on us to accept His invitation."

"So, I know you said you had sex with Rhonda, and you did with Briana since you were supposed to have a child together. Do you believe in waiting for marriage now, or does that make a difference for you?"

"I've decided I want to wait."

"Really? I mean, what about having fun? I'm not saying bang anything that moves, but if you're committed to someone, what's the point of waiting? There's nothing wrong with having some fun along the way."

"Well, that's just it. I believe you should wait if you *are* committed to that person. Many people talk about test-driving the car before you buy it. Here's my thing. Why should someone be looked at as if they were an appliance? I think it devalues humans in general and cheapens the experience of sex. And that's the same principle I applied to Rhonda.

Just have a little fun along the way since we were *together*. Well, how did that work out? Not so good.

"And looking back on it now, I wish I didn't have sex with her since she didn't even like me. The people that think saving oneself for marriage are backward thinking – and yet, having sex before marriage is more backward to me. If the secular way of thinking was more correct versus God's design, there shouldn't be so many divorces then. Plus, if everyone is humping like rabbits nowadays, why aren't more people happy? I thought sex was supposed to be satisfying. That's my take on it. Sex itself isn't a bad thing. God created sex. It's when sex is used outside of God's parameters of marriage is where the problems lie. If other people choose to have sex before marriage, I won't judge them for it. But I'm choosing to wait."

"You know, I never thought of it that way. So... like... hypothetically, if *we* were together, you would want to wait?"

"Yes, I would. I think God deserves that respect, and so would you because you're more than an appliance or a booty call, Janine."

"Well... thanks for saying that. No man has ever looked at me in that way before. I don't know what to say."

"It's what I believe. Some people think that if you wait for marriage, what if you find out your partner isn't good in bed? The fact is that both people should talk about those things, like if they're engaged, for example. What they want or don't want. Sexual activities between a husband and wife need to be consensual. Neither one should feel uncomfortable or pressured into doing something they don't want to do. And the thing is, as time goes on and the marriage grows, the sex will be good. Before you know it, you'll be married to someone for forty or fifty years, having old people sex, and it will still be as hot and steamy as ever!"

They both laughed at that. They finished eating their food and ordered dessert. Janine ordered cheesecake while Roman ordered crème brûlée.

They were halfway finished with their dessert when Janine asked, "Can I say something to you?"

"Sure," said Roman.

"I appreciate the fact that you can talk about stuff like this. So many Christians don't want to talk about things like sex or even have an intelligent conversation about it. Or if you bring it up, they look at you like you're the spawn of Satan. My folks never even talked to me about sex, how babies are made, or anything like that."

"I know you've said you have a rocky relationship with your folks. But you never know. They may come around someday."

"Well, if they do, it probably won't be tomorrow or the next day. They wouldn't even let us trick-or-treat. They don't even believe in dinosaurs! Now, what do you make of all that?"

"Halloween for me is eating a chocolate bar and watching a scary movie. If parents want to dress their kids up and take them out to get candy, I'm fine with that. I don't get into the dark aspects of it, however. But Christmas can be as bad as Halloween."

"What do you mean?"

"Some Christians despise Halloween, which is fine if they want to. Yet, some only care about the decorations and the presents during Christmas. Christmas has become way too commercialized. The baby Jesus is an afterthought. And I'm not sure if this is true, but some even argue that a Christmas tree has pagan roots. So, if you want to be technical here, the people that complain about Halloween should also complain about Christmas in a certain sense."

"Huh... that's interesting. Okay, so what about dinosaurs then?"

"Let me say this first. Whether an individual believes in dinosaurs or not isn't the thing that grants them entrance into Heaven. I believe dinosaurs existed. Some Christians don't. That's fine. Whatever a person believes as far as dinosaurs go is irrelevant. Kind of like hoop snakes."

"Hoop snakes?"

"Yeah, they're a rare and endangered species. When one feels threatened, it bites its tail and rolls away. It's a defense mechanism that they use to evade predators."

"Interesting," said Janine and then paused.

She noticed that Roman was keeping a straight face. She couldn't tell if he was telling the truth or making a tall tale.

"Anyway, check this out."

Roman grabbed his phone and brought up a photo for Janine.

"Take a look at this picture, Janine. I saw this on TV a while ago. What do you see?"

"Lightning."

"Take a closer look."

She looked closer but couldn't figure out what Roman was trying to tell her.

"It *is* lighting," Roman continued, "but look at it closer. The main bolt hits the tree, but then there's a leader that goes upward. Also, to the left, you can see one streaming up from the telecommunication pole."

"So, what's your point?"

"My point is God is much bigger than what atheists and even some Christians give Him credit. Yes, He is the God of creation. But He's also the God of science, as seen in this picture. He's the God of history, math, chemistry, etc. So, whether he made dinosaurs or not... I don't know. I wasn't around then."

"You're a lot smarter than you look sometimes. And I mean that as a compliment."

"Eh, it's what I do. Hey, check out that sunset."

"Yeah, it's as pretty as the one we saw that night we were smoking cigars and playing Cribbage together."

Roman paid for their meals and left a generous tip. They put their masks on so that they could leave the restaurant. They hopped in the Rolls-Royce and drove back to Janine's house. After he parked the car in the driveway, he decided to bring out the surprise.

"Hey, are you doing anything right now, Janine?"

"No, why?"

"Good. I have a surprise for you."

"Oh yeah?"

"Yeah, let's go to the backseat. It's in the middle there."

"What is it?"

"You'll see."

They both got out of the car and got into the backseat of the vehicle. Then Roman said, "Check this out."

He opened the built-in refrigerator that was in between them. Once he opened it, Janine saw a bottle of Veuve Clicquot sitting with two champagne glasses.

"Man, this car has everything! No wonder they're so expensive."

"That's not all."

He turned on the feature that made the stars appear on the ceiling. She noticed that there were also shooting stars.

"That *is* cool. You sure do know how to set the mood."

Roman smiled at Janine as he poured the champagne into each glass, filling each half full. They each took a few seconds to enjoy the quiet piano music playing through Roman's phone while sipping their champagne. Also, the stars that were glowing inside the Rolls-Royce made it peaceful. The night felt complete.

"I enjoyed spending this evening with you," Janine said.

"I have as well. For the first time, I've felt more alive than I ever had in a long time."

"Me too. I feel comfortable around you. You're so easy to talk to."

"Thank you. I feel the same about you. It's like I can be myself around you."

"I wish the night didn't have to end so soon."

"Who said it does?"

They both gazed into each other's eyes for several seconds. They could feel the waves of passion and energy from each other. They slowly leaned toward each other for their first kiss. It was gentle and tender. They paused to look at each other again briefly. Then they continued kissing each other more passionately and deeply while gently caressing each other's faces and the back of their heads. They could each feel the attraction that they had for each other. All the magic from this evening and the friendship and trust they had built were felt through this romantic moment they shared. They both felt safe with each other and in each other's arms.

After a couple of minutes of kissing one another, they stopped. Roman put his right arm around Janine and held Janine's hand with his left one. They sat there for a while in the stillness inside the Rolls-Royce. They were both happy. But they knew that sooner or later, the time would come that they would have to part ways. Plus, it was getting late, and Roman and Janine felt they could drift off to sleep.

"I hope we can do this again sometime," Janine said.

"Absolutely. I enjoyed sharing this evening with you."

"Me too."

They both got out of the car, gave each other a big hug and another passionate kiss, and went their separate ways. They were both content with how the date night went. Each of them learned a valuable lesson that night, too. People are still people regardless of where a person may be on the political spectrum or their sectarian lineage. They have the desire to bond, interact, and be loved. Maybe the problem doesn't lie so much within people's differences as in their selfishness. That would be a lesson both Roman and Janine would learn during their first fight together. But would they know that unconditional love is a bond that can't be broken?

CHAPTER 12

The house was getting close to being finished. Janine was happy about everything they had accomplished together. Also, she was delighted that Roman had taught her the ropes of house projects. She was pleased that their friendship was blossoming. Roman continued to improve his driving skills with her manual transmission vehicle under Janine's instruction. They continued to play Cribbage and go out on dates together. She also continued to pick his brain with questions she had about God.

However, she was anything but happy today. She was downright miserable. It was the last Friday in August, and it was oppressively humid outside. For starters, the oppressive heat made Janine cranky. Today was the day Janine's period decided to show up as well. And to top it off, she was quitting smoking and dealing with the job she despised.

She looked at Roman and the Bible as inspiration. If Roman could put his trust in God to quit gambling and stop using smokeless tobacco, she figured she could do the same by quitting cigarettes. She knew that the road ahead wasn't going to be an easy one for her. She had been a smoker now for a little over twenty-three years.

She needed to go to Roman's house because she had left her phone at his place. She planned on going there to pick it up, and that was it. She wasn't in the mood for socializing or much of anything today. She knew she was in a foul mood and wanted to be left alone. Plus, it was late afternoon. She didn't want to stay at Roman's house for long. Janine drove to his house and knocked on the door. He shouted to her that the door was open. He figured she would show up since he knew she had forgotten her phone. He had it on the coffee table.

He was watching *Benny Hill* on the TV. He had planned to do outside work, but it was too humid today. Not to mention Roman wasn't feeling his best either. He was trying to relax on the couch while dealing with an outbreak of shingles.

"Hey, Janine."

"Hi there."

"I assume you're here because you forget your phone?"

"Correct."

"It's right here on the table."

"Okay."

She walked over to grab her phone. She noticed Roman didn't have his nasty bottle of tobacco spit, so she knew he was committed to kicking the habit. She hoped she could do the same with cigarettes. She grabbed her phone off the coffee table and started to leave. Roman noticed this and paused the episode of *Benny Hill* with the remote. He knew something was up with Janine since she wasn't talking much.

"Janine, are you okay?"

"Yeah, I'm fine."

"You don't sound fine. Anything you want to talk about?"

"You know... it must be nice to sit at home and watch TV while some of us have to go to work and not give a shit."

"Um... what's that supposed to mean?"

"It's like all I do is get treated like dirt at my job. I mention an idea, and the boss doesn't want to hear it. But if a *man* mentions it, then the boss approves of it. I can mention something beforehand, and I'm not taken seriously because I'm not a man."

"I'm... I'm sorry to hear that. I wish there were something I could do to help you."

"That's it?"

"Well... I know saying 'sorry' won't change things at your job, but I can't help but feel bad. I'm sorry I'm not feeling my best today. I have..."

"Not feeling your best? You're at home watching your British show again. With no job to worry about. What the hell do *you* have to worry about? Some of us common folk must work for a living! It must be great to sit around and do whatever you want, whenever you want, and not give a fuck about anything."

Roman could feel a bit of uneasiness starting to fill the room. He didn't want to fight since his shingles were agonizing. He could feel the pain from the sores as they were on the side of his body. His blisters were open and oozing. He noticed that the sky was getting darker outside. Thunder was rumbling off in the distance. He tried to stay calm and talk to Janine in an indoor voice, but she wasn't having any of it.

"You know, all you people say is trust in God," Janine continued. "Trust in God. He hasn't made my situation at work any better, nor has He made it better with my parents. It's easy for you. *Your* parents were good to you. Meanwhile, my parents always sided with my sister. She couldn't do any wrong. And here you are. All you do is stay home sitting on a pile of money and drive around in that Rolls-Royce!"

Roman got up in pain and stood up slowly. He slammed the TV remote on the floor in anger. When it hit the floor, Janine was startled. Her heart started to beat a little fast as he slowly approached her. She could tell she had struck a nerve within him somewhere. The thunder outside started to get louder as the storm moved closer. His eyes were locked onto hers. She could feel the imminent wrath upon her, making her more uncomfortable.

"Let me tell you something right now. Do you think I'm sitting around on money while not doing anything? Look at this," he said as he lifted his shirt.

"Am I *just* sitting around not caring? Or is it because I'm having an outbreak of shingles? Do you want some of these? I think not.

"Do you think I keep all this wealth to myself? Who's funded the church that the Kojićs and I go to and help this community with the ongoing opioid problem? Together we helped get a food kitchen started there.

"So many times, churches dump all their money into missions overseas to spread the gospel. Good for them! But on the same token, those churches forget that the local communities need to hear the word of Jesus just as much as the international community.

"Not to mention, I've also donated my time and money to help fix your house without expecting anything in return. I haven't asked for a *penny* in return! *Have I?* I wanted to enjoy your company and give you a set of skills to have in the future in case you need to do any more home improvement projects. How ungrateful you are! You come into my house and insult me, making me out to be some sort of evil capitalist!"

"I never *said* you were an…"

"I don't want to hear it from you!"

Lightning flashed outside and filled the living room. Janine could feel her body tense up more as Roman yelled at her. She hated getting yelled at. She also felt tense because the thunder was getting even closer, becoming more frequent.

"You think you can walk on my property and start a fight with me? *Do you?"*

He paused for several seconds to see if she would respond.

"What's the matter, cat got your tongue? You'll leave if you know what's good for you."

Janine's eyes started to tear up. She didn't know what to say other than she felt wounded on the inside. She knew she shouldn't have started the conversation as she did while swearing at him, but she also knew that being talked to in that manner wasn't right either.

"Go on, Rhonda! LEAVE! Go take your propaganda somewhere else!"

Lightning illuminated the living room again as the storm got louder.

Janine ran out of Roman's house sobbing. She got into her car and drove to the Kojić house as quickly as possible to beat the weather. She got to the doorstep and knocked on the door. Theresa answered it.

"Oh, hi there! Say, what's going on?"

Janine didn't say a word. She stood there for a few seconds, crying. Lightning soared from above, followed up by a crash of thunder.

"Come on inside."

Janine stepped inside the house. Theresa and Janine went into the kitchen and sat down. Miroslav and the children were playing a board game in Jason's bedroom.

"So, what's going on? Did something happen to you?" asked Theresa.

"Roman and I… we got into a fight… it's all my fault," Janine said, still crying.

"Well, before we jump to any conclusions, tell me what happened."

Before Janine could tell her story, Miroslav walked into the room and said, "Oh, hi, Janine. What's going on?"

"I go into a fight with Roman."

"Oh no… I'm so sorry to hear that. Do you and Theresa want to talk alone? I can make myself scarce if you want me to."

"No, that's okay. I don't mind if you stay."

"Very well. I will let Sarah and Jason know I'll be here for a few minutes."

Miroslav told the children he needed a few minutes with Theresa and Janine. He came back and had a seat next to his wife.

"So, tell us what happened," Theresa said.

"Well, work has been killing me. I've been thinking about finding another job, but I don't know where I will go. Plus, I'm trying to quit smoking."

"Really? That's wonderful that you want to quit smoking," Miroslav said.

"Thanks; I want to call it quits for good. But with that, the job, plus the crimson tide showed up today, if you know what I mean… all that compounded on me. I sort of took out my frustrations on Roman."

"So, how did he respond?" asked Theresa.

"Not well at all. Things escalated between us. I know I personally attacked him, and I shouldn't have done that. I let my emotions get the better of me. However, I didn't like how he yelled at me."

"Well, he has admitted to us in private that he struggles with anger and how to handle it at times," Miroslav said. "But the fact that he yelled at you doesn't make it right, either. I think I'll go over and have a chat with him."

"You're not going to get revenge on him, are you? I don't want to start anything."

"No, no. Nothing like that. I have my ways of getting through to him. Trust me. I'm not going to add anything between you and him to make it worse. Every wise man grounded in his faith has a wise mentor to help him walk with Christ."

"Roman may not be perfect, but getting to know him has been a wonderful experience. He's a genuine person, and he loves God. He also loves people, too. I want what he has. I've been reading the Bible more and more at night, and I'm considering accepting Jesus. Roman may be a complete bonehead at times, but I feel he has this way of living it out versus only talking about it or putting on a show to look good for others. He's the real deal."

Miroslav and Theresa looked at each other, then at Janine. They were silent for several seconds. Then Theresa broke the silence.

"So… you want to accept Jesus into your life?"

"I'm thinking about it," said Janine. "I'm tired of how things are in my life, and I want something different. Something better. Something that's promised. Something that I can feel loved regardless of what I've done in my past."

"Well, that's great! We're so proud of you, and we'll assist you in any way."

"I do appreciate that. I'm going to need all the help that I can get. I don't know anything about being a Christian."

"Neither did I growing up," said Miroslav. "And neither did Roman, for that matter. But here we are today. You can do this, Janine. We'll be there every step of the way for you. Some say they want to get their life right and then attend church. I say go to church first so you can get your life right. Roman is in that process right now as we speak. Remember, Christ didn't die for us at our best. He died for us at our worst."

"Thank you so much. Can I ask one thing? What Is the Trinity? I thought we only worshiped one God, not three of them."

"Think of the Trinity this way. Take water, for example. You have water in the form of liquid, frozen, and vapor. It's in three different forms, but it's still water. You see what I'm getting at?"

"Huh... well, that's an interesting take on that. I never thought of it that way before. That puts it in a little clearer perspective. Now... back to Roman. I do have to say one thing. Roman is a great guy but has a bizarre sense of humor."

"Including his cheesy jokes. You know the Yugo cars, Janine?"

"Yes."

"Well, one time, we played Monopoly with our kids. Roman joined us. He owned Boardwalk and Park Place with hotels. I hit Park Place and then Boardwalk on my next turn. You know what he said to me?"

"What?"

"'There *you go* again! How *unorthodox* of you. See what I did there?' You know he was referring to the car because I'm from Yugoslavia and grew up Orthodox Christian."

"Oh, brother," Janine said as she laughed.

"Yeah, and don't forget his toilet humor," Theresa added. "You know he asked me to pull his finger once, and I fell for it. I didn't know he was going to fart. And he did it too!"

"You didn't know about that prank?" Janine asked. "Well, I guess you know not to do that again! I've come to the conclusion that Roman's person of being is Jesus Christ meets Ren and Stimpy."

Theresa and Janine laughed at that statement. They had to explain to Miroslav the type of humor featured on *Ren and Stimpy* since he wasn't familiar with that show growing up.

"Some of his jokes are corny or disgusting, and he may have some strange antics, but Roman has a big heart," Theresa continued. "His humor is unconventional, but I don't question his faith. He might not act like a stereotypical Christian, but he didn't grow up as a believer. He accepted Christ not long ago, so he will not know everything. No one can know everything, for that matter. And if Christians are going to judge people like him, there's no way to be a light for someone. We are called to live in this world and be an example. If we don't, there's no way to lead people to Christ. That's our duty as believers.

"I think with the death of his girlfriend Briana and losing their child, especially how it happened, I'm sure even though Roman has reconciled all that, there are days where it still hurts him."

"I kind of had a feeling it would. So, when do you think you'll talk to Roman?" Janine asked Miroslav.

"I would say…" he was interrupted by what sounded like a bomb going off.

A blinding light filled the entire house taking everyone off guard and causing them to feel alarmed. Everyone knew what had happened after it occurred. They ran to Jason's room to ensure the children were okay, knowing they had also been taken off guard. From Jason's room, they could see Roman's property. They could see that one of the trees in his backyard was no more. Lightning had obliterated the big pine tree and was split partially down the middle. The wind started to pick up with brute force within seconds. The wind was so strong it began to push the tree over that had been struck by lightning. Everyone watched it fall over.

"Let's go to the basement," Miroslav said.

Everyone went to the basement to take cover. No tornado was spawned from that thunderstorm. But what had happened was that a microburst showed up instead. It uprooted two more pine trees on Roman's property. Although the downdraft from the microburst didn't occur directly over Roman's property, straight-line winds roared for several minutes and dumped heavy rain. Both Roman and the Kojics lost power for several hours. Power was restored during the wee hours of the morning.

Janine spent the night at the Kojić house even though she hadn't brought an overnight bag or anything. She felt better staying with them. She had gone over to their home for moral support. She was happy that she had gotten things off her chest.

But the following day, she knew she had to make an early start to go home to see if there was any property damage from the storm. She also wanted to see if her cat Willow was okay. She trusted the Lord to resolve the conflict between Roman and herself. And Miroslav was the right man to assist in the job, for he would go to Roman with love, not condemnation.

CHAPTER 13

Roman's situation wasn't good. He had his work cut out for him with three trees down. They needed to be chopped up and stacked for wood. He knew he could clean up the mess, but he wasn't looking forward to it. He wished he could do something fun with Janine, like teach her how to use a chainsaw. He enjoyed doing those kinds of activities with her and having that interaction. But he had a bigger mess to clean up than the trees that fell over. Roman needed to patch things up with Janine, but he wasn't sure how to do it. He wasn't even sure if she wanted to talk to him again. The isolation had set in. He felt like a complete failure. He felt the urge to go to the gas station and buy a tin of tobacco pouches or a lottery ticket. Who would know if he did? He was tempted, but he didn't give in to the temptations that were haunting him.

The day after the microburst, Roman stepped outside to the backyard and examined the property while holding a cigar. His house was in good shape. He didn't need to work on the roof since he had a metal roof instead of shingles. But there were the trees. He stared at the big tree that was hit by lightning.

"Good grief," he muttered as he shook his head.

As he made his way back to the deck, he scuffed the side of his body on the top rail of the deck. This caused Roman to shout out in pain as it grazed the shingles on his body. He slowly took a seat in anguish and thought about the work ahead of him. He looked to his left at the two smaller trees that had blown over from the winds. He took a cutter and a lighter out of his pocket to smoke. He cut the end of his cigar and lit the front end of it as he started puffing on it. He could relax by himself. Or so he thought.

"Znao sam da si ovde."

Roman heard a voice to his right. He turned around fast, but he knew it was Miroslav since he spoke in Serbian.

"Yeah... I guess the smoke gave me away," Roman said with some pain.

He still felt the pain from scuffing himself on the top rail.

"As you can see, mother nature took a dump on me. Now I'm evaluating all this. Anyway, what's going on, Miroslav?"

"I wanted to check up on you to ensure you were okay. After all, we saw that lightning bolt hit that tree there."

"Yeah, it sure scared the crap out of me. It was wild. I was looking out the backdoor, and it happened right before my eyes. I'm not scared of thunderstorms, but seeing and hearing that made me jump out of my skin. How about you guys? You made it through the bad weather, I assume?"

"Yeah, we all stayed safe. But anyway, I figured I'd check up on you to see if you survived."

"I appreciate that... but... I..."

"You what?"

"I don't know if I will survive another storm I created."

"What do you mean?"

"Do you have a few minutes?"

"I sure do. And if you ask me to stay for a cigar, I'll say 'yes.'"

"Okay, great," Roman said with a smile.

Roman went inside to get Miroslav a cigar. When he returned to the deck, Miroslav cut his cigar and lit it.

"Šta te muči, prijatelju?"

"Well, I'm bothered that Janine and I got into a fight. A bad one. I raised my voice to her, and now I feel terrible. Granted, she came over and started to attack me personally; but it still didn't give me the right to do what I did. My shingles are also killing me, so I don't feel good. But it's still no excuse. I don't know what to do."

Roman was looking down at his feet while fidgeting. Miroslav knew that Roman genuinely felt terrible about the situation and wanted to make things right.

"Have you talked to Janine?"

"No. I'm afraid she'll never want to talk to me again."

"How do you know?"

"Well, I guess I don't know for sure. I mean, has she said anything to you guys?"

"She came over right before the microburst happened. I'm guessing she left your house after the fight since she came to our house in tears."

"Oh, great. I can only imagine the things she must have said about me."

"I suppose you *can* imagine what she said. But just because we imagine things doesn't mean they happen either."

"What do you mean?"

"Well, you've already convinced yourself that you have no chance of winning her back."

"Well, I'm sure I don't... do I?"

"I think you should hear the evidence first before reaching a verdict. Sorry, that's the lawyer in me. I must tell you that Janine has been much happier since she met you."

"Really?"

"Yes. I've known Janine since Theresa and I were both dating. Let's see, I've been married for eight years and have known Theresa for about twelve years. So, I've known Janine for almost as long. I'll tell you this. You should have seen her face when she showed us the picture you drew of her."

"She liked it that much?"

"Are you kidding? She *loved* it! She was smitten with joy. And the times she's been over now, all she does is talk about you in a good way."

"Geez… I never thought I made that big of an impact on her. I mean, I always like being around her and doing activities together."

"And she does too. I'm glad she's met you."

"So back to my original statement, you know, the things she said about me last night when she was at your house. What *did* she say?"

"You know what she told Theresa and me?"

"No, what?"

"She's considering accepting Jesus into her life. And she gives you much credit for leading her to Him."

"Wow… I mean… I… can't believe that. That's awesome! As I said, I never would have guessed I made that much of an impact on her. But at the same time, I don't understand. I mean, I wasn't exactly that nice to her during our fight either."

"She wants to work things out with you. She doesn't want to give up on you. She knows you're a genuine person. That's exactly what she said about you, that you're a genuine person."

"I don't know what to say."

"You weren't expecting that, were you," Miroslav said plainly.

"No, no, I wasn't. But how do I make it right? I try not to lose my temper, but I can't help it sometimes. You and Theresa seem like you have it all together."

"Yeah," Miroslav said as he chuckled. "We do *now,* for the most part. But it took years and *years* of work. Things weren't always a bed of roses for us, especially during the beginning of our marriage."

"What was a big problem for you guys?"

"I'd say one example would be differences. Not only some cultural differences but also our upbringings. Theresa had a stable home, whereas I did not have that growing up. Even though her father's side was Catholic, he didn't attend church much as a child until he met Theresa's mother. So, the Flahertys grew up attending a Protestant-aligned church, whereas I attended the Serbian Orthodox Church as a child. I switched over to becoming a Protestant later in life. We still do some Orthodox traditions in our house for fun. I certainly don't have anything against the Orthodox Church, and I applaud the Orthodox Church for all its hard work. However, we didn't attend church much when I was a child. Since the communists strongly discouraged church when my folks were growing up, they didn't keep up with it much in our house.

"Anyway, marriage is not for the faint of heart. Every day you both need to do the work. And it's not fifty-fifty either. Each person needs to give one hundred percent. It's an all-hands-on-deck approach. In the beginning, I knew both of us were not doing that. She placed great emphasis on family, whereas I didn't. She couldn't understand why I felt the way I felt. She didn't have the same experiences I did."

"So... can I ask you a question?"

"You want to know about my life in the Balkans, don't you."

"How did you guess?"

"I knew this day would come. But I don't mind sharing with you," Miroslav said as he readjusted himself in his seat.

"I haven't shared this information with many other people. Theresa is the only one who knows other than my blood relatives for obvious reasons. My children don't know the graphic details yet. I figured I'd wait to tell them later. I say let them enjoy the innocence of their youth."

"Does Janine know about your past?"

"She does not. I'm not against telling her, but it hasn't come up in conversation. It's nothing I go out of my way to share voluntarily. So, you want to know about my life growing up... I shall tell you.

"I lived in what was called Yugoslavia, as you already know. Where I lived exactly was a town called Glina, which is now in present-day Croatia. We didn't live right in the center of town, however. We lived in a country-type setting. Our family lived off the fat of the land. We had our livestock and crops for food as well. It was a simple life in that aspect."

"What was your family like?"

"My mother's name was Lidija. She was a very loving woman. She was outstanding. She knew how to take care of us children. My father's name was Dobrica. He wasn't evil but could be rough, especially when he drank too much. My mother and us kids hated it when he drank. He wasn't overtly abusive, but he could get belligerent. Sometimes, he would pick on me because I was a scrawny kid. However, we did have some good times, and he taught me a lot. But I could have done without his drinking. Plus, he smoked cigarettes inside the house and at the dinner table. It would have been nice if he could have done that outside.

"Although I will admit, he could be funny sometimes when he drank. One time he got drunk, and my folks were arguing about something. Suddenly, he pulled down his pants, mooned my mother, and said, 'Come on and get some. Come on and get some, woman!' I died laughing, seeing my father making a spectacle of himself while spanking his butt. My mother heard me laughing and told me that it wasn't funny. She took a wooden spoon and smacked him on the butt with it."

Miroslav and Roman laughed at that.

"So, then what happened?" asked Roman.

"Oh, she hit him with that wooden spoon a few times, and he laughed at her over it. I'll never forget that. She kept hitting him with it and chasing him around the house. She also chased me with the wooden spoon since I laughed at her. We eventually ran outside. He was in front of me, running while holding a beer bottle with a cigarette hanging out of his mouth. He exclaimed to me, 'Run for your life, Miroslav! She's going to kill us all!' As we were running away from Mom, a pig got loose and ran in front of us. We had to catch the pig while trying to outrun Mom. Since I know you like *Benny Hill*, that incident reminds me of the ending scenes from *Benny Hill* when they all chase each other around. My mother had to put up with some things you could say," Miroslav said with a smile.

"That *is* funny," Roman said while laughing. "What did your parents do for work?"

"My mother stayed at home and raised us. She did all the housework, and I helped with indoor and outdoor chores since I was the oldest. I was the man of the house when my father joined the Army when Serbian Krajina was formed. He wanted to fight for the cause. His drinking addiction had a lot to do with the ethnic tensions. I think he knew what was coming. Before he joined the military, he was a blacksmith."

"Really? That's cool."

"Yeah, he worked in his shop on our property. I would help him when my mother didn't need assistance with my siblings and other chores. He made all kinds of things. Tools, knives, you name it. The man could have done all that work in his sleep. I guess he would have been a bladesmith too. If he were still living, he could have easily won a contest on *Forged in Fire*. Word got out that his skills were so superior that even Slobodan Milošević visited us."

"Really? You met him in person?"

"I sure did. I was maybe nine years old or so. He bought a high-end knife that my father made. He mainly talked to my parents, but I remember he patted me on the head and wished my family and me well. He told me always to fight the good fight no matter how scary the enemy looks. You know… He even gave me an autographed picture of himself, which I still have."

"That's crazy. I remember hearing about him growing up."

"I thought about selling it for money, but given that it's Slobodan Milošević, I doubt many people in this part of the world would buy it. And I'm not sure how much it would be worth anyway. So, I'll probably keep it for history's sake and the fact that I met him in person. People can judge me however they want to for that. I don't care.

"Now, as for my siblings… I was the oldest of three children. My sister Zorana is in the middle at three years younger than me. She's a great sister and friend. Then there's Cvetko. He's the youngest. Seven years younger than me, to be exact. He was so precious when he was young. What a sweet boy. He brought so much joy to our family. He could even make Dad go from grumpy to melting his heart on most days.

"Honestly, except for my father's drinking, my childhood wasn't that bad. And he didn't drink all the time either. We worked together as a family to make ends meet at our house. We didn't have everything we wanted, but we had everything we needed. Our family wasn't wealthy, but the food was always on the table.

"As you can guess, Yugoslavia eventually broke up. We lived in Glina, now modern-day Croatia, as I mentioned to you. However, for a few years, it was in Serbian Krajina."

"Now, what is Serbian Krajina?"

"Ah, yes. It was a self-proclaimed state that broke away from Croatia. It wished to be unified with Republika Srpska and when Yugoslavia became a federal republic. Republika Srpska is in Bosnia and Herzegovina, in case you were wondering. You know, the government was communist before Yugoslavia broke up. However, I don't think the ethnic tensions came from nowhere. I think it was always there, and the government had the power to suppress it.

"So, because the government discouraged that kind of speech, sure, on paper, the tensions weren't there because the communists said so. But it was always right beneath the surface. My father always hated Croats. He told us kids that they should never be trusted and that they should all be damned to Hell.

"So then, of course, the wars broke out. The Serbian government tried to protect us, but the Croats eventually won. They destroyed and annihilated everything and everyone in the area. The mainstream media won't tell you that, however. People don't believe me or accept it when I say the Serbs were victims of ethnic cleansing. They act like I'm spreading misinformation or disinformation. Do you know what the easiest way to get in trouble nowadays is? Tell the truth... Now, doesn't that sound familiar?

"The ethnic cleansing has stopped, but it's still like wartime for the former Yugoslavia. Sure, the heavy artillery isn't being used. However, this wartime edition still carries bitterness and hatred toward others because they are different. In a sense, it's *to be continued,* as they say. It's fighting a war using other means. It can be as simple as using words or the silent treatment toward the so-called opposition.

"Even what's going on in America as we speak. You *must* hate someone because they *don't* wear a mask and *don't* get their vaccine. You *must* hate someone who *got* their vaccine and *wears* a mask. Then you have men versus women, Republican versus Democrat, and black versus white, for example. I *do* see some parallels between America and the former Yugoslavia. Instead of progressing, we've regressed, in my opinion. People have used social media as an outlet to spread hate as well. True love has no room to flourish in a toxic environment without reconciliation. Satan has pegged people against each other and loves every minute of it."

"Déjà vu," Roman thought as he distinctly remembered having a similar conversation with Janine about wartime while they smoked cigars and played Cribbage together.

"So… what happened to you and your family?"

Miroslav took a long drag on his cigar. He stared into Roman's eyes. Roman knew what he was about to hear wouldn't be good. He braced himself as he repositioned himself in his chair. He started to feel uncomfortable.

"As I mentioned, my father left to fight for Serbian Krajina. He was young enough and still in great shape. My parents were very young when I was born. They were in their early twenties. I was fourteen years old when my life drastically changed. I'd only see my father occasionally when he joined the service. I didn't know at that point if he would come home safely or be killed in action."

"Did he make it?"

"No… he died in combat. He died fighting for what he believed in. He was killed in battle in early May of 1995. I don't know exactly where it happened. That hit our household hard. Dad could be a pain sometimes with his drinking, but we all loved him, and I *know* he loved us. What an incredibly hard-working man he was.

"Anyway, Serbian Krajina was overtaken once the Croats came in during Operation Storm. Now the war was up close and personal. I could hear military combat off in the distance during the evening. It was a sleepless night… the next morning brought its own set of horrors."

Roman noticed Miroslav had a look of torment on his face. He didn't want to press him to continue his story. He figured it would be best to wait for him to go at his own pace.

"That day, I was supposed to cut grass. I may have been scrawny, but I was strong and quick. Pulling my weight around our house made me strong, especially working outside. I was supposed to cut grass with a scythe that day. However, I had a late start to the morning because my stomach was mad at me. Once I finally quit using the bathroom, I knew my job awaited me… or so I thought. My sister Zorana and I were startled by the high-pitched screaming we heard. I told my sister to wait inside.

"I quietly ran to the shed to grab the scythe I used to cut the grass. But now, I intended to use it as a weapon to protect my family. My whole body shook uncontrollably, and I had a big lump in my throat. That screaming I heard…"

Miroslav paused as a tear came to his eye. He took a deep breath before he continued with his story.

"I heard my mother screaming for her life. She was yelling profanities. Even though my body shook, I ran toward my father's shop. I reached the edge of the shop, and then I peeked inside… I saw them. I saw three Croats in military uniform. And what I saw was unspeakable."

Miroslav paused again and took another drag off his cigar. He sat there silent in his chair. Roman stared back at Miroslav feeling his adrenaline kick in. He knew the story was going to get ugly fast. It was evident that Miroslav was holding back the tears, but he still shared the rest of his story.

"My mother was the victim of a war crime. Two of the Croat soldiers held her arms, so she couldn't move as she lay on the table face up. She couldn't break free no matter how hard she tried. I knew she wanted to kill them for what they were about to do to her. She struggled, but it was no use. After the third soldier punched her in the face a few times, he pulled down his pants and lifted her skirt up. He forced himself upon her. As he started to rape her, the other two men laughed at what was happening.

"Rage overtook my body. I knew I had to act quickly. I was armed with a scythe, but I knew they had guns, which a scythe would have been no match for. Then I found my opportunity. Whichever one did it, they left a gun by the doorway. At this point, I didn't care about dying. I wanted those people to die for what they were doing to my mother. In a flash, I grabbed that gun. I was in luck since it was fully automatic. I shot several rounds at the Croat, holding my mother's right arm first since there was a clear firing lane. I killed him instantly. I could hear my mother screaming as I opened gunfire upon the Croat soldier. I didn't hit her once by accident. The man that was raping her ducked down quickly. The other one took out a pistol and returned fire on me. I got out of the way in time before he could hit me. Since I was outside, I saw a shovel leaning up against the side of the shop. I quickly grabbed it and threw it across the shop entrance to serve as a distraction. The soldier unloaded the remaining bullets as he saw the shovel tossed into the air. I then heard him cursing after he knew he would have to reload. But he wasn't quick enough. I exterminated him too. And then there was one: me and the rapist. I walked inside with the gun pointed at him before he could grab his. He was the one who stupidly left his firearm by the doorway. He didn't have enough time to grab another weapon since he had taken cover from me, opening fire. Plus, he lost time since he had to pull his pants up. I told him that I'd shoot if he made a move."

"Not to interrupt, but how could you talk to him? I thought Serbian and Croatian were two different languages."

"They are, but they're very similar. Back in the day, the communists called it Serbo-Croatian. That will be a conversation for another day.

"As I entered my father's shop, he got on his knees and begged for his life. He was crying, not because he felt terrible for what he had done, but for the fact that I caught him. My mother eventually saw it was me. She looked like death. They roughed her up badly. She had a black eye on her left eye to the point where it was closed shut and leaking. Her face was bruised up badly as well. She didn't say anything, however. I looked the rapist in the eye for a minute while maintaining eye contact. As he inched closer to me, begging for his life, I kept moving away from him while staying inside the shop. I didn't know what tricks this criminal had up his sleeve. So, I pulled the trigger... and nothing happened. I was out of bullets.

"Then he smiled at me with the evilest grin. He knew he had me right where he wanted me. He told me that we'd settle this in another way. He opened a window and placed the guns outside. Then he grabbed a pitchfork from the corner of the shop. He was confident that he would kill me through a painful death. So, he charged at me hard, but he didn't get me. As he pulled the pitchfork out of the wall, I ran out of his way to the opposite side of the shop. I didn't want to run out the door because my mother would have been stuck with him. I knew I was quick. However, he was a lot bigger than me. He was one big slab of muscle. I knew if he got a hold of me, he would have squashed me like a bug. My only thought at that moment was what those tines would feel like penetrating my organs. I couldn't let him do me in because then I wouldn't be able to save my mother.

"He picked up a brick and threw it across the room with all his might. He did this to serve as a distraction. That brick hit me perfectly on the nose with sizeable force. I could feel the tears building as my face reacted to the impact of the brick. The blood started to flow out of my nose since my nose was broken. As he charged me again, I ran to the other side of the shop. He almost stuck me to the wall since I could barely see with all the tears in my eyes. After he pulled the pitchfork out of the wall again, he told me that if he got a hold of me, he would rape me like he did my mother. I was in a prime position now to make my move. I grabbed a knife that my father had made and slowly walked back toward the door while facing him. My eyes never left him even though I still had difficulty seeing. I wanted to make him mad so that he could charge me hard. If he stuck the tines in the wall, I could stab him. I yelled at him and said, 'Long live the Serbs!'

"My trick *almost* worked. He charged me with everything that he had. But as I walked backward, I tripped over a hammer. I fell backward and lost my knife. He was coming for me. That big man was going to do me in. I had to form a plan in my head in a split second. I jumped up in a split second and stood with my back against the wall. I held off for the very last second. I jumped out of the way as he approached me. He ran with such force that he buried that pitchfork halfway into the wall. He was so mad that he didn't kill me. He kept trying to pull that pitchfork out of the wall with substantial vigor. At that point, I made my escape outside."

"You mean you let him go?"

"*Hell no!* As I wiped the tears out of my eyes, I swung the door open as he tugged on that pitchfork. I didn't give him a chance to react. With all my strength, I cut off part of his left arm with the scythe I had sitting outside. He screamed as blood shot out of his arm like a fire hose. He fell to the floor, and I kicked him square in the face. Blood was flowing out of his nose now. I ordered him to get up and apologize to my mother for what he had done to her, which he did. He begged for his life again. I told him that what he had done to my family was irreversible. I told him, '*For the Serbs and my family, you shall pay for this!*' With my scythe in hand, I swung that thing with as much force as possible. I cut his head clean off with one swipe. A pool of blood followed as his head went flying.

"Did killing him and the other two men bother me? No, it didn't. I was defending my family, and doing so was no crime. I know my father would have protected us if he were home. I didn't ask for the Croats to show up and perform war crimes on my family. They made their choices... but so did I.

"I ran over to my mother lying on the table. She tried to sit up a little as best as she could. When I was next to her, I was able to see the damage that was done. She had one stab wound in the chest and two in her stomach. Blood was running out of her mouth, and she had difficulty breathing. I suspect the rapist stabbed her when I initially opened fire. I knew right then and there that she was going to die.

"She grabbed me by the collar of my shirt and said, 'I love you, son. You take care of Zorana and Cvetko for me.'

"'I love you too, Mom,' I said as I began to cry. 'You're not going to make it are you...'

"She said, 'No, my son. I'm not. But you listen to me. I want you to hear my words before I die. I...' She was interrupted by coughing up more blood. 'I want you to follow Christ. That's your ticket to Heaven. Follow Him and accept Him into your life as I have... It's all I have left now... I love you, Miroslav.'

"She died right there on the table in the shop. I yelled, *'Mom! Mom!'* as I was crying, but it was no use. Reality had reared its ugly head. My mother was dead – a victim of a crime against humanity. But you want to know something? My mother was a hero. She was a strong woman and will always be. I've noticed that they make strong female characters invincible or possess superpowers in pop culture. Or they make them unbeatable superheroes. I know it's for entertainment purposes.

"But I'll tell you this, Roman. My mother lost the battle. The Croats beat her, bludgeoned her, and raped her. Then she died. But she *still* has the victory because they didn't rob her of her integrity. They couldn't take that from her. And in those dying moments, she accepted Christ as her Savior and Lord. I know she did because Christ was never really talked about much in our house. Sure, we grew up going to the Orthodox Church occasionally and doing all the traditions, but the relationship aspect of Christ wasn't there. My mother lost the battle... but she won the war. And despite her being murdered, she *is* and always will be a strong woman in my mind. My mother had the victory that day through Christ. That was my first real encounter with Christ when she told me about Him in her last moments of life.

"My mental anguish had only begun. Now both my parents were dead... *Cvetko*. I didn't take him into account thus far. I ran back to the house to see if he was there. My sister saw me with blood spattered on my clothing. I didn't go into the graphic details at that moment. However, I had to tell her that our mother was dead. She broke down and wept, as did I again. I asked her if Cvetko was with her, and she told me he wasn't. I ordered her to stay inside because it wasn't safe to go out. I ran back to the shop to grab the weapons and ammo that the Croats had. I brought Zorana back a pistol and a rifle. I kept the other gun for myself. This time I made sure it was fully loaded.

"I frantically looked outside on our property to see if Cvetko was anywhere in sight... but he wasn't. He wasn't anywhere. I called out for him, but there was no answer. The only other place I could go was my grandparent's house next to our property. That would have been my father's parents. They had stayed with us overnight due to the shelling and combat we heard off in the distance. I know they returned to their house early the following day since they had to feed the chickens and pigs.

"I knocked on their door only to discover it was already open. I went inside their house. I called out for my grandparents, but no one answered. My heart started to race again. I started shaking. The place was too quiet. Something didn't seem right as I noticed a couple of broken glasses and a chair knocked over by the kitchen table. The tablecloth was on the floor as if someone had pulled it off. Then I saw a couple of droplets on the tablecloth. It was blood. The Croats were here before they showed up at our place. I could only imagine the horrors at that point of what they could have done.

"I heard a noise from upstairs. It was whimpering. I knew it was my brother. I swiftly made my way upstairs. I ensured I was quiet while going up each step in case I was again met with the enemy. Before I got to their bedroom, I raised the gun to my shoulder and checked my surroundings. I entered the bedroom with my weapon drawn. I didn't see the enemy. But I saw a bump in the middle of my grandparent's bed, shaking. I knew it was my little brother, but what was he doing under the bed sheets? I approached the bed slowly. He was crying loudly at this point. I think he heard my footsteps and was afraid that I was a Croat. I was terrified. My body was shaking uncontrollably like it was earlier. What did they do to my little brother?

"As I approached the bed, I could see from the outline of the sheets that my grandparents were lying in bed. I did find it odd that their big winter blanket was on the bed since it was August. I didn't want to look under the sheets, but I knew I had to. I set the gun up against the wall. I got next to the bed and took hold of the sheets and blanket. I took a couple of seconds to brace myself. My hands couldn't stop shaking, but I had to gain composure. Then I lifted all the sheets and the winter blanket in one quick swoop. My little brother screamed in fright due to the element of surprise. As for me, I gasped at the sight that I saw. I stared at what I saw with both hands covering my mouth. My grandparents were lying in a pool of their blood. The Croats had taken knives and cut their throats open. I was devasted. The same monsters that took advantage of my mother also killed the innocence of two older adults... my grandparents.

"Cvetko crawled over to me and hugged me with all his strength. He had blood on him too. I lifted him off the bed to the floor. I continued to hold him in my arms as we both cried together. I asked him what had happened. I had an idea of what he would tell me, but I wanted to hear it from him. He was the witness, and I wasn't. I also asked him if the Croats had touched him in any way. They didn't punch or kick him. The Croats didn't touch him inappropriately, either. But he *did* tell me they held him in place. They forced him to watch the graphic execution of our grandparents. He said they forced him to go under the bedsheets with his dead grandparents and not to move, or they would kill him – what an excellent way to treat a seven-year-old," Miroslav said with resentment.

"Anyway, we quickly made it back to our house. Zorana and Cvetko were so happy to see each other. We told Cvetko to hurry, wash up, and change his clothes. After he bathed, I quickly examined him. I wanted to see if they had physically harmed him in any way. I also wanted to know if they told him to keep quiet about it. But I didn't see any evidence of physical harm.

"We ended up burying Mom and our grandparents at the back of the property. We didn't have fancy caskets on hand, but we put the three next to each other and wrapped them up in blankets before burying them. It was the best we could do with the limited materials on hand. Not to mention, we were pressed for time. We knew we had to escape; otherwise, we would be next on the chopping block."

There was a pause between Miroslav and Roman. Roman had barely touched his cigar as he sat there motionless like a statue. He was in shock as to what he had heard from Miroslav.

Finally, Roman spoke, "I... I don't know what to say to you. Saying 'sorry' will not bring your family back. But I feel bad that you had to experience this, especially at a young age. Nobody, especially a child, should ever have to go through what you and your siblings did."

"I'm not going to lie; it *does* bother me from time to time. Every year Croatia celebrates Victory Day in August. Sure, it was a victory for *them*. The Serbs of Krajina paid for that victory with blood on the Croats' hands. The same way Serbs paid for it during World War II when Croatia was a puppet state to Nazi Germany.

"Many Croats that committed genocide during Operation Storm in Serbian Krajina received no punishments. No trials, no arrests, and no justice for the Serbs. People will argue with me and say, 'Oh, that never happened. They never did what you claim.' Of course, they didn't do it... on paper. Since no one found out that they killed my grandparents and raped and killed my mother, their consciences are clear... again, on paper. The so-called experts also will say, 'Well, the Serbs *chose* to leave Serbian Krajina. They could have stayed.' My response to that propaganda is this. I can *choose* not to file my taxes next year, but that will get me in trouble if I don't. The same applies to this. We could have chosen to stay in Serbian Krajina, but we probably would have paid for it with our lives.

"But I manage all this better than I used to. I used to blame all Croats and hated them. All of them. I hated them because I felt like the Croats got away with everything while acting like choir boys. But that didn't make me feel any better. So, I don't carry that prejudice around anymore. The Bible says, 'But I tell you, love your enemies and pray for those who persecute you.' I had to give all this to Jesus because it's much easier to quote that phrase than to live it, especially in my case. It's something I really must make a conscious effort to do. But if I give this to the Lord daily, He brings me comfort during my struggles because I still mourn the loss of my family. I'm not happy that my family was murdered and the Croats did wrong, but the Lord is my shepherd. And I choose to follow Him and His ways. I might not have any personal gain, but God is not a bargaining chip. I serve God because He served me first. He loved me first.

"It also didn't matter how often I drank or how much in one sitting. I could never find those answers at the bottom of the whiskey bottle. That's why I don't drink anymore. It was getting way out of hand. And I'd rather admit to someone that I went to counseling to seek help with my PTSD versus trying to do it all alone, only to crash and burn. I'd rather admit I need Christ to help me rather than go it alone.

"People say Christianity is for the weak. They don't know it takes a stronger person to follow Christ and stay committed to Him. That takes a lot more strength than doing whatever you feel like. Some people have told me that I should stay mad at God. If He were real, He wouldn't have allowed these things to happen to you. We've all heard that before. It's tempting to buy into all that, but I look at it this way. How could I be mad at God if there's a claim that He doesn't exist? Were we all afraid of COVID-19 a few years ago? No. We were not because it wasn't around then."

"I agree with that. I wish people would look at following Christ more like how you put it. And I'm happy you've shared all this with me. You have a great story, and don't you forget that. So, were you and your siblings able to escape?"

"Yes, we did. At that point, it was time to make our escape. After we buried our family, I changed out of my bloody clothes and washed myself up. I made sure we all had food and water for the road. That's all we could take besides the clothes on our backs. The only other thing I took was our family photo album. I'm glad I grabbed that album. I found an envelope with a wad of dinars inside of it. We hopped into our Yugo 45, and off we went. You can't fit much else in a Yugo. Most of the people from Serbian Krajina wanted to escape to Republika Srpska or Yugoslavia. They wanted to be with the Serbs. However, that caused a pile-up of people trying to escape going east. People were also killed by the Croats while they were stuck waiting. The Serbs were like sitting ducks. But again, the media won't tell you that part.

"On our end, our escape happened rather quickly. I chose to go in the other direction. We made it to Slovenia in the nick of time. They closed the borders minutes after we got there. Luckily, we had an aunt and uncle that lived in Austria. Once they found out we had to apply for asylum, they took us in. Many other people had to request asylum, as well. They fled persecution because there was no sensible way to return to where they came from.

"Eventually, I made it to America on a student exchange program. My sister and brother also decided to come to America several years later. I told you before that Zorana lives in Carlisle and Cvetko lives in Harrisburg. Anyway, coming to America is where I studied law at Yale. It helped that I had scholarships to get in there. I worked hard to get accepted into law school and worked even harder to graduate."

"That's neat. Yale has an outstanding reputation in schools that teach law, from what I know. So let me ask you this. What made you choose to become a criminal defense lawyer versus a prosecutor? I figured, given the circumstances you saw growing up, you would want the bad guys to go to jail."

Miroslav chuckled and said, "Well, that's true. Justice needs to be served. But, then again, *justice* needs to be served."

"What do you mean?"

"If someone didn't commit a crime and is still found guilty in the public eye or the courtroom, that's not justice. I can guarantee that since the Croats took back Serbian Krajina, they blame the Serbs for everything. I mean, I was a teenager when all this happened. I didn't go to people's houses and attack them because they were of different ethnicity. That would be like if you moved to the south and people hated you because you're a northerner. You weren't even alive during the Civil War, were you?"

"No."

"Exactly. In society, we forget that someone is innocent until proven guilty beyond a shadow of a doubt. It seemed like people had little to no interest in defending the Serbs during the Yugoslav Wars. Crimes committed against the Serbs seemed to be viewed as irrelevant by both the media and the legal system. It's like we didn't matter. That's why I decided to become a criminal defense lawyer. Certain people hated me because I was a Serb. My guilt was presumed without a fair trial. I saw that as an opportunity to be a voice for people. And I hope someday the Serbs will have their voices heard.

"When a person dies, they will be judged by God. Notice that I said 'judged' and not automatically condemned. When a person has Jesus, He has already paid for that person's sins. Think of it like the game you and Janine play. In Cribbage, you only get dealt a perfect hand by chance. When a person accepts Jesus, they will be holding the Perfect Hand because they chose to. So, if He is gracious enough to give us that chance and hear our side of the story, I feel called to do the same for others. I'm not saying everyone must be a criminal defense lawyer, but for me, that was the path God called me to take."

"Yeah, I see what you're saying. Instead of giving people the benefit of the doubt, I feel like people run around and condemn everyone with a guilty verdict."

"Absolutely. So, think about everything we've talked about. I want you to sit on this. Whatever happens between you and Janine is your business. I'm not going to make you do anything. All I ask is to think about our conversation that took place tonight. And don't presume Janine's guilt right off the bat. Give her a chance to tell her side of the story. Listen to her with an open heart. From there, you can make your own decision."

"All right, man, I will. I'll give her the benefit of the doubt next time we talk."

"Sounds good, brother. Well, it looks like our cigars are almost done, or at least mine is. I should probably head for home."

"Yeah, it's getting late anyway. Say, can I ask you a question about Croatia?"

"Sure. What's up?"

"What do a Croat and a beer bottle have in common?"

"Oh no," Miroslav said as he tried not to laugh. "Here we go again. The circus is back in town. All right, let's hear it."

"They're both empty from the neck up! Get it? Get it?"

Miroslav couldn't help but laugh at Roman's joke.

Miroslav said, "That sounds like a joke my father would have told me growing up."

"I couldn't help myself."

"And there you have it, folks. Another dragon slain by the mighty wizard."

They both hugged each other and parted ways. Roman eventually finished his cigar and got settled in for the evening. He thought about that night. He cringed at everything Miroslav told him about the war crimes against his family. But he rejoiced that Miroslav used his story to speak against prejudice and hatred rather than holding onto it. Roman examined his life now. Maybe he could work on some things in his own life. Perhaps Miroslav's story and wisdom served as a gentle reminder to Roman.

Maybe he was too hard on people who identified as liberals or people from New England. He challenged himself on his original beliefs and saw his heart open. He didn't have to agree with everything they believed in, but he decided not to carry that resentment around anymore. In his mind, it was time to practice what he preached in that specific area. Roman also made a deal with himself to take the time to appreciate the little things in life. He couldn't imagine what it would be like if someone killed his mother or grandparents, nor did he want to think about such things. But now he knew Miroslav's story. He saw where Miroslav's life was now and saw him as a walking testimony. The truth he spoke to Roman that night was the kind of truth Roman wanted to be intentional about. He would wait for this opportunity once he saw Janine again. But it would come with yet another trial.

CHAPTER 14

It was around dawn when Roman woke up. He decided to start cleaning up his yard from the storm last week. He ate a good breakfast, knowing he would need the energy to do the job. He didn't plan to finish everything today but figured he needed to start somewhere. Since he had his vaccine, his outbreak of shingles was mainly cleared up now, which meant he felt better. He brushed his teeth and got dressed. He made sure to wear pants and long sleeves for safety. He made his way out to the metal building, where he kept his yard equipment. It was a decent-sized building. He had room for all his tools and more significant equipment like his sit-down lawn mower and UTV. Plus, he had a place for his toolbox where he could work on things like sharpening his lawnmower blades and whatnot. He kept the inside of the building clean and organized, like his house. Roman topped off his chainsaw with bar oil and fuel.

After making sure his chainsaw was good to go, Roman grabbed his safety glasses and earplugs and got to work. He started with the two smaller trees first. He finished cutting up the first tree and took a break. The high humidity made the air exceptionally uncomfortable and stagnant. Roman knew it would be best not to kill himself working today. He paused for a water break, and then he moved the blue tarp from the woodpile so he could begin stacking. He stacked wood for several minutes, then paused. He looked at his phone and saw his brother had sent him a funny meme that had the man from the Dos Equis commercials. Roman laughed out loud at it and sent his brother a reply text. He set his phone down on the woodpile and paused. He couldn't stop sweating from the oppressive humidity.

Then he heard a noise coming from the woods. He looked over to see what was going on. He couldn't see anything, but he heard something moving about. The noise grew louder as two objects appeared before him, roughly twenty-five yards away. They were two black bear cubs roughhousing with each other. But Roman knew better than to stop and admire how cute they were. For he knew the mother was in proximity of her young. And he was right. Before making a run for it, he saw the mother emerge out of the woods behind the cubs. She froze in her spot, and so did the cubs. Both the mother and the cubs looked directly at Roman. He could feel the mother staring a hole right through him. He knew she perceived him as a potential threat. Luckily for Roman, he was not standing in between her and her children.

He wanted to exit the area to go inside his house. He reached for his phone but bumped it into a crevice of the woodpile. Waves of fear radiated from his body. He felt that he would never leave the situation alive. He knew if the mother bear charged, he wouldn't stand a chance since he was unarmed. His chainsaw wasn't within reach either. He locked his eyes on the mother bear as he fumbled with his right hand, trying to dig up his phone. He was finally able to reach it. He felt a slight prick on his hand as he pulled his phone out of the woodpile. The prick he felt was between his pointer finger and thumb. It felt like a poke from a sharp splinter of one of the logs. He made himself look more prominent and slowly walked back to the house.

"All right, bear. I promise I'm not going to hurt you or your cubs," he said in a low but assertive voice.

He slowly waved his hands above his head and said, "I will go back inside and leave you guys be."

He walked backward slowly toward the house while gently waving his hands above his head. The mother bear kept her eyes on Roman the whole time. Roman did the same to the bears. His eyes never left them, either. What felt like a three-hour event only lasted a couple of minutes. He finally returned to the deck and quickly opened the door. He promptly shut the door and locked it. While inside, he checked his phone to see if Craig had responded to his text from earlier. There were no messages, so he set the phone on the toaster oven. He had never put his phone there before but wasn't thinking clearly. He was still startled by his encounter with the bears.

"Man, that was a close call," he said.

After he got himself a glass of water, he sat down on the couch to take a break. He needed a break anyway from the bear encounter and high humidity. He felt cramping in his right hand from where he got pricked from inside the woodpile. He figured the pain would subside, but it didn't. After a little over an hour or so, it grew worse. The pain became excruciating, as though knives were stabbing him repeatedly. His muscles were also starting to spasm involuntarily. His body was losing control.

"What's... what's *happening*... to me? I must find my phone to call for help."

He got up from his chair in the living room, but it did him no good. He took a couple of steps and collapsed. He hit the side of his head on the floor. He started to cry in pain. Cold sweat flowed out of his body as his skin became increasingly pale. He feared the wrath was upon him again, like the microburst last week.

"God... *GOD!* I'm sorry... *I said I'm sorry!* I didn't mean to hurt Janine. If this is the end of me, I accept your decision."

Now he was sobbing. He had no recollection of leaving his phone on the toaster oven. So, calling for help was out of the question now. More importantly, he feared he would never have the chance to make it right with Janine.

Over the years, he blamed himself for Briana's death. Had they not gotten into an argument about his gambling problem, she wouldn't have stormed off and driven on the road for her last time. Now Roman found himself in a similar position. He was leaving someone on bad terms… again. Satan enjoyed every minute of this torment at Roman's expense.

His abdomen started to stiffen up with a board-like rigidity. There was nothing he could do. He tried to get up repeatedly but to no avail. He thought of all his good times with his family. The memories he had of Briana. And then Janine. How he loved being around her. The happiness she brought him. How proud he was of her. He didn't care that her politics were left-leaning. He loved her. But he knew it was too late now. He thought for sure he was finished and made his peace with that.

Janine had tried to call Roman, but it went to his voicemail. She finally sent him a text saying she was going to swing by. It had been eight days, and they had only spoken once since their fight. They were planning on burying the hatchet at Roman's house. She wasn't supposed to be there until after dinner, but she couldn't wait anymore. The waiting around was killing her. The fact that she received nothing but silence on her phone after trying to reach out to Roman made it worse for her. She was tempted to go to his house anyway, whether he would approve of it or not. Despite *his* right-leaning politics, she loved him. She knew it would be worth it to make things right. So, she finally got the courage to get in her car and drive.

She made it to Roman's house and knocked on his door. She heard a response from Roman, but it wasn't what she expected.

"Help! SOMEBODY, PLEASE HELP WHOMEVER YOU ARE!" Roman yelled.

"Roman? *ROMAN!*"

This time there was no response. As Janine knocked on Roman's front door, his breathing became labored. She knocked on the door harder and screamed his name again. As she put her ear to the door, she heard Roman vomiting. She pulled on the doorknob frantically since she was starting to panic. But fortunately for her, the door opened, and she looked shocked. Luckily for Roman, he forgot to lock the front door when he stuck his bills in the mailbox that morning.

She ran in and saw what was going on. The place was not a pleasant sight. She noticed the vomit on the floor. He was lying on the floor next to his vomit, uncontrollably shaking. He was extremely pale, and she could see he was sweating excessively. And his eyelids looked mildly swollen. He looked like death. He looked at her for a couple of seconds while still shaking.

"Janine… is that… is that you?"

"Yes, Roman, it's me!"

"Oh… I uh…" he tried to get up but threw up on the floor again.

Janine did her best to prop Roman up with his back against the couch. She tried to brace herself for it, but she was too late. She managed to dodge most of it, but some of his vomit ended up on the side of Janine's shirt.

"Janine… I'm sorry. I…"

"Roman, please don't worry about that now. What's happening to you?"

"*I SAID I'M SORRY!* Please… Please don't hurt me!" he yelled while still crying.

Roman tried to move away from her for fear of Janine hurting him, but he didn't get far for obvious reasons.

He continued the conversation and said, "I'm sorry… I did what I did to you."

"I'm not going to hurt you," Janine said as she started crying.

Unlike last week's fight, she knew Roman didn't yell out of anger this time. Either way, this situation she found herself in was agonizing. She knew something was wrong but didn't know what. She knew that this wasn't an act. From what she noticed, Roman was not with it mentally. She suspected that drugs were to blame for this but didn't want to jump to a false conclusion.

"It… well my… my hand. My right hand started hurting. And my stomach… my…"

He couldn't finish his sentence as he threw up again violently for several seconds.

He resumed his train of thought and said, "It's almost like my appendix... but I had that removed years ago. I guess... I guess my time is up."

She saw his right hand. It was severely inflamed. Her eyes grew a little bigger as she looked at it. It occurred to her. He was bitten by something. It looked like a bite mark that resembled that of a spider.

"A black widow. That's what did this," she thought.

"I'm calling for help, Roman. I'm not going to leave you, I promise."

"What? You're going to... leave?"

"No, I said, 'I'm *not* going to leave!'"

She called 911 for help and told them what was going on. She cleaned the bite wound with soap and kept ice on it, to Roman's dismay. She patted his head and held him to try and keep him calm.

"Please... *PLEASE...*" he said as he was interrupted by irregular breathing.

She jerked back a little bit from reflexes to brace herself in case he was going to vomit again.

He resumed the conversation he started and said, "Don't leave me. I... um... I love you, Janine. I didn't... not want things to end this way."

"I love you too, Roman. It's not going to end this way. They'll take you to the hospital and care for you when they show up."

"But... what if the Soviets..."

"Nobody is going to hurt you, Roman. I'm not going to let them. If they try to, they'll have to go through me first. Now, I'm going to say a prayer for you."

Janine continued to hold him close to her with excellent care. He threw up on her again, but she didn't care at this point. She wanted to be there for him to the best of her ability, even though he continued to shake uncontrollably with varied breathing. She began to pray while trying not to cry too much. She was scared for Roman. She didn't know how long he had been in this condition at home alone.

"Dear Lord... I thank You for Roman... I pray that You bring him back to health. I pray that the hospital and its staff take excellent care of him." She began to cry more and continued praying, "I pray that You can ease his mind, so he doesn't think anyone… will hurt him… the former Soviets of all people… I pray that You let the man I love live a long and happy life." She was sobbing as she kept praying, "I pray that maybe one day we can grow old together. Please… please don't take Roman from me… He's a man after Your own heart, and I love that about him. I love how kind he has been to me, and I like his sense of humor. I don't want to lose him… Amen."

Janine continued to cry as she held Roman next to her. Even though it felt like an eternity, the ambulance showed up. After the EMTs took him away, Janine took it upon herself to clean up the area. She cleaned up all the vomit. She went home and showered since vomit was on her clothes. She eventually made her way to Fulton County Medical Center, where Roman was.

Roman had been sleeping. He slowly woke up groggy and saw an object smiling at him while sitting on his belly. He rubbed his eyes with his fingers. It took him a few seconds to fully wake up. He recognized it immediately. It was the poop emoji in the form of a stuffed animal. He smiled as he held it, but he wondered who put the poop there. The second he looked up, he saw her. It was Janine. The woman he admired was there for him when he needed help. He knew he would have to talk things out with her. However, he felt like the conversation would go well. She approached him and sat on the chair next to the bed.

"A woman that saves a man who doesn't treat her right has every right to take a dump on him," Roman said as he held the poop emoji up. "See what I did there?"

Janine laughed and said, "Well, I know you have a gross sense of humor with your farts and everything, so I got you that as a present."

"Thank you for that. And… *thank you*… for saving my life."

Roman readjusted himself in the bed, so he wasn't lying down. He propped himself up with the pillows so he could sit up.

"Listen, Janine. I'm... I'm sorry for talking to you like that. You didn't deserve that. And what's worse. I threw you out of my house during that terrible weather. I'm so ashamed of myself."

Janine could tell Roman felt horrible about that. After he said his apology to her face, he hung his head down in shame.

"Roman..." Janine began.

He looked up to give her his undivided attention.

"Roman, I forgive you for that. I should say I'm sorry too. I had no right coming into your house, starting a fight, and swearing at you. You were trying to take it easy with your shingles outbreak; I should have been more sensitive to that. I took my anger out on you because of work. It was also that time of the month. Plus, I've decided to quit smoking."

"Really? That's great! Good for you, Janine. I think that's awesome. I know how hard it is to give up something you're addicted to. I'll support you in any way that I can."

"I appreciate that... Roman... I..."

"What is it?"

"Can I tell you something?"

"Of course, you can. I sure wish I had something to eat and drink, though."

Janine pulled out a Gatorade from her purse to give Roman, and the grand surprise came. It was Roman's favorite. His beloved White Castle sliders. She pulled those out of her purse too.

"Wow! You got me White Castles sliders! What a babe you are!"

"Eh, being a babe is what I do best."

"I mean, look at these sliders! The sheer ambiance of it all! All the nostalgia behind a White Castle slider leaves the audience craving more!"

He bit into the slider and made yummy noises.

"Wow! I taste the victory in that bite! If I were an elk during mating season, I would be bugling at full force. I swear these things are like an aphrodisiac!" Roman exclaimed as he pinched his nipple.

Janine was smiling as she shook her head.

She said, "If only they could have added you into that movie *Harold & Kumar Go to White Castle*. I'm not sure how much you can eat since your body has been through the wringer, so don't feel like you're obligated to eat."

"Yeah, I'll take it easy, even though it's hard to say 'no.' So, Janine… let me ask you something about your beliefs."

"Sure."

"Would you rather take a dump on the Trump or be ridin' with the Biden? See what I did there? It rhymes perfectly."

"I see *someone* is starting to feel better."

She saw how something so tiny could make someone so happy, which made her happy. Before coming to the hospital, she was terrified of the conversation she would have with Roman. She helped Roman out of bed so he could go to the bathroom. After that, he made his way back to bed with her assistance. He wanted to be focused without any distractions during their conversations. They both ate their sliders first before they dove into any serious discussion. Now it was time to talk.

"So… you wanted to tell me something?" Roman asked. "The fact that you're a thief?"

"I beg your pardon?"

"I saw you steal the Bible from my bookshelf that day when I drew your picture."

Janine felt her heart sink into despair. She thought she was done for in Roman's eyes.

"It's okay. I wanted you to have it. I wanted you to have that communication with God. Not to mention I lied to you about hoop snakes. They're not real."

"Yeah… I kind of figured that."

"Now, what was it that you wanted to tell me?"

"Yes," Janine said hesitantly. "Let me have the floor for a bit without interruption. You know, for so long, I hated men. I couldn't stand their pride and egos. How they look down on women and think we're all stupid and can't do certain jobs. And then I met you. I'm not going to lie; I thought you were a nut case. Or as you Boston people would say, 'wicked retaaded.'"

They both laughed at that. Roman always got a kick out of Janine trying to mimic his thick Boston accent.

"Anyways, I saw you. I got to know you. And we probably won't agree on most things politically... but I *can* say you're the kind of man I've longed for."

"Really? But we're so different, you and I."

"Not so much. For example, we may view the pandemic differently. However, you still respected my feelings about it... I know you think wearing a face mask is garbage and doesn't work, but you didn't fuss at me or try to change me. You chose to do that because you regarded my feelings. You supported me. And at the same time, you taught me how to have fun again and not live under a rock for the rest of my life. I was so stressed over the pandemic that I didn't see my sister and her family for almost a year. That's about a year I'll never be able to get back. Don't get me wrong, some of your notions were unconventional, like farting out confetti and what have you," she said, trying not to laugh, "but what you taught me was not to live my life in such fear that I'm not even living. And that's how you make me feel when I'm around you, Roman. I feel alive again.

"All the things I told you about my parents. You didn't fight against me. You listened to me. Or even the questions I had about God. All you did was answer them and be my friend. You lead by example. Even the times I was confrontational with you. You still were there to be my friend. You wanted to be my friend during the bad times, so you'll have me during the good times. And speaking about you leading by example, I want to accept Jesus into my life."

"You do?"

"Yes, I do. But I'm not doing it for you. I'm doing it for Him."

"That makes me feel better. Knowing that you're doing it for the right reasons is what I wanted to know. You're not doing it to impress me. You're doing this for *Him* and no one else."

"I want to… but I don't know if I can."

"Really? What's stopping you?"

Roman saw that Janine looked uncomfortable. He knew she was holding back on something but didn't want to pressure her for a response. She took a deep breath and finally continued with the conversation.

"I have to tell you something," she said with a tear in her eye as she put her hand on Roman's arm.

"I… I have herpes," she said with pain and guilt as she stared into Roman's eyes.

"Remember I told you about George from McKeesport?"

"Yes, I do."

"Come to find out… he cheated on me. I didn't even know he did it until my first outbreak of herpes. I was so freaked out because I knew I had only had sex with a few guys before George. All those times I had sex, protection was used. I didn't understand until he confessed his actions behind my back. The woman he slept with gave herpes to him, which he gave me in turn. I felt so hurt and betrayed. It was the *one time* I didn't have George wear a condom, and I paid for it. And I'll pay for it for the rest of my life too. Once you have herpes, you can't get rid of it. I feel like less of a person since I have an STD. Theresa and Miroslav don't know that I have herpes. Neither do my parents. I don't know if God will accept me into His Kingdom because of this… nor do I think you'll want me as your woman."

From there, Janine broke down and cried right beside Roman's bed. He gently put his arms around her and let her sob for a couple of minutes. As he thought of what to say, he wanted her to let go of the years of baggage she had been carrying. Roman was no stranger to past hurts. He remembered at that moment the days he would blame himself for Briana's death and their unborn child.

Janine finally looked up at Roman and said, "You don't want to be with me now, do you… I'll understand if that's the case."

"All right… let's take a step back and look at this before doing anything rash. Believe it or not, I have herpes too."

"Wait… you do?"

"Well, not exactly. You have herpes simplex, which is transmitted sexually. I have herpes zoster, which is shingles. They're like cousins but require different treatment since they're still technically different."

"Oh, I didn't know that was the case."

"Yes. So, I know a little bit about the pain you experience. However, it doesn't happen to me downstairs. Now, back to the point. It sounds like you feel that God won't accept you because society places a stigma on people who have STDs. Correct?"

"Yes."

"Janine… you are beautifully and wonderfully created by God. You told me you want to give your life over to Christ. So do it. Don't worry about the fact that you've had sex before marriage or if you have an incurable virus. You can't change that now. What matters the most is what you choose to do in life moving forward. He wants you and wants to see you in His Kingdom whether you have herpes or don't have herpes."

"What about you?"

"What about me?"

"Would you ever want to be more than friends with me?"

"I've given that much thought."

He saw Janine put her hand over her lips. He knew she was feeling the suspense.

"I would be honored to have you as my woman. My beautiful lady. You've shown me that you want Jesus in your life and are searching for God's Kingdom. I know you're not blowing smoke at me. You've made me so happy. I love spending time with you. And you've softened my heart too."

"How so?"

"I think past experiences hardened my heart toward the politics of

212

living in the northeast, if you know what I mean. Sometimes my resentments steered me off course. But you've been very kind to me, and I owe you that same respect."

"Do you think God will accept me if I'm a Democrat?"

"Of course, He will! When He sent His Son Jesus to planet Earth, He did it for love and redemption. Jesus wasn't a Republican or a Democrat. Jesus isn't a politician. Jesus is Jesus. That's who He is, and that's whom I follow. I mean, look at the Apostle Paul. Before he was Paul, he was a murderer. Then God worked in Paul tremendously. Because of that, Paul was able to further God's Kingdom here on Earth. Remember, once you put the Lord first, He will guide you. You can discern what's right, whether it's with your political stances or anything else. Politics take a backseat when the Lord leads a person."

"What about the fact I'm a feminist? I know some church people think feminists are communist heathens."

"You can still believe in woman's equality. I do. Jesus Himself believed in liberating women."

"He did?"

"Absolutely. Ever read about the woman caught in adultery in the Bible?"

"You know, I did. It's in the book of John. I enjoyed the redemption aspect of it."

"There you go. As you can see, you can still be a strong and independent woman. You simply use it for a different purpose. You use it to serve the Lord. You can use it to help other women around you. You use it to serve your family and others, as well. Only when one walks with the Lord is the one who experiences true independence.

"Let me say something else. It was only at the beginning of this year that I accepted Christ. It's our duty as believers to invite everyone to church. Everyone from all walks of life. If we don't extend the invitation to a non-believer, where will they ever hear the gospel? Some seasoned Christians think believers need to act a certain way. I'm not saying a believer should do whatever they feel like because then there would be no point in professing to be a believer. But when someone is brand new to Christ, we can't expect that person to do a complete turnaround overnight. That's why it's good when the church offers study groups and get-togethers. Then someone can see how people of faith *should* live."

"I see what you're saying. So, you're okay with the fact that I have herpes?"

"Honestly... I am. And I do appreciate you being upfront and honest about this and not leaving me in the dark. Now, I'm not going to pop the question to you today, but we could work around that if we got to that point. We could still have sex in marriage, but we would have to use condoms. I don't want to get herpes, but that wouldn't stop me from putting my 'P' inside your 'V.'"

"You're so... freaking weird!" Janine said as they laughed at Roman's comment about sex.

"So, did you see the lightning bolt obliterated my tree?"

"I sure did. We all did. After our fight, I went to the Kojić house since I was upset. We didn't see the bolt, but the bright light filled the house. It was so loud. I can only imagine what it was like from your point of view."

"Um, I may have done a pants check on myself, you could say. I saw it happen as I was standing in the kitchen. Thunderstorms don't scare me, but I jumped about a mile once I saw and heard that. Then the wind picked up, and I hid in the basement. I didn't know what was going to happen."

"We didn't either. We all went down to the basement, too. So, when do you think that black widow bit you?"

"You know it took until about now to figure it out. I was cutting up one of the trees with my chainsaw. I took a break for a sip of water when a mother bear approached me with her cubs."

"Oh wow. That must have been scary."

"Yes, it was. The two cubs ran out of the woods and stopped playing around once they saw me. A couple of seconds later, the mother bear emerged. You don't want to be around a mother bear with her cubs."

"Did the bear charge you?"

"No. Thank goodness no. As you can imagine, I was scared. I tried to grab my cell phone off the woodpile but bumped it instead. It fell into the crevice of one of the logs. As I reached for it, I felt something prick my hand. I thought nothing of it. I thought maybe I had grazed my hand on a splinter of wood. Plus, I was so focused on not being attacked by the bear. I slowly returned to the house so I wouldn't look threatening to the bears. Once I was inside my house, I sat down. And that's when all the side effects from the venom kicked in."

"That was scary seeing that. I was terrified. I didn't know if I was going to lose you."

"I didn't know what was going on either. It felt like my appendix ruptured, but I knew it wasn't that since I had it removed years ago. So, I was confused at first, but then I figured it out once I was in the ambulance. And thank you again for saving me. I owe you one."

"You don't owe me anything. You led me to the Lord."

They gave each other a long but gentle hug since Roman was still in some pain.

"Say," Roman said, "I've been meaning to get baptized. I talked to Theresa and Miroslav about it. Would you want to get baptized together?"

"I would love that. I think that would be great. Maybe my sister could baptize me, and Miroslav could baptize you."

"I was thinking the same thing. Earlier this year, I had mentioned to Miroslav that I wanted him to baptize me."

"I have an idea. You have that pond on your property. Could we do it there?"

"That would be wonderful. That's what I've wanted to do all along."

"Me too."

"Hey, can I ask you a medical question?"

"What's that?"

"Povuci moj prst?" Roman asked as he extended his finger to Janine.

"Seriously, dude? Miroslav taught you that, didn't he."

"Ah, come on, Janine. It's a medical emergency!"

"Right… sure it is."

"Nobody will know if you do. Besides, I think flatulence is covered under HIPAA. Besides, I'm liable to experience spontaneous combustion if I hold it in. I could explode right in front of you into a million pieces!"

"Oh, all right, fine."

As she pulled his finger, he farted. It was followed by a sigh of relief and a goofy smile.

"Thanks, Janine. Man, that was a keeper. It smells like a swath of roses. Don't look away, either. It's important to maintain eye contact when a person farts. You know, the family that farts together stays together… or is it prays together… either way, Jesus knows. He sits at the right hand of God. Not to be confused with the Red Hand of Ulster."

"Yeah… faats together. I'm in love with an idiot. I'll take that Red Hand and smack you upside your head with it."

Janine and Roman were happy to have made peace with one another. They also grew their friendship into a relationship with one another. They knew the other one would have their back. Their trust and love were built on the same foundation. Christ would be their cornerstone.

CHAPTER 15

Roman was eventually released from the hospital and was set to go home. Janine picked him up so he would have the means of getting back home. Roman had told her that his parents would spend a couple of weeks with him. They wanted to know he was going to be okay. While Janine and Roman were at his house, they were waiting for his folks to show up during the late evening.

"Do you think your parents will like me?" Janine asked.

"I know they will. They're good people. You won't have anything to worry about," said Roman.

"I'm sure someday you'll meet my parents too. I don't know what they'll think. Knowing them, they'll probably like you more than they like me."

"I know that's a rough situation for you. Do you think they'll show up when we get baptized together?"

"I think they would, but they may think I'm doing it to be fake. I don't set the bar high as far as expectations go with them. They do what they do, and that's that."

"I think I hear my parents pulling up the driveway now."

Roman went to the door to greet his parents. He knew what to expect. He knew they would be all over him since they knew what had happened. But he knew it wouldn't be in the form of negative attention.

"Roman!" his mother exclaimed.

Roman didn't even have a chance to say "hello." She immediately gave him a hug and a couple of kisses. His father also greeted him with a big bear hug. Janine already had a good impression of his parents. She wished her parents were warm like his parents were.

"Mom and Dad. I'd like you to meet Janine. She's my girlfriend. She's the one that saved my life."

"It's so nice to meet you, Janine. My name is Carol. Thank you for saving my son's life."

Carol gave Janine a big hug. She could feel the love that came from Carol's hug. She noticed that Carol was wearing a tank top. Carol had the Ulster Banner tattoo on her right arm below her shoulder. It was complete in fine detail, right down to the crown and the Red Hand of Ulster. Years ago, the Ulster Banner would have struck a nerve in Janine. Now, it didn't matter to her.

"Yes, thank you for saving our son's life," Roman's father said. "He means the world to us, and we also think the same of you for doing what you did. My name is Roger."

"It's very nice meeting you both," Janine said as she shook Roger's hand.

"Did you both already have supper?" asked Roman.

"Yes, we ate on the way here at a restaurant called Hoss's," said Carol. "It was pretty good. We liked it. Did you guys eat?"

"Yes, we did. You guys need help unloading your car?"

"We should be all right. I'll take care of it," said Roger.

"Which way is the bathroom?" asked Carol.

"It's over that way," said Roman.

Once Roger unloaded the car, everyone sat in the living room. Janine didn't feel as nervous as she thought she would. She already felt very comfortable around Roman's parents. She was looking forward to getting to know them better.

"So, how did this all happen? Did you get bit while putting on a shoe?" Carol asked Roman.

"No, it bit me on my hand between my pointer finger and thumb. See here? You can still see it," Roman said.

Roman showed the mark on his hand to his parents. His mother cringed at it.

"That *is* something, son," Roger said. "Did you see the spider on you?"

"I didn't. You won't even believe this, but if you look out of the sliding glass door, you'll see the remnants of the trees. Well, lighting hit that big tree and annihilated it."

His parents got up to see what Roman was talking about. They stepped outside on the deck since it was dark to look closer. Then both his parents came back inside.

"Wow, that must have made a hell of a crash," Roger said.

"It sure did. I jumped out of my skin when it happened. So, I cut up the tree next to that big one. As I took a break from work, I was approached by a mother bear and her two cubs."

"I don't know what I would have done if I saw bears. I probably would have freaked out," Carol said.

"That's pretty cool you have that kind of wildlife on your property," Roger added. "I remember you showed us a picture of the bear you shot. Good thing the mother bear didn't go after you. I assume she didn't anyway."

"No, she didn't. Otherwise, I'd probably still be in the hospital for that one. Anyway, I wanted to escape that situation as quickly as possible. I reached for my phone. It had slid into the crevice in the woodpile, and that's when it happened. Although I didn't know that it had happened since I was so distracted by the bears. I made it inside the house, and then the troubles began."

"Wow, well, we're glad you're still here," Carol said. "We're sorry we couldn't come sooner to visit you while you were at the hospital. We found out your grandmother was officially diagnosed with Alzheimer's, and we needed to help her with some stuff. We wanted to tell you in person once we knew we were coming down here. So, there's been a lot going on."

"I'm not surprised she has Alzheimer's. I talked to her recently when you both were visiting her. You probably remember that the conversation started well but went downhill quickly. Is she in assisted living or something like that?"

"Yes. We had to get that set up for her. She can't do it alone anymore. Not to mention, she's been widowed for several years."

"I need to make a trip up there to see her before it's too late."

"That would be great if you could visit her. Craig hoped he could spend as much time here as we were. Even though they're not showing up until Sunday, at least Craig and his family will get to celebrate with you and Janine. Plus, you'll get to spend time with each other again."

"I'm glad they'll be here, even if it's only for the day of the baptism and the following day. It's better than nothing. Now… um… you guys aren't upset that I'm getting baptized along with Janine, are you?"

"Upset? Why would we be upset?" asked Carol.

"Well… I know we didn't go to church in our house, pray, or anything. I didn't know if you would hold it against me now that I've chosen to live a different life. I hope you'll still love me."

"Roman," Roger said. "There is *nothing* you could do to make us turn our backs on you. We know you went through Hell when Briana died, and we saw it crush you into a million pieces. Now, your mother and I don't practice any religion, but we're not going to fault you for doing so. We want you to know that we stand by you."

"Do you think Craig and his family would too?"

"Absolutely. I'm sure his kids may have some questions about what you're doing and why you're doing it. But I doubt they would come at you in a threatening way."

"Well, that's good. I can breathe a sigh of relief now."

"So, tell us a little about yourself, Janine," Carol asked. "What do you do for work?"

"Well, I am a truck driver locally. I don't do long-distance or anything like that. Roman and I first met at my sister's house. She lives right next door over that way," said Janine.

"Oh, is that Theresa and Miroslav, the ones Roman has told us about?"

"Yeah, that would be them. I'm Theresa's older sister."

"So, you *never* told me you and Janine were together," Carol said with a big smile.

"It happened not that long ago, *Mom.*"

Janine giggled at the fact that Roman was blushing.

"Well, we're happy for both of you. But we probably should be getting ready for bed," Roger said. "We did our best to get here earlier, but we got stuck in construction traffic on the highway. Toward the end of the week, we'll do anything to help you and Janine prepare for your baptisms. I can even take care of those trees for you."

"That would be greatly appreciated. I may need some help since I still feel weak."

"We'll also have more time tomorrow to catch up," said Carol. "Are you going to be here tomorrow, Janine?"

"Yes. I'll be here probably around the dinner hour."

"That's great. We're looking forward to getting to know you more. And thank you again for saving our son's life. Someone who does that for our child is considered family to us."

"Well, I do love him. You raised a good man even though he's goofy sometimes."

"That is true," Roger said as he laughed. "Speaking of goofy. Did you get Janine to watch *Benny Hill* yet?"

"Oh, don't start with that again! Not at this hour. He's such a raunchy man! If you think I'm watching him the whole time I'm here in Pennsylvania, you have another thing coming!" Carol exclaimed.

Both Roman and Janine giggled at his parents' banter. They continued to listen to Carol fussing at Roger about *Benny Hill* as both Roman's parents started to make their way down the hall.

"We could watch *Beavis and Butt-Head,* if that makes you feel better, Mom. Besides, I remember you telling me and Craig one day that you and Dad watched *Fritz the Cat* and *A Clockwork Orange* at the drive-in back in the day."

"Well, that's… that's beside the point! Now, if there's more talk of *Benny Hill,* I'll throw you and your father in the cellar with the rats!"

"Hey, Carol?" asked Roger.

"What is it?" asked Carol

"My fingers are killing me. Will you relieve my arthritis by pulling my finger?"

"Oh, here we go again with that!"

"Like father, like son," Janine said, smiling.

Once Roman's parents got to the bedroom, Carol slammed the bedroom door. Roman and Janine each busted out laughing as they could indistinctively hear Carol fussing at Roger in the bedroom.

"Your parents are super nice," said Janine.

"They are. I love them very much. So, we got a big day coming up soon. You excited?" asked Roman.

"I am. I'm more excited that we'll be doing this together. Sharing the moment with God will be special."

"It sure will be."

They kissed each other and parted ways for the evening. Roman wanted to get some sleep and rest during the upcoming days. His father would take care of all the tree work so Roman wouldn't have to do it. Roman knew he would have to help prepare the house to the best of his ability and figure out a menu. He knew it would all get done with everyone's help. All he wanted was a good night's sleep.

———————————•———————————

The day had come for both Janine and Roman. It was their time to shine. The weather was perfect. Bright sunshine filled the sky, and there was no humidity. Roman's parents, along with Craig and his wife and children, were there to witness this event. On Janine's side, Jason and Sarah would be spectating, while Miroslav and Theresa would perform the baptisms at Roman's pond. A few people from Bible study attended the baptism as well. Janine felt a little nervous. She was fearful of her eventual interaction with her parents, but she remained calm. She relaxed when Roman approached her.

"Come this way, please. I want you to meet someone," Roman said to Janine.

They both walked over to Craig and his family.

"Hey, big brother!" exclaimed Roman.

"What's up, my man? Bring it on in!" Craig said, overjoyed as they both hugged each other.

"Thanks for having us here, my man," Craig continued, "We're honored to be here to celebrate this day with you. Not to mention we're glad you're alive!"

"Me, too. Thank you for being here."

"So… is this the lucky lady?" Craig asked suavely.

"Yes, it is. Janine, this is my brother Craig. Craig, this is Janine."

"A pleasure to meet you," Craig said, extending his hand.

"You, too. I've heard only good things about you."

"You better watch my brother. He's a real lady's man."

"Oh, stop," Roman said as he blushed.

"Janine, this is my wife, Chelsea."

"It's finally nice to meet you. Thank you for being there for Roman. He has a big heart. We're glad that you two have met."

"It's a pleasure meeting you too. I hope we can get to know each other more when you're here."

"That would be great. We'll be here all day tomorrow."

"That's great. I have a vacation day that I'm using from work tomorrow."

"Awesome! We'll get to see you then."

"*Uncle Roman!*" both his nieces exclaimed.

They ran over and both hugged Roman at the same time.

"Meredith! Emily! Good to see you both!"

"It's great that we can see you again," said Emily.

"I know. I've missed seeing you both."

"Once I get my license, I'm driving down to see you!" exclaimed Meredith.

"Sounds good to me. I'd like you both to meet Janine."

"It's nice to meet you both," replied Janine.

Janine and both girls extended their greetings to each other. After that, she decided to leave Roman so he could spend some time with his family. She needed to use the bathroom anyway. Walking back to the house, she stopped dead in her tracks. She stood there frozen in time. She came face to face with her parents. It was over two years ago when she last saw them in person. It was even longer when Janine remembered the last time she had a decent conversation with them. She quickly felt the uneasiness inside her head and stomach but decided to approach them. She didn't care what they may say to her. She wasn't going to let them ruin her special day.

"Hi, Mom and Dad. I'm glad you both could make it."

"You didn't think we would show up, did you?" her father asked dryly.

"You guys are free to do whatever you want," Janine said as she rolled her eyes. "I'm not going to tell you what to do or not to do."

"Can we say something?" her mother asked.

"Sure. Go ahead."

Janine was waiting for the criticisms to make their way into the following conversations. But Janine didn't care. She was accustomed to both her parents pointing out her peccadillos.

"Well, what is it?" Janine asked.

"We wanted to say we're sorry, Janine," her father said.

"Wait, what?"

"I know you weren't expecting that for an answer," her father continued, "but we're here today because of you."

"I'm afraid I don't understand."

"Your father and I have heard from your sister about how things have been going in your life. And we're proud you've made this decision yourself."

"So, you're saying you only wanted to see me because I'm doing something *you* like since it's a church thing? Is that right?"

"We like what you're doing because *you're* doing this," her father said. "No one else told you to do it. Not us. Not anybody. We admit that your mother and I didn't do right by you. We weren't there for you as we should have been. I know it's been a long time that's passed by, but we wanted to let you know that we're both sorry for not being more loving parents to you. That's something we could have done a better job with. We hope you can forgive us. We both love you, Janine."

Janine stood there dumbfounded. She didn't expect to hear this conversation from her parents. All she could do was stare at them. She wanted to figure out if they were both pulling her leg on this or not. She finally decided to respond to what her father said.

"You know what? I could completely cut both of you out of my life and think nothing of it. It's been a long time, so what will a couple more decades matter? I could choose to take this position regarding my parents."

She saw her parents looking more vulnerable with the words she used against them. She could see them getting smaller and smaller by the second.

"Or I could choose something different," Janine added.

At that moment, Janine could see an immediate confidence boost in her parents' demeanor as they stood there silently.

"That's right. I'm going to choose something different. Let me be honest with you both. Our relationship will take much work to get it back on track. I'm not going to sugarcoat that. But I do believe in forgiveness. And true love is loving someone when it hasn't been *easy* to love them. True love is loving someone when they may not deserve that love. We, as humans, don't deserve it. But God freely gave us that love because He loved us first. That's how I intend to live my life to the best of my human ability. People in this world think the grass is always greener on the other side. Well, instead of going my own way, I'm going to take care of my grass and maintain it. That way, my lawn *will* be green."

It was a proud moment for the Flaherty family. The three of them went in for a group hug. The peace agreement that Janine had chased for years had finally shown up. It showed up on the day of her baptism of all days. Janine showed her true faith even before it was expressed publicly.

Now was the time to show it publicly. From there, Janine stepped into the water first with her sister Theresa. She asked Janine to repeat the confession of faith. That's when Theresa baptized her sister. Everyone clapped for Janine. It was an honor for each of them since they were sisters. Next up was Roman. It was Miroslav's turn to dunk him into the water. Roman repeated the confession of faith that Miroslav gave him. He was then baptized into the water, and everyone clapped for him.

Roman showcased some of his culinary talents to everyone who attended the baptism. He smoked two pork butts for pulled pork and the turkey he shot during the spring on his Backwoods Smoker. Although he started smoking the food early in the morning, his smoker was well-built, so he wouldn't have to babysit it too much. Janine, Roman's parents, and the Kojićs made the sides.

Everyone enjoyed each other's company at the feast. It was the perfect day for a celebration – a day of redemption. Roman was excited that he got to do this and that his family didn't think any less of his decision. As for Janine, she felt like a significant weight had been lifted off her shoulders. The love of Christ shined within her. She felt like she had her old life buried. Once those hatchets were buried, she had been raised to the newness of life from Roman's pond.

CHAPTER 16

t was the first day of spring day of 2022. Roman and Janine dressed like they did when they went to Gold Mountain Estate in Altoona. But they weren't planning on going anywhere for fancy dining. They dressed and drove the Rolls-Royce to Mandarin Gardens in Chambersburg. They wanted to get dressed up for the fun of it. The restaurant had a quiet atmosphere. They also brought the Cribbage board so they could play in the restaurant. It was a good time, but Roman could tell that something was slightly off with Janine's mood. She didn't say much to Roman.

"Is everything okay?" Roman asked.

"Yeah, I'm fine," Janine replied.

Roman thought about what to say to Janine next. He discarded two cards into Janine's crib. The game was halfway through, but Roman wished it was done so he could talk to her more. After the game was finished, he decided to break the awful silence.

"I don't want to be pushy," Roman said, "but if it's something I did, would you tell me?"

She finished chewing her food and swallowed it.

After she washed it with green tea, she said, "It's nothing you've done… I don't know… I'm still thinking about quitting my job. It's sucked for so long, but I'm not sure I can take it anymore."

"What's going on at work?"

"The management there is so horrible. They keep getting worse and worse. Of course, they don't like me because I'm a woman. They don't want a woman driving a truck because that's *'a man's job,'*" she said in a manly voice, using her fingers as quotation marks.

"I've worked hard for that place for sixteen years now. When I started there, it was great. Not perfect, but still great. But then the owner died, and his son took over. From there, it went downhill. When Bill Oglebay died seven years ago, I think the company died with him. His son recently sold the company to someone a couple of months ago. He sold it to some British dude, I heard. I saw him walking around in a three-piece suit wearing a top hat. He also wore a monocle and had a handlebar mustache with a goatee on his chin, like the one Colonel Sanders has. He looked like a real character. That's the only time I've seen him so far. I don't even know his name."

"Do you think anything will get better at Oglebay Brothers?"

"I doubt it. I mean, it's only been under new ownership for a little bit. I guess I can't say for sure. I don't have a crystal ball, you know. But it's very doubtful anything will get better there. If the new owner lives in England, I doubt he will care what's going on at Oglebay Brothers.

"I have considered a job change, but I know another place would be apprehensive about hiring me. It's hard being a woman in this job field. I don't mean to play the card, but it's true."

They both paused to eat more of their Chinese food.

Janine started the conversation again, "You know what I wish I could do?"

"What's that?" Roman asked.

"I wish I had the money to open a truck driving school and get more women into this job field. So many people around this area are starving for jobs. If you're not a farmer, you're driving to Harrisburg or even Washington, DC, to go to work. The jobs aren't here. I don't know… it's something I've always been passionate about. I want to help other women and people in general. I'd love to be able to open a school and even be a teacher at a truck driving school. That way, I can help people get plugged into jobs. I know it's an unrealistic dream, but it's something I think about."

"I admire your passion for wanting to help other people, Janine. And you're right; I think women should be able to get into trade-type jobs without being marginalized. So, you get treated differently at work because of who you are?"

"In a sense. For example, we were at a meeting at work, and I brought up an idea about recording fuel usage to the supervisor. We had a clipboard next to the pump with the log information. You fill up the truck at the end of the day and record how much diesel you used to fill up. I mentioned that we should do it on a computer so the logging sheet doesn't get soaked by the rain, or sometimes hornets would make a nest near it. I also mentioned they could move it to somewhere inside if they didn't want to use a computer. He didn't seem to pay me any mind.

"Then, a couple of minutes later, a coworker brought up the *same thing* I mentioned, and somehow, he thought it was a *great* idea. He didn't care about it when *I* said it. I've had a few run-ins with my supervisor. His name is Jerry. I've known him since grade school, and we have had a checkered past. I've stood up for myself, which he hates. I know he hates being put in his place by a woman and someone beneath him since I'm not in management.

"As you can see, management cares nothing about me or other men. Crazy Larry had a heart attack at work, and they had to call the ambulance and everything. The jerks *still* had the nerve to give him a point against his attendance even though he had a heart attack. He could have died, and they wouldn't have cared. He's such a nice man too. A little out there, but he has a heart of gold.

"Then I know Aminadav had put in for scheduled days off for Yom HaShoah. They denied him those days off even though he had already requested it well in advance. They told him to do that stuff on his own time and that he was needed at work. You're telling me you couldn't give this man time off so he could spend it in remembrance of those that died in the Holocaust? And he *did* have family members that were exterminated in the camps. I think they don't like him because he's Jewish.

"It's funny how the people who work there, like myself and the two other people I mentioned, are the ones who work the hardest. We volunteer to work the most overtime, yet we're the ones that get picked on the most. Then the ones who do the least work reap the most rewards."

"My gosh, Janine. That's awful how you suffer in this kind of work environment. I'd go crazy if I had to work in that."

"I'm surprised I haven't already. I know that's what triggered me to smoke more in the past. I started smoking in high school, but it got way worse once ownership changed and the reins were handed over to the son. So, I'm not sure what I'm going to do. As I said, I wish I could be a teacher and start my truck driving school, but it's only a dream."

"I can't say if things will change for the better or if you'll get to pursue your dream. I'll I can do, is keep praying for you."

"You think you'll start working again?"

"You know, I've been thinking about that lately, and I think I will. Sitting at home isn't cutting it anymore. And now that I'm in a better state of mind, I feel ready for something new. What that looks like, I'm not sure. I enjoy working part-time at the meal center that Miroslav and I started at church. Maybe I'll do more work with the church. As I said, I'm not sure yet, but I'm ready for whatever God lays on my heart."

"I know you'll find something. You're a good man."

"Thanks, you're a good woman. And don't let this place steal your happiness."

"I'll do the best that I can."

They both finished their meal at Mandarin Gardens. After their date, they parted ways for the evening. Once he was back home, Roman sat on his couch, thinking about what Janine had told him. Roman couldn't help but feel bad for her. He knew he had to make a move without her noticing it. But what could he do? That's when Roman crafted an idea.

A significant change would be coming for Oglebay Brothers. He would have to wait a little bit to get his ducks in a row.

———————————•———————————

The following two weeks went by quickly. Roman didn't talk to Janine much during those two weeks. He wanted to prepare for what he had in store for Oglebay Brothers. He was clean-shaven and shaved the hair off his head completely. He wore a suit and a tie for the occasion. Today was the day judgment would fall on Oglebay Brothers.

Janine had finished up her route for the day. It was an average day collecting the trash in the residential neighborhoods as far as the workload went. Everyone was supposed to go to the conference room for a meeting. Nobody had any idea what the meeting was about other than meetings were usually dull. Nothing good came from them. Most of the time, management wanted to hear itself talk and pat itself on the back. Janine was the last one to get back to the worksite. She could see everyone making their way to the conference room.

As she washed her face and hands at the sink, she heard a voice behind her say, "Meet me in my office when you're done."

She rolled her eyes at the voice. She knew it was Jerry. She was never in the mood to talk to him, let alone speak to him in his office. She dried off her hands and face and went to his office.

"What's going on?" Janine asked.

"Close the door, please," Jerry commanded.

Janine closed the door and then crossed her arms across her chest. She already felt herself becoming annoyed simply by being there.

"Maybe this is the day he quits. That would be nice," she thought. "Or maybe he'll fire me. That wouldn't make me sad one bit."

"So, how have you been, Janine?"

"Good."

"You know, let's keep this between you and me. I don't want this to get out to everyone at work."

"Are you coming out of the closet, Jerry?"

"You always had fire and spice in your personality… I like that."

He got up and stood between Janine and the entrance door. She backed up a little when he stood up. She didn't know what was going on. She never saw him this calm. Usually, he would get all sore when Janine would make a joke about him. But he didn't this time which caught her off guard. She felt herself tensing up a little.

"What does he want?" she thought.

Although she stood taller than Jerry by a few inches, he was built big with muscle. He could use that to his advantage if need be.

"I have to say, Janine. You've been here for a long time. I know we haven't gotten along the best, but when you show up to work, you go to work. You don't fuck around as these other assholes do. I don't even know why I keep some of them, especially that kike, um, whatever his name is."

"His name is Aminadav! He has a name, and it's not an ethnic slur!"

"Wow, what a temper. There's that fire again that I like. As I said, these other people don't do *nearly* as good of a job as you do."

"Well, I know a few of them are your buddies. I also know we went to school with some of them."

"Yeah, but that's beside the point. The point is we're talking about you right now."

"Okay… so what do you want?"

"Well… how's about I put in a good word to give you a raise? After all, with our proud company under new ownership, it would be fitting to start things off right and make a good impression with the new owner. After all, that's what the meeting is about today. It's about new beginnings. Not to mention this guy is loaded with money. I mean *loaded.* So, I'm sure we could get you more money in your paycheck… if you do something in return."

Jerry put his hand on Janine's arm. He slowly ran his hand down her arm to her hand and wanted to hold it. She quickly batted his hand away and looked at him in disgust.

"What do you want me to blow you or something?"

"I thought you would never ask," he said with a big smile. "If you do that and fuck me one good time, I'm sure you could get at least thirty dollars an hour working here. That's a lot more than you have now. I bet you're an animal in the bedroom."

"You're disgusting! I would *never* sleep with you even if you paid me a million dollars! You wouldn't even know what to do with a woman since you have a small dick. Your dick must be small if you think trying to pressure an employee will get you laid. Now you let me out of this office. Otherwise, I'm reporting you for sexual harassment!"

"You *are* a dumb Irish bitch, you know. I can't believe you would turn down that kind of money just so…"

"I said let me out of here!"

She shoved Jerry hard onto his office desk. He fell over onto the floor. His pride was hurt now. This time he wanted her to pay for it. All the years of conflict between them reached the tipping point. His blood was boiling as he got up and quickly returned fire. He belted his hand across her face. The impact of his hand striking her turned her head to the side. Janine was a strong woman, but she felt the impact of Jerry's hand. She felt helpless at that moment, trapped inside his office. She had nowhere to go or hide from this monster that was her supervisor. She would do anything to prevent Jerry from having his way with her. She hoped it wouldn't come to that, but she feared the worst. He walked over toward Janine and was ready to tee up on her face again. This time it would be in the form of a punch. He grabbed her by the collar of her work uniform and arched his arm back. Janine braced herself. She was prepared to feel a ton of bricks hitting her face.

But Jerry stopped mid-swing and dead in his tracks. He didn't move as Janine saw his eyes grow big. At that moment, a familiar click could be heard. It was the sound of a hammer being cocked on a revolver.

"Back away. You do as I say, and nobody dies," the voice said calmly.

Jerry backed away from Janine. He slowly moved himself to the other side of the office. Janine couldn't believe it. It was Roman. She didn't recognize his new look but could hear that thick Boston accent ten miles away. Roman had seen what went on in Jerry's office. His office window was big enough for the whole world to see. Jerry wanted a big office window to see if anyone was standing around at the end of the day and not working. This time, the joke was on him.

"What do you think you're doing?" Roman asked Jerry.

"I wasn't fucking doing anything. Who the fuck are you, anyway?"

"Me? Do you ask who I am? Why… I am the punishment of God. If you have not committed great sins, God would not have sent a punishment like me upon you."

Roman aimed his revolver at Jerry's head. Jerry began to tremble in fear. Both Roman and Janine could see him shaking in his skin. He got on his knees and started weeping.

"I think Genghis Khan said that," Roman continued, "but I would have to do a fact check. Huh… what do we have here? What a big tough guy. First, you hit my woman in the face. Then you start swearing at me and lying to my face. And now, look at you. Now you're blubbering like a baby."

"Look, man… I don't want any trouble."

"No trouble, you say? What gave you the right to hit Janine in the face? *And then, you lied to me about it on top of that!*"

"Please," Jerry begged. "Don't shoot me, please."

"My best friend who lives next to me found himself in a similar situation. Someone raped his mother and then begged him not to shoot him. You know what my friend did?"

"He shot him, didn't he?"

"No. He sliced his head off with a scythe instead. The man knew how to wield a scythe for sure. Perhaps we should go to his house and visit him since you told me not to shoot you."

Jerry broke down and sobbed. Roman stared at the scene Jerry was making for several seconds. What he saw in Jerry was utterly despicable. He saw nothing redeemable about Jerry at that moment.

Janine put her hand on Roman's shoulder and calmly said, "Don't shoot him."

"Well… okay. I wasn't planning on running into this kind of a show today, anyway. However, I was prepared for the following. Jerry… stand up."

Jerry stood up. Roman still had his gun aimed at him. Roman pulled a piece of paper from his pocket and put it on the desk.

"So, here's the deal, Jerry. I'm not going to shoot you. However, you'll sign this paper for me like a good little boy."

"What is it?"

"It's your resignation. It was typed up a few days ago. I've heard some rumblings about how you mistreat your employees. That's bad enough, and you will be held accountable for that. Striking a woman, my woman, and sexually harassing her is completely unacceptable. It has no place in the workplace or outside of it, for that matter. These are things the owner and this company *will not* tolerate! I know the owner very well, and he brought me on to investigate things within this company. Now sign this resignation letter, or I will press charges on you. Do I make myself clear?"

"Yes. Yes, you do."

Jerry signed the paper, and Roman signed it below Jerry's signature. Roman took the form and put it in the filing cabinet. Roman grabbed an envelope from his pocket and held it by his side.

"You understand that a resignation means you're not qualified to receive unemployment benefits since you're leaving on your terms… on paper, that is. See what I did there? So here. Take this," Roman said as he extended the envelope to Jerry.

He gingerly took the envelope out of his hand.

"What is it?"

"It's your severance pay. It's precisely twenty thousand five hundred eighty dollars in cash. *Don't* open the envelope until you get in your car. You take this money, and you get lost. I never want to see you on the premises again, nor does anyone else. If I catch you on here or find out you're harassing the employees outside of work, especially Janine, you're a dead man. If you *ever* lay a hand on Janine again, I promise you that a scythe blade will go right through your neck. Do you understand me?

"Yes."

"Good. Before you go, you apologize to Janine for what you did to her."

"I'm sorry, Janine."

Janine didn't say anything. She nodded her head and stood there quietly. She couldn't wait for Jerry to be gone for good. Jerry scrambled out of the office and headed for his car. She was happy that he was terminated but still felt unsettled. She had a bone to pick with Roman over the severance pay he gave Jerry.

"How could you do that, Roman?"

"Do what?" he asked in a confused manner.

"I can't believe you would let that creeper walk out of here with all that money!"

Roman extended his hand forward to symbolize "stop." He cleared his throat with a smile and said, "Allow me to explain, my lady. I gave him twenty thousand five hundred eighty dollars, but I didn't specify whether it was American dollars or not."

"So... what did you give him then?" she asked with a devilish grin.

"Monopoly money! Here, I'll prove it to you. Come over here."

They both walked to the window. Roman quietly opened it. He knew Jerry's car was parked by the window. Then he and Janine ducked down so they wouldn't be seen.

"Wait for it... wait for it," Roman said as he lifted his pointer finger.

They both waited through the pause of quietness that lasted several seconds. And then they heard it. They heard Jerry realize that his severance pay wasn't what it was all cracked up to be.

Jerry yelled at the top of his lungs, *"I HATE YOU, ROMAN, YOU MOTHERFUCKER!"*

"And there it is, folks!" Roman exclaimed joyfully.

They both laughed at Jerry's expense.

"Okay, that *was* pretty good," said Janine. "And thank you for stepping up for me back there."

"Hey, anything for my best friend." They both hugged each other. Then Roman continued, "Besides, you helped me out when I needed it too."

"So, I need to ask you two things. First, do you have a neighbor that knows how to use a scythe?"

"Yes, I do. His name is Miroslav."

"Are you serious?"

"Yeah, we were talking one night, and he shared his life during the breakup of Yugoslavia. It was challenging to listen to but necessary for me to hear. He has a great testimony."

"I'm sure he does. Someday I'll get to hear it, I'm sure. Did he kill someone with a scythe?"

"Yeah, he chopped off a man's head because he raped his mother. His family members were victims of ethnic cleansing."

"That's horrible. I believe what you told me, but I had no idea he had to go through that. So… now the second thing, how did Jerry know your name?"

"He may not have known it was me. But he knows that Roman is this company's new owner."

"You mean the guy from England I saw walking around with the top hat?"

"Yes, that's me also."

"I don't understand."

"I thought about our conversation at Mandarin Gardens a couple of weeks ago. I've thought about it a lot, which is why you haven't heard much from me. Before our conversation that day, I knew you weren't happy with the work environment. But until I saw this crap today, I had no idea it was *that* bad. Has he done that to you before?"

"Honestly, that was the first time he did that to me or offered me a pay raise for sexual favors. We did have our verbal spats in high school together, but nothing of this nature."

"Well, I'm glad he's gone now. I don't think we'll have any more trouble with him. Anyway, back to answering your question. Remember how you said you saw a British man walking around dressed up?"

"Yeah."

"That was me. I dressed in disguise and talked to them with my perfect British accent. That's why I completely shaved today and talked in my normal Boston voice so he wouldn't recognize me."

"Wait, *you* bought the company?"

"Yes, I did, and Miroslav is a co-owner. We hatched this plan a while ago. We split the company right down the middle, fifty-fifty."

"I mean, I know he has a ton of money being a lawyer, but you bought this place with your own money?"

"I mean, not to brag, but I drive a Rolls-Royce if that tells you anything."

"Well, you got me there. How much money do you have?"

"Lots and lots of it. That is how I've been able to be charitable with the church starting the meal center and outreach for people addicted to drugs. I also made a charitable donation to White Castle. I told them about my crazy idea that they should open an amusement park. They loved it! They decided to send us food to help with our meal kitchen at church. And the next order of business will be your school."

"My school?"

"Yeah, you know how you wanted to be a teacher at a truck driving school?"

"Yeah."

"I can see to it that your dream becomes a reality. I'm not doing all this to buy your love. I'm doing this for the community because this is the direction God is leading me. Pennsylvania has been good to me, so I will be good to it."

"Wow... I don't know what to say. That's so amazing. All I've wanted to do is help others. It's like we can be business partners."

"That and..."

"And what?"

Roman got down on one knee and could tell Janine was taken off guard.

"Janine, fairest lady of land… will you marry me?"

She gazed at the ring that he produced as he popped the question to her. Her eyes lit up like diamonds staring at the diamonds. She could feel her heart melt. For all those years, she pushed away men with distrust. Who could say anyone could blame her for that? Many of the men she encountered were either dishonest and lazy like her ex-boyfriend George or piggish like her former supervisor Jerry. Janine didn't care that Roman was a few years younger or several inches shorter. She didn't even care if he acted like a class clown sometimes. She knew immediately that she could see herself spending the rest of her life with Roman.

"I do!"

She extended her left hand out. Roman put the engagement ring on her ring finger. He got up, and they kissed right in the office as they wrapped one another in their arms. Their love was valid for one another. They had total trust in each other. They both knew each one had the other's back. They both knew that if a life-threatening event were to arise, the other would be there to protect them. Their romantic moment had to end, though, for there was still a work meeting to attend.

"I meant to tell you there was supposed to be a scheduled meeting," said Janine.

"Yeah, that was my doing too. I've probably kept everyone waiting. But I had to ask some hot chick to marry me."

Janine smiled, and they both made their way to the conference room. Janine took a seat. Roman walked in and saw everyone. He could tell they were waiting impatiently for this meeting to start. So, Roman decided to keep it brief.

"Good afternoon, everyone. I'm Roman, the new owner of Oglebay Brothers, and I'm sorry to keep you all waiting. My business partner Miroslav was unable to attend today. I'll be speaking on his behalf since he is the co-owner of this company. Something came up right here in the workplace… Jerry, your supervisor, has been fired."

Roman could tell people were shocked. Most of the workers looked relieved.

"I'm going to be clear with everyone here, so no mistakes are made on this subject. Workplace harassment *will not* be tolerated in any way, shape, or form. Doing the work everyone does is hard enough. It's a physically and mentally demanding job. Not to mention you deal with the public. The last thing anyone needs is someone to give you a hard time. That culture Jerry bestowed upon this company is going away. Anyone caught harassing someone else will be subject to disciplinary action or even termination. If you think I'm kidding around, then try me. I got the supervisor kicked out, so I'm not messing around."

Roman could see their faces and knew he had everyone's attention on this. He didn't shout at the employees but spoke sternly to them.

"With that said, our company will be looking for a new supervisor as soon as possible. The second order of business is that everyone here will get a pay increase with better benefits. It's sickening to see that you guys get paid not much more than someone at McDonald's makes. If this company is going to be competitive, then I feel like it's my duty as an owner to pay the employees a competitive wage and the benefits to boot. Anyone from one to five years will get a bump in pay to twenty dollars an hour. Anyone here for five years or more will get up to twenty-five dollars per hour. I've had people in the company go over the numbers with me, and it's very doable. We'll do our best as a company to give raises once a year. This pay increase is only a starter. Pay grades and years of service will be examined more, but I wanted to give you all some quick relief. Everyone deserves better pay than what you get now. With inflation on the rise, you'll need it. Your pay increases are effective the following payday. A yearly boot allowance will also be allotted once a year. You'll receive a two hundred dollar stipend, which you can claim this coming Monday.

"Okay, now for the third order of business. Here are the benefits. We, as the company, plan on giving you a better healthcare plan with a lower deductible. These benefits kick in for first-day hires. The employee will be responsible for a fraction of the cost. You'll also keep your dental benefits, and we will add vision care. People who wear glasses or contact lenses need to see where they're driving while behind the wheel. Once we get some plans and premiums together, we'll give you all the information to look at.

"We're also going to be more generous with vacation days. It's sickening to me seeing how little vacation you guys get. What's the point of making money if you can't enjoy the fruits of your labor? Most of all, I don't want anyone to miss out on family life. Family life is precious. You don't want to work your life away only to discover you never had a relationship with your family. So right off the bat, new hires will get two weeks of vacation. After three years of service, you'll get three weeks and four weeks after eight years.

"I'm also kicking around the idea of doing either holiday luncheons or dinners. Maybe even company events so we can take time to have fun. I've been told I'm pretty good at barbecuing and using a smoker. I'm just putting that out there for everyone. I believe it's important to celebrate the company's achievements together. Without everyone in this room, business wouldn't be possible. The employees are a company's backbone and must be treated like that. Are you all with me?"

Roman looked around the room. He could tell these people had never seen the light of day working at Oglebay Brothers.

"All right... fourth order of business. We're going to expand this company to make more revenue. We want to recognize that our employees are valuable. However, we're going to need income to do that. That's where I come in. We'll be looking into opening a truck driving school in Huntingdon. That's a work in progress. I'll keep everyone in the loop about when the facility is finished. We also want to open a waste-to-energy and recycling facility in McConnellsburg. The ground will be broken for that project in the next several months. The last thing we're looking into is the idea of hazardous waste removal, such as asbestos siding from people's houses. As I said, I'll keep everyone up to date with things as they happen. Any questions on anything?"

The room was silent for a moment. Then Aminadav got up and started clapping for Roman. Everyone else started standing up and clapping one by one. Roman felt relieved that his speech was received well.

"Thank you, thank you very much, everyone," he said as everyone continued to clap for him. "I appreciate your hard work and look forward to getting to know you all more in the future. But please, go home and relax tonight and enjoy your weekend."

The standing ovation continued as Roman exited the building. All he wanted to do now was go home and take a shower so he could relax for the rest of the evening.

Once back home, Roman showered and decided to settle for a few minutes in the living room. Before he could figure out what he would eat for dinner, there was a knock on his door. He went over to see who was there and answered it.

"Oh, hello there, future wife."

"Hey there, future husband."

"Come on in."

They made their way to the living room and sat beside each other.

"I wanted to say that I can't thank you enough for doing this for me… and everyone. Everyone was so happy with the meeting."

"Oh yeah?"

"It's been a long time since that place was worth working for. It was somewhat decent when Bill owned the place, but the benefits were only mediocre. Then, things started to disappear slowly when his son took over, yet they expected more work out of us."

"Well, I look at it this way. There's a shortage of workers in America right now. I want to get people back to work, but I also want to incentivize them to go to work. I feel that this inflation will not go away for a while. And if companies aren't willing to treat their employees right, who would want to work at a place like that? I sure wouldn't."

"So you and Miroslav are the two owners now, huh?"

"Absolutely. We put our heads together because I wanted to do something that would help people in our society. I have a passion for helping others like yourself. We can now start building this business from the ground up. It will serve as a good investment for the Kojić family and us. Let's say we wanted to surprise you."

"Well, I'm sure blown away by all of this. Now, where did you get all your money from?"

"I knew this day would come. I was only going to tell you if I were to marry you. Now that you're going to be my wife, you have the right to know. I won the lottery a few years ago."

"You did?"

"Yes. That's the truth."

"How much did you win?"

"After Uncle Sam took his share, I got slightly under half a billion dollars."

"Holy cow! That's a payout for sure!"

"To say the least. I had all that money, but I wasn't happy. The death of Briana and our child was still looming over my head. I have to say that moving down here was the best thing I ever did. It made me clear my head and not be around those sad memories. It's allowed me not to feel like I must continue gambling to cope with my losses.

"Living here has given me purpose. Sure, I have money, but I can use it for good, such as the things I've done with the church and now building up Oglebay Brothers. I appreciate life more than I ever have. But most of all, God has led me to a beautiful woman. I love you, Janine. And I'm so happy that we met."

"I love you too, Roman. So... this future wedding of ours..."

"Ah, yes! Any ideas of what you want?"

"Call me crazy, but I don't want a big, extravagant wedding. I'd rather spend more time on the honeymoon since the wedding is only one day. If anything, I'd rather elope and call it good."

"I'm fine with that. Where would you like to go on our honeymoon?"

"I've always wanted to go to the beach. It's funny, I know you're from New England, but I've always wanted to go to Maine."

"Maine was not that far from us, but we went there only once. Maybe we could do the beach for part of the time and then do a cabin in the woods for the other part of the time. I've always wanted to go to Greece or Israel, too."

"That would be fun. It would be warmer there too. Either way, we don't have to decide right now. There's something else I wanted to talk to you about as well."

"What's that?"

"It bothers me that Russia has decided to attack Ukraine. I hate seeing the images on the news of what the Russians have done. And it's not justified at all. I can't help to think of what Miroslav went through as a child and how the horrors of war affected him. I wondered if maybe we could adopt a couple of children from Ukraine at some point."

"I would love to do that. I'm on board with that idea."

"Plus, Jason and Sarah could have cousins. I think that would be special."

"Me too."

Janine and Roman held each other on the couch for a few minutes and then decided that they would do take-out from Pizza Star for dinner. They played Cribbage together that evening while they went over more plans regarding the future. The thing she wanted most was finally going to become a reality. She would get to help other women in the community to seek employment. Roman knew this was her passion and wanted her to be at the forefront of the school. He wanted her to be the driving force that got people into the door at Anderson Brothers Driving School.

Janine and Roman decided to elope in the summer of 2022 and were pronounced Mr. and Mrs. Anderson. Eventually, they would have a small celebration with their immediate families after their honeymoon. They ultimately decided to go to Ireland and each region in the United Kingdom, spending a week in both countries. Both got to see where their family origins came from. And, of course, Roman got a photo opportunity next to the statue of his favorite comedian… Benny Hill.

Eventually, both the school and the waste-to-energy plant would be completed. Janine would subsequently leave her position as a truck driver and pursue her dream of being a teacher at the truck driving school. It was agreed upon that the company name would be changed to Anderson Brothers. Not everyone knew how to pronounce Kojić, so Anderson was the decided name. From the grace of God and the generous hearts of the Kojić and Anderson families, they could give many job opportunities to the surrounding communities that otherwise wouldn't have existed. Janine decided to lead a women's group at church. She had a chance to share her testimony of "holding the Perfect Hand." Because of that, she led a few women to the Lord. One of them was Diana. Janine's testimony inspired her. This motivated her to say "no" to drugs and "yes" to the Lord. For most of her life, Janine was a loner. Now, she could rejoice in having genuine connections, especially with Diana.

The Andersons continued to show loving kindness by following through on what they discussed. They adopted two children from Ukraine who had been displaced due to the war. They were a brother and sister, Krystiyan and Ivanna Shevchenko. She was nine years old, and he was seven years old. The Shevchenko children found themselves in a similar situation that Miroslav did when he was a young teenager. Although their stories varied, they were victims of war crimes and bitter hatred, like Miroslav was years ago. Having Miroslav as a neighbor helped the children immensely since they could relate to his experiences growing up in Serbian Krajina. Both Janine and Roman loved their children to no end. They loved each other as husband and wife to no end. They showed their love to their families and the community in south-central Pennsylvania to no end. They did this because they kept God's commandments. For His love has no end.